Reading Hoshino's novels is like traveling to a strange land all by yourself. You touch down on an airfield in a foreign country, get your passport stamped, and leave the airport all nerves and anticipation. The area around an airport is more or less the same in any country. It is sterile and without character. There, you have no real sense of having come somewhere new. But then you take a deep breath and a smell you've never encountered enters your nose, a wind you've never felt brushes against your skin, and an unknown substance rains down upon your head.

–Mitsuyo Kakuta, award-winning author of *Woman on the Other Shore: a Novel*

Adrienne Hurley's beautiful translation of Tomoyuki Hoshino's *Lonely Hearts Killer* is a much-needed contribution to the very small body of translations of radical contemporary Japanese fiction that has little or no connection to the nostalgic, pop uncanniness of Haruki Murakami, and belongs to an entirely different universe from the SF worlds of anime and manga. Here is a novel that believes in radical political action, and that stubbornly sticks to its vision to the bitter end.

–Livia Monnet, Professor, University of Montréal, author of *Critical Approaches to Twentieth Century Japanese Thought*

Lonely Hearts Killer considers the ways in which seemingly 'meaningless' symbols and structures profoundly affect society, calling into question the power of the dangerous fictions which are constantly perpetrated on us, as well as the mass hysteria that lurks below the surface.

–Nate George, filmmaker, Beirut, Lebanon

LONELY
HEARTS
KILLER

LONELY HEARTS KILLER

TOMOYUKI HOSHINO

TRANSLATED BY
ADRIENNE CAREY HURLEY

PM PRESS 2009

ISBN: 978-1-60486-084-9
LCCN: 2009901379

PM Press
P.O. Box 23912
Oakland, CA 94623
PMPress.org

Printed in the USA on recycled paper.

Cover: John Yates/Stealworks.com
Inside design: Josh MacPhee/Justseeds.org

This novel was originally published in Japan by Chuôkôron Shinsha under the title RONRII HAATSU KIRAA.

Contents

TRANSLATOR'S INTRODUCTION
Adrienne Carey Hurley

Eric Shih, a young activist working for the Chinese Progressive Association in San Francisco, was the first person I heard respond to a news story by saying he felt like he hadn't taken his "crazy pills." Having heard this expression countless times since then, I suspect Eric is far from alone in feeling like "crazy pills" are necessary to accept the official versions of reality presented to us on the nightly news. Tomoyuki Hoshino's *Lonely Hearts Killer* is a novel for those of us (like Eric) who are not living under the influence of officially prescribed "crazy pills" — and those of us who are desperately trying to get off them.

In the pages that follow, Hoshino takes us on a journey through our own world amplified. I say "our own" world because while much of the novel seems specific to contemporary Japan, readers living in North American or other G8 (or even G20) states will surely encounter familiar problems, questions, and developments. Hoshino draws on the everyday and headline news stories to create an alternate reality that is often every bit as realistic as it is fantastic. Because we experience violence, hope, oppression, resistance, discrimination, mutuality, emotional distress, love, and catastrophes of all sorts in our own world, readers should expect the same (and quite a bit of it) in this novel.

The novel takes its title from actual events that inspired films such as the 1970 cult classic *The Honeymoon Killers*. Martha Beck and Raymond Martinez Fernandez were dubbed the "Lonely Hearts Killers" of the late 1940s and were executed in 1951 after a high-profile trial. Beck and Fernandez had posed as siblings and contacted women through "lonely hearts" personal advertisements and killed some of them. Coverage of the pair invariably focused on elements of their lives deemed different or strange. Beck, a survivor of physical and sexual abuse, for example, was routinely criticized as "fat" and sexually deviant in the press. The "foreignness" of Fernandez, the Hawaiian-born son of Spanish parents, also figured prominently in the sensational news reports. No explicit mention of Beck or Fernandez is made in Hoshino's *Lonely Hearts Killer*, but readers will notice similarities in how the mass media in the novel relay sensationalized information about individuals, relationships, and incidents to the public. By the end of the novel, some readers might even draw comparisons between certain characters and the real-life pair whose story inspired the title.

Hoshino's interest in "incidents" developed in part through his experience working as a journalist for a conservative newspaper, the *Sankei Shimbun*, for two years after his graduation from Waseda University (with a degree in literature) in 1988. In the late 1980s Japan's "bubble economy" was about to burst, and political scandals dominated the headlines. One such scandal was the notorious Recruit Incident of 1989, an insider-trading debacle that involved many politicians, including several former prime ministers, and newspaper CEOs. Occasionally, headlines about political and corporate corruption would be eclipsed by sensational coverage of cases such as the brutal killings of four girls under the age of ten by Tsutomu Miyazaki, who was arrested in 1989 and executed in the summer of 2008. 1989 was also the year when Japan marked the end of the previous emperor Hirohito's Shôwa era and the beginning of his son Akihito's Heisei era. Culturally, the release of the *anime* megahit *Akira* in the summer of 1988 and the death of the singer and postwar superstar Hibari Misora (the "Queen of Shôwa") in the summer of 1989 seemed to suggest that times really were changing. This was surely a heady and disillusioning time for a young student of literature to work for a large (and fairly nationalistic) newspaper. In an issue of a Japanese literary journal dedicated to his work, he recalls simply, "I traveled to the Kôshien Stadium in the spring [of 1990] to cover the national high school baseball championships. I took a few days vacation on my way back, and, while kicking around the streets of Osaka, lost my desire to carry on as a newspaper reporter." (*Bungei Tokushû: Hoshino Tomoyuki*, Spring, 2006, 81-82, translation mine) He left the Sankei in October of that year and soon after left Japan to spend the better part of the next four years in Mexico, where he would begin his journey toward becoming a novelist.

The politics and ethics of information and storytelling are central to *Lonely Hearts Killer*, as is the case with much of Hoshino's other fiction. Whether it's in the footage of a 9-11-esque event on the television in his novel *The Worussian-Japanese Tragedy*, the dissociative break a newspaper reporter experiences in *Sand Planet*, or the two teen killers turned "terrorists" loosely modeled on figures from the news in *The Treason Diary*, cameras, journalists, and "incidents" are everywhere in his work. In *Lonely Hearts Killer*, Hoshino invokes a wide range of "hot" issues drawn from contemporary Japanese tabloid news (the lives of Japanese royalty and internet suicide pacts) and transnational right-wing punditry (anti-immigrant xenophobia and support for martial law), as well as incidents from Japan's present and past. For example, roughly two-thirds of the novel takes place in a mountain lodge that may evoke images of the headquarters of the Aum cult that carried out the attack on the Tokyo subway system in 1995.

A mountain lodge was also the site of one of the most "shocking" incidents of the 1970s, the *Asama Sansô* Incident. In February of 1972, five members of the Japanese United Red Army (*Rengô sekigun*) fled a remote mountain training retreat where some of their comrades had been purged, beaten, and lynched. In what was surely a desperate moment, they sought refuge in a mountain lodge and held the manager's wife, the only person there at the time, hostage. The lengthy stand-down with the police was simulcast on Japan's national television network, NHK. *The Choice of Hercules*, a 2001 film starring Kôji Yakusho, depicts the stand-down with the leftist "terrorists" from the police point of view. The motives of the Red Army members are never mentioned in the film. They are all but invisible, shown only very briefly, with their faces almost completely hidden in the shadows. They are not real. Their stories do not matter. While never mentioned in the novel, the *Asama Sansô* Incident and NHK's coverage of it are part of the televisual and filmic history that is layered into *Lonely Hearts Killer*. Hoshino's focus, unlike that of the commercial film, is on figures that might otherwise be relegated to the shadows.

The individual chapter titles are also replete with allusion. The title of the first chapter, "The Sea of Tranquility," refers not only to the actual lunar landscape described in the story, but recalls the title of Yukio Mishima's final tetralogy, *The Sea of Fertility (Hojô no umi)*, named after another "sea" on the moon and closely associated with Mishima's dramatic suicide. Mishima was a novelist and playwright who remains one of the most translated and studied figures in modern Japanese literature. His personal life, politics, and sexuality have generated perhaps even more interest than his work, and his death made news around the world. In 1970, Mishima and four members of his private militia, the Shield Society (*Tate no kai*), entered the office of General Kanetoshi Mashita of the Japanese Self Defense Forces (SDF). Purporting to be there for a visit, they held the general hostage while Mishima read a speech to SDF members assembled beneath the balcony outside Mashita's office.

His speech was not met warmly, but according to his plan, Mishima returned to the office and committed (rather anachronistically) *seppuku* (ritual self-disembowelment), as did Masakatsu Morita, one of his militia members. Because Mishima's speech called for a reaffirmation of the emperor's powers and a remilitarization of Japan, many have interpreted his suicide as a political act, as a call for a right-wing *coup d'état*. Others have interpreted it as a love suicide for Mishima and Morita, an aesthetic act, or simply the result of "lunacy." Mishima's fiction, interviews, essays, and other writings provide ample evidence to fuel a variety of such speculations. Like some of the characters in *Lonely Hearts*

Killer, Mishima appealed to and tried to make use of the mass media, which has continued to generate profit off the promise of lurid spectacle, violence, sex, and "deviance" exacted from his story.

The second chapter, "The Love Suicide Era," is named after the news media's label for the fictional period of time covered in that chapter. The term "love suicide" (*shinjû*) itself evokes a long literary tradition of pathos-filled tales of romantic impasses such as the eighteenth century *Love Suicide at Amijima* by Monzaemon Chikamatsu in which a couple unable to overcome economic and social barriers end their lives together. The term might also call to mind the real-life deaths of writers like Mishima and Osamu Dazai, who died in 1948 after several unsuccessful love suicide attempts. (Readers should not expect to find romanticized or elegiac accounts of suicide in this novel.) The third chapter and mountain pass where the retreat is located are named after Luis Buñuel's 1951 film *Subida al Cielo*, which while released under the title *Mexican Bus Ride* in the U.S. would be more accurately translated as "Ascent to Heaven." This film features an autonomous, somewhat communal village in the mountains of Mexico. Various media's reach into the story includes other references to films, such as *The Lady from Shanghai*, the internet, cellular phones and text messaging, radio, and, of course, television.

The country where events unfold in the novel is at once identifiably Japan and not Japan. Although the proper noun *nihon* (Japan) is not used in *Lonely Hearts Killer* and the word *nihongo* (Japanese language) appears only once (when Iroha is badgered by a reporter), the story takes place in a nation referred to as the "Island Country." The real names of places in Japan, such as the Shinjuku district of Tokyo or the Isetan department store chain, are referred to by their usual names. Titles of famous Japanese newspapers, literary journals, and magazines are only slightly altered, often in humorous ways. The conventional words for China and Chinese (*chûgoku* and *chûgokugo*) are replaced with words based on the root usually reserved for Chinese food and Chinese neighborhoods (*chûka*), such as *chûkago* (an invented word something akin to how "Chinaese" might sound in English). Hoshino plays with national identity in ways that beg larger and very serious questions, many of which turn on notions of terrorism.

Some anarchist and anti-authoritarian fantasies involve what official discourse terms terrorism. While the word terrorism might not immediately lead some readers to think of Japan, many of you will recall the Aum cult's 1995 sarin gas attacks on the Tokyo subway system. Some of you may be old enough to recall the Japanese Red Army's activity in the 1970s and events such as the *Asama Sansô* Incident. Less familiar to some readers will be the stories of Japanese anarchists, such as those who hoped to abolish the emperor system in the first decade of the twentieth century. All of these legacies, particularly the latter, are called forth in *Lonely Hearts Killer*, a novel in which metropolitan paranoia over terrorism, suspicion directed at separatist or autonomous community formations, and yearnings to transcend national identity coalesce in a story that can be read as nightmarish, predictive, cautionary, and even utopian.

While Hoshino makes no explicit mention of his-torical anarchist desires to abolish the emperor system in this novel, his characters inhabit a society we might understand as the worst case scenario early anarchists in Japan imagined developing out of Japan's aggressive imperial expansion. Put simply, that worst case scenario might be summed up as life under neoliberalism. Neoliberalism has reached a level of dominance that renders it practically invisible in the sense that belief in it feels good, fair, and "natural" to many people. Like the emperor system, neoliberalism is presented to us as a matter of faith. Early Japanese anarchists would be par-ticularly dismayed to see neoliberalism's tough incursions into precariously situated communities, such as the forced removals of homeless people from public parks in Japanese cities prior to international sporting or other events. Several recent "removals" have targeted autonomous homeless com-munities in which members provided community food and health services for one another. The "removals" are justified as economically "rational" due to the increased possibilities for profit-generation through special event-related tourism. They are touted as beneficial for all even when the process is violent and homeless people themselves are put in more dangerous and isolated situations. It warrants mention that violent attacks on homeless people, including lynching and murder, have increased along with the "removal" programs.

The "sacrifice" of precariously situated homeless populations in Japan, the mass incarceration of people of color and immigrants in privately run U.S. prisons, or the criminalization of poverty in the form of anti-loitering laws are justifiable according to the neoliberal demand that nothing inhibit the flow of capital. If certain people are not good for business, removing them from city streets where they might make shoppers and tourists uncomfortable and sequestering them in privately operated prisons, for example, frees the state – and us – from having to acknowledge inequities or address people's social needs and also creates more avenues for profit generation. Through his fiction, including *Lonely Hearts Killer*, Hoshino gives us very different ways of looking at these contemporary problems. He also invites us to reflect on how difficult it can be to resist neoliberalism, the emperor system, and other forms of authority (or divinity), and he challenges us to imagine more for ourselves than battles over sovereignty or national identity.

These treasonous musings are perhaps the unfinished business of twelve anarchists and socialists who were executed in 1911 in what is known as the High Treason Incident. They were executed for *thinking about* killing the emperor – of having criminal intent without the crime. At the time it was a capital offense just to think about harming a member of the imperial family. Later, it was revealed that the case against the executed twelve (as well as their alleged co-conspirators whose sentences were reduced) was manufactured. The government's disingenuous prosecution should not, however, lead us to downplay the seriousness of some of those anarchists' abolitionist dreams. In those final years of the Meiji era, some anarchists believed that only by abolishing the emperor system could a society without authoritarian differential power begin to grow.

These abolitionist fantasies were relayed to the general public at the time through tabloid news reports on the personal lives and "habits" of anarchists. As literary and cultural theorist Chizuko Naitô explains in her award-winning recent study *Empires and Assassinations*, news reporting on anarchists in the early twentieth century fostered public fear of anti-establishment organizing, and even more prominently characterized anarchists as debauched deviants who were engaged in a scandalous "lifestyle." She cites many newspaper articles, one of which entitled "The Unseemly Habits of the Kashiwagi Anarchists" appeared in the June 25, 1907 issue of the *Tokyo Asahi Newspaper* and included the following "evidence" of anarchist dissolution.

> First, one need only look to the time when Suga Kanno and Arahata lived together illicitly in a house in Kashiwagi. They would roll out of bed around ten o'clock in the morning and loaf around all day doing nothing. Before long, night would fall and suspicious-looking student types would throng into the house, reciting utterly subversive lines, carrying on, stamping their feet, and debating every night until two or three in the morning... (Naitô, *Teikoku to ansatsu: jendaa kara miru kindai nihon no media hensei*, Tokyo: Shinyosha, 2005, 287, translation mine)

As Naitô elaborates, this anarchist "lifestyle" was depicted as an illness by the media, and women engaged in the "lifestyle" were singled out as especially sexually deviant. And if their personal lives were so unconventional and "sick," surely, as readers were led to believe, their political goals must be every bit as pathological and twisted. The underlying message was: only "sickos" would want to kill the divine emperor. In *Lonely Hearts Killer*, characters in pursuit of alternative and autonomous communities are similarly portrayed with contempt and curiosity in the media. However, Hoshino makes sure we can't rest easy with media storytelling.

A report such as the one Naitô discusses might seem laughable to us today. (Many of us will also think the scenario described sounds like fun.) It might even be easy for those who do not consider themselves to be anarchists to understand why some people wanted to dismantle the emperor system at the turn of the last century given the changes underway in Japan at the time. But why now? Why is the emperor system still a problem in our neoliberal age? While no longer as blasphemous an act as it could have been only two generations earlier, critiquing the emperor system remains largely verboten in the world of Japanese literature. Yet many young Japanese people in particular, especially those who do not consider themselves nationalists, are baffled by any suggestion that the emperor is important (as either a positive or negative figure). Hoshino explains what led him to explore such questions:

> After writing [*Lonely Hearts Killer*], I was asked the following by my students and young writers. "We don't understand why you'd want to problematize the emperor. Is the emperor really that big of a presence in the lives of people over thirty?"
>
> I felt the same way when I was younger. But then I wondered what would happen to the people of Japan if right here and right now the emperor system were abolished? (*Bungei Tokushû: Hoshino Tomoyuki*, 18, translation mine)

The experience of having been a new reporter at the time when Hirohito (whose responsibility in the Pacific War remains contentious) died must have affected the development of this "what if" question he also tells us about in the preface to this English edition. Hoshino's fictional answer is not pretty in the short term even if abolitionism itself is a desirable outcome. Hoshino moves us in the direction of abolition almost imperceptibly at first. He does so with reports of the death of the young emperor, the unprecedented succession of his sister (a topical development given the debates about female heirs in Japan's imperial house), and questions as to "what comes next" in a society increasingly defined and motivated by its obsessions with "security" and "unity."

A novel that asks us to imagine the end of the Japanese emperor system and perhaps even the collapse of Japan as nation state surely qualifies as anti-authoritarian. Hoshino's fiction is also often characterized by critics and readers alike as "difficult," which I take to mean his plots are sufficiently layered and complex so as to preclude a quick or simply "fun" read (although, as you will see, it is quite humorous at times). The greatest "difficulty" this novel presents may be its portraits of the institutions vested with the most authority today. Governments, mass media, policing apparatuses, and hipster coffee shops tend toward the grotesque in this work. These institutions and the brutality they engender elicit interpersonal brutality. The institutions and not the characters who commit shocking acts, Hoshino seems to suggest, are monstrous. In this sense, he couldn't be more unlike Yukio Mishima (to whom he has been compared). Mishima often located the grotesque in the individual (see for example, *The Sailor Who Fell From Grace With the Sea*). The characters in Hoshino's novels might also be "sick," but they are not plagued by inner badness or congenital ailments. Rather, they live in a literally crazy-making society. The novel thus asks us to think about defection – how do we get ourselves out of crazy-making societies?

This brings me to the subject of another earlier Japanese writer to whom Hoshino is not often compared, the proletarian novelist Takiji Kobayashi. Takiji (he is known, for some of us affectionately, by his given name) was tortured to death by the military police in 1933. Conventional wisdom might tell us these two writers could not be more different. Takiji's direct style of realism is considered simple, straightforward, and, to his detractors, sentimental and propagandistic. Hoshino, on the other hand, is considered "difficult," heavily influenced by magical realism, and expressly "literary." Yet these stark contrasts don't hold up to close inspection. One can find stunningly rich and very literary descriptions (of colors, smells, sounds, etc.) in both of their works. Neither has skimped on adjectives. Each writer also dares to explore complex feelings about uncomfortable and tender subjects. Above all, both writers demonstrate a great deal of trust in their readers. They take us through painful journeys, showing us what is wrong or crazy and how some characters respond, but leave to us the work of imagining what comes next. While we always have agency as readers (to imagine different endings, sequels, etc.), some writers (like Mishima) suffocate us with their visions. Hoshino and Takiji insist on participation and dialogue, on a more mutual relationship between text and reader. In his preface to this English edition, Hoshino makes this clear.

This is not to say that Hoshino makes our job as readers easy. We have to stop and think a great deal. For example, his names for nations and relationships are deliberately disorienting, as are his ways of referring to emperors. The emperors in *Lonely Hearts Killer* are referred to throughout as *okami*. *Okami* means "emperor," the "higher-ups," or "the powers that be," but also "proprietress" or "female manager" (of a restaurant, bar, etc.). While *tennô* may be the more common way of referring to the emperor in Japanese, *okami* lends itself to several themes developed in the novel. *Okami* is written phonetically in *katakana* throughout, which leaves available room to invest it with multiple meanings. If written as the term for an emperor in *kanji* (Chinese characters), the character for "above" or "top" would be used, underscoring political and social hierarchy and differential power (*jôge* or "top-down" relations). The homonymous "proprietress" also proves significant, as one character notes, when the young emperor is succeeded by his sister. The structure of the emperor system and the sense of a "continuous" and "uninterrupted" national and cultural identity it suggests have often been invoked to assert "Japaneseness." To some, nothing could be "more Japanese" than the emperor system. The narrator of the first chapter, Inoue, tells us that nationalist youth are calling for a "Restoration" (harking back to the Meiji Restoration of 1868) not long before the *okami*'s death. Mishima seemed to hope for the same. In this novel,

Hoshino directs us toward very different possibilities, but he leaves us at the point where we must make significant interpretive leaps and choices for ourselves.

After considerable handwringing, I decided to translate *okami* as "Majesty." "Highness" might have worked just as well. Neither, as is the case with so much in a novel written by someone who bends and stretches words in unexpected and new ways, is a perfect match. Readers familiar with classical Japanese, for example, might quickly recognize the character names Kisaragi and Udzuki as quirky. They are pre-modern names for the months of February and April. Surely anyone translating serious literature faces similar dilemmas. Do we leave more untranslated and rely on explanatory footnotes? How closely should we adhere to the original sentence structure? Because *Lonely Hearts Killer* is so rich and so complex in the original, I opted for minimal explanation. Hoshino demands quite a bit of his readers, and it seemed only fitting that the translated version reflect that. For my students and me, figuring things out in this novel has been part of the fun.

In an ideal world in which more resources were invested in sharing and communicating the relevant than the comforting or commercial, you would have several translations of this novel to compare and the time to read them all. As it stands, English language readers are not afforded the opportunity to read much contemporary Japanese fiction that challenges stereotypes or demands serious self-reflection. The comforting and the pleasantly distracting sell in Japan and the United States, and many publishers fuel and maintain the parameters of the "marketable" by feeding us that which we are coached to want. I translated this novel because I felt a profound sense of urgency. I wanted my students to read it. I felt (and still feel) like people need to read it. I wish my students had many translations of works by "difficult" Japanese writers like Hoshino and Yoriko Shôno. We are all fortunate that PM Press has made this novel available to English language readers at a time when many bigger presses do not trust that we will want to read and can handle "difficult" literature.

AUTHOR'S PREFACE

For all of you reading this in English.

I had several motivations in writing this work.

Among them was the question: what would happen to Japanese people if the emperor system was abolished today and the emperor disappeared from Japan? I'd been holding onto this question for twenty years, ever since my student days. There are few people in contemporary Japan who think of the emperor as Japan's *raison d'être*. Yet I've felt that if the emperor system suddenly vanished, Japanese people would start racing towards emperor-nationalism – much in the way that people thronged to Judeo-Christian nationalism in America after 9-11. For me, this work was an attempt to make sense of how national identity functions and exists beyond awareness at the unconscious level.

Another motivation was hypothesizing what would have ensued had the Columbine High School incident occurred in Japan. The profound impact that incident had on me stemmed from the likelihood I saw of something similar happening in Japan too. Japanese youth are placed in the same kind of environment as Eric and Dylan (although I suppose this isn't limited to youth). The only difference would be that such an incident wouldn't result in as many deaths because of Japan's strict system of gun control. I wondered then: what form of violence might Japanese Erics and Dylans resort to? This novel is an exploration of that question as well.

I feel like Japanese and American societies, and our entire world today for that matter, have gone mad. When the majority is overtaken by madness, it becomes all the more difficult to explain what madness is or how it manifests. For that reason, I turned to the novel as a venue for trying to make the madness visible.

Unfortunately, serious literature is faced with extinction everywhere in our world, including in Japan. People want to believe they are not crazy, and readers seek out tales that allow them to avoid confronting the madness. And writers respond to such desires and demands by offering comfort.

I don't believe that is the role of the novel. I think the novel is meant to help us understand that we are crazy. After all, we must begin by recognizing our state of affliction if we don't want to surrender to the madness.

This work is arranged in three chapters. The narrator of the second chapter critiques the narrator of the first chapter. The narrator of the third chapter gives perspective on the narrator of the second chapter. By the same token, I ask you as readers to think about the enigmatic narrator of the third chapter.

Tomoyuki Hoshino
March 30, 2008

Translated by Adrienne Carey Hurley

LONELY HEARTS KILLER

Even when His **Majesty** died I wasn't fazed, not even *un poquito*. Devastated youth were showing up in droves according to the TV and newspapers, and we were bombarded with the predictable over-the-top sympathetic blathering and condescending pep talks, but I was the same as ever, going about my business as usual. Put simply, I busted out my video camera. As was my habit when hitting the streets, I put the video finder up to my eye in lieu of glasses and recorded everything I saw just as it was. And I saw what you'd expect: people in His **Majesty**'s forest mourning, repeatedly dabbing their eyes with handkerchiefs, chanting to the Amitabha Buddha, making the sign of the cross, and preaching in the streets. I was called out by some thugs, all dressed in school gear and old enough to know better. "Hey you, what the fuck do you think you're doing, bringing a camera in here like that? People are in mourning." "Heartless." "Disrespectful!" "Inhuman." They told me off while beating me up. But I got those bastards on film and affixed the caption: "After His **Majesty**'s death, there are still strong young men in their prime." I shaded out just their eyes and had the footage streaming on my webcast site. It was pretty unusual for me to be victimized like that; my presence is negligible, and my camera is small enough to fit in my hand, so it's rarely the case that anyone takes notice of me.

What struck me as really strange came on the Monday two weeks after His **Majesty** died when I went in the Isetan department store in Shinjuku. The number of customers wasn't significantly less than usual, but it was incredibly quiet. The silence didn't register with me at first. It just felt like society as a whole was grieving and the atmosphere was somehow heavier, but before long I noticed that couples, families, and friends were not saying a word to each other. They shopped in silence. Employees were not barking out sales pitches and, when they did have to explain something, kept their words to a minimum. Inoffensive classical music played in the background, and beyond that there was nothing to hear except the sounds of shoes shuffling, merchandise being handled, the escalator running, and the electric hum of the lights.

With this new awareness, I looked around to find that no one was having conversations on the trains either. All the more unnatural was how few people were sending email or talking on their cell phones. I hardly received any messages or calls on my own cell. And virtually no one was reading *manga* or books; all the passengers were basically lingering in a daze. I couldn't stand the feeling of being inside a train with other people who were doing nothing but staring vacantly. I wasn't afflicted with whatever had a grip on them, so I opted to get off a stop early and walk. I anticipated more of the same on the streets, but residential neighborhoods were always relatively quiet before anyway, and on the busier streets, the noise of passing cars would make the eerie silence less noticeable.

The silence spread steadily over the net too. The volume of my incoming mail decreased as the number of un-updated homepages and e-zines on hiatus increased. Message boards saw a drop in contributors, and while it was all well and good that a "His **Majesty**'s death" thread was added to a satirical forum, some pathetic guy, who was probably just role-playing to provoke a reaction, unfurled his grandiose diatribe only to have it bomb in the end when no one responded.

It felt like the number of words in the world was decreasing. I can't explain it well, but it was as if there was nothing to talk about — no topics begging to be discussed, no need to chat. The motivation to mutter unnecessary things was gone. I was already someone who thought small talk was meaningless, so I didn't really care, but now that meaninglessness was overpowering, and I remained silent. It wasn't like this after the deaths of Their Previous **Majesties**.

And that must be further proof that His Young **Majesty** was different.

His **Majesty** died a sudden and premature death. Without the slightest warning sign, his lifeless figure was found as if he were asleep, still tucked in bed in the morning. It was determined that he suffered a heart attack while sleeping, but the cause of the heart attack remained unknown. Or at least there was no official announcement. There were no signs of suffering, and people said he must still be dreaming. At the time, I lightheartedly thought I'd like to have the kind of dream that makes you not want to wake up.

Their Previous **Majesties** had all conformed to the national life expectancy and lived a long time, declining little by little and fulfilling their geriatric quota of normative years. We had become accustomed to heirs succeeding after the age of sixty. As a result, the length of time they served as **Majesty** was never all that long. They reflected the aging population of today's world, and people were halfway resigned to this pattern.

After this quietly unchanging series of plain and similar **Majesties,** we finally got someone young. His Young **Majesty** who just died was born after His Previous **Majesty** had passed forty, so he himself was only around forty when he succeeded. His Previous **Majesty** hadn't planned to produce an heir late in life so that the next generation would succeed at a younger age. He just happened to remain single until his forties and finally married only after the health of his father, His **Majesty** before that, was uncertain. Only the deceased knows his true motivations though.

His Young **Majesty** succeeded in mid-life and was like a breath of fresh air. He introduced an atmosphere of newness and made it feel as if we'd been unburdened of the collective death our aging population had shouldered and like our whole society was rejuvenated. He wanted to make a powerful statement at his succession ceremony and stirred up a whirlpool of solidarity and inspiration with his ad-lib proposition. "We must all live life in our own way and, instead of studying the face of another, hold ourselves to be precious and meet one another with respect in this Island Country. Isn't a 'big-as-life' society like that what we all should be building?" The content of his speech was good enough, but for many who heard him, it was His Young **Majesty**'s way of speaking that was truly as "big-as-life." More and more people, especially those in their thirties and forties, felt like they could trust His **Majesty**, that he understood them all. Particularly since he was still single at that age and, moreover, didn't give off any marrying vibes, the growing sector of the population made up of middle-aged singles, divorcés, and even those who live as couples for appearance's sake felt a sense of connection that one could say was more than a bit self-serving. He took on a meaning different from Their **Majesties** before him.

That alone would have made his untimely passing, merely three years after his succession and at the age of forty-six, tragic. People had been so certain that His Young **Majesty**, who seemed so lively and so full of possibilities, surely would have changed things that a bitter sense of having lost out, of having suffered a setback now loomed. Most of all, among those of His Departed **Majesty**'s generation, there were many who expressed being as distraught as if their dearest friend had preceded them in death. Unlike the somber and expressionless periods of mourning and remembrance following the deaths of Their Previous **Majesties**, there was no question that this time the majority of the population was crushed and heartbroken.

But what was it that started to pull people my age into the abyss? According to the news, even after the period of official mourning was over there were youth in their late teens and twenties who had been oblivious to His **Majesty**, but who now were not returning to their jobs or schools, and in some places work was at a standstill. Headlines about "memorial general strikes" were popping up everywhere. They said this phenomenon differed in nature from the sense of loss experienced by the grieving middle-aged generation in that young people had become like imbeciles whose core had been forcibly ripped away from them. They withdrew into their shells, occasionally brooding over something, groaning, stupefied, or simply staring blankly.

For example, the case of the young mid-level commercial company businessman K (28) appeared in the newspaper *Sun Rising*. On the morning when the death was announced, he wasn't particularly shocked or saddened, and since his company was closed on account of the tragedy, he was thinking he might go catch a movie, but while sipping his coffee, he glanced outside his window and saw a class of elementary school students going to school. At that moment, "it was like coming off an all-nighter when everything is hazy," and the energy was sucked out of his chest. He couldn't even get up out of his chair when he finished breakfast and was struck by "a feeling akin to chronic and extreme sleep deprivation" that produced aching from his back through his chest, and he fell asleep just like that. Three days later when his company reopened, he asked his mother P (56), with whom he lives, to phone in to let them know he would be absent. P knew that the death of His **Majesty**, in whom her son had invested little emotion, could not be the reason why he had fallen into such a severe depression. The son who was "always cheerful and eager to talk about everything" became completely silent, so she couldn't know what he was feeling and was left to conclude that surely "layers and layers of accumulated work-related stress had happened to find a means of release on the occasion of His **Majesty**'s death."

Having read about this, my dad looked at me and said, "I've got nothing to worry about."

He went on, "This guy's on the recovered side considering he could respond to the interviewer. Even over at my company the seriously ill kids aren't like that; their parents and friends say it's like they're in critical condition and near death. There's one of them in my department too, a really easy-going young guy, but sometimes he comes out with something so sharp it makes you go 'huh?' He's a good kid, cooperative and upbeat. Well, apparently he's been sleeping straight through and doesn't wake up. Even if his family forces him awake and makes him eat, he falls right back asleep after eating. I'll be damned if the only cause of that is stress from work." He looked over at me again.

My mom added, "It's the ordinary ones who are most at risk, like with any latest trend."

"What I'm worried about is what you could call the results of overprotective, or just plain anal parenting. These kids haven't experienced the dark side of people, and that makes them weaker."

"We're not that naïve," I said a little sarcastically. "And isn't it the other way around anyway? I'm not sure what you mean by the 'dark side' of people, but whether it's dark or light, plus or minus, isn't it the inability to divide things in categories like that that would make someone zonk out and just want to sleep?"

"I don't understand the connection between not being able to tell plus from minus and sleeping." My mom looked like she was earnestly trying to understand.

"Okay, to put it simply, everything's the same, no ups and downs or nuances, just flat. Front and back or left and right are all the same. In a world where you don't know which is which, the ideas of looking forward and moving ahead or looking behind and falling back are pretty meaningless, right? In that kind of situation, all you can do is sleep."

My dad asked, "So, you're saying everything looks gray?"

"Maybe it's because the world's been a dark place since they were born." My mom was still trying.

"Whether it's gray or light or dark doesn't matter. They don't understand those concepts. They don't get it."

"Well, aren't you special then? You can do what you like without caring about how you're closing off your own future."

"It's not as if I'm filming just because I like it. I just can't settle for a job like some people, so I take pictures."

My dad was about to fly off the handle and quickly brought himself under control, but I could see it in his face. "I'm relieved that you don't want to give up who you are, but that doesn't mean it's okay to be conceited."

My mom interceded in a stern tone, "You may be free-lancing, but does that give you the right to think you're better than other people? I'm not saying that confidence isn't important, but it's not necessary to make fun of other people."

"I overstated it when I said *settling* for work. It just set me off when you were focusing on what's involved in making a living."

"Well, you aren't really in the position to make an issue over that now, are you?"

"I know that making a living so you can eat and survive can be a real issue, but a job isn't only about that, right? That's why I also wanted to say that, on the other hand, you can't pick a job just because you say you like it either." I was wasting energy and gradually not even understanding what I was saying myself. My folks are liberal and genuinely invested in trying to be attentive to my life choices. Still, it's almost tragic how much they don't understand. Tragic to them — I don't give it much thought. Parents respond like parents. That's why they kept trying to make their point.

"Shôji, you also need to understand what it's like to be stressed out when you have to do something that isn't fair or perfect. Everyone faces this, and we're all just doing our best to cope."

I unconsciously sneered and said, "My chronic stress is not having stress then, huh? There's just no winning."

"That's enough. Just remember your promise." My dad was suppressing the anger about to flare up again. The promise was that I'd move out and live on my own in three years. The implicit message being that if by then I couldn't make enough to eat, I'd have to give up the camera and get a real job. I'd thrown in the towel and vowed to honor at least the part about moving out in three years.

"I know what you are trying to say, Dad. How will I ever amount to anything by doing what I please without experiencing some of the hardships out there? Won't I be destroyed when coming up against the walls society has in place? Won't you be responsible for my weakness because of how you raised me? You'll wish you'd been stricter with me, right? Isn't that it?"

"Listen, I wouldn't complain if you kept arguing as long as you stopped criticizing the whole world from the safety of your little bubble here. I want you to give a damn about your future, to be strong and push ahead when it comes to choosing your path in life. That's all."

"People who think in terms of pushing ahead or being pushed aside are simpleminded. For them, life must seem like a competition, like a fight to the finish. But it doesn't matter if you win or if you're a total loser, because none of us can die even if we want to. Isn't that why so many people are shocked by the premature death of His **Majesty**?"

I said that just for the hell of it, but if you think about it, I really was right. By assuming the debt to my family for room and board — and this is coming from the vantage point of someone who takes the meals they serve me for granted — I forfeited the right to choose starving to death from the get-go. Therein lies the cost of leeching off your parents. Among the average households of today, you'll find situations like mine everywhere. Parents allow themselves to be consumed while their kids sponge off them for years, and all the while both sides are thinking something isn't right. But since the circumstances are supposed to be part of a temporary and transitional phase, everyone defers the debt collection and hides any fears that they are losing their power to resist. Barring any major outbursts of conflict, year after year passes uneventfully. The upshot of all this being that the cost of staying alive is silence. You reap what you sow, and I can't forgive myself for having capitulated to these terms.

What I'd really like is to document myself having this sort of conversation with my folks on film. I'd want to make it like the story of some stranger out of a cartoon world. Of course, filming won't turn it into someone else's story, so I don't bring my camera into the space I share with my parents.

When it comes down to it, I have no real sense of participating in society. I sell a fraction of what I film for close to nothing, and the only reason I'm not going to die is because I live with my folks in Tokyo's Nerima neighborhood. What keeps me alive isn't myself, but rather society's energy reserves. I don't know how it's all amassed, but I eat up the money and energy society has stored, and that allows me to live.

It's the same for everyone — whether you are a temp, a working stiff, or a slacker. Even if you aren't living at home, you get some kind of allowance or get to borrow money for what your parents hope will lead to a successful career. As long as you aren't too picky, someone my age can find all sorts of part-time job opportunities. The notion of starving to death even though you work hard is unreal, like a faraway dream. The fact that there are so many part-time jobs waiting out there is not the result of any efforts on our part either. We've inherited them. That's why when someone tries to stress to us how self sufficiency is important or how you've got to work to eat, their words don't seem real. I can't even believe in things like "reality" enough to get to that point, let alone feel satisfied.

On the other hand, my generation, which is relatively few in number, is also being crushed under the feet of the elderly who do not work and who make up more than forty percent of the population. They let us eat, but they deny us access. The reason I think I'm missing an authentic sense that I'm alive is because in this world, which is teeming with old people, there's nowhere to participate.

But if I really think about it, it wasn't as if I'd ever participated in society before becoming an adult of working age anyway. Whether it was at West Funabashi elementary in Chiba, in junior high, or even at my public high school where, on the soccer team, I worked to make it to the National New Year's Tournament, I got along well enough with kids in my classes and my teammates, and I didn't stick out, but I wasn't participating either. The proof is that while I always had a clique with lots of people around me, there's not even one person I'd call a friend or still trust today. I was a tag-along. You could say everyone was a tag-along though. Kids who had a close friend they trusted were the freaks, and honestly, those kids also had very nasty personalities. Well, the reality is that they were so energetic and alive that I experienced them as having nasty personalities, and that says a lot more about how strange I was. It wasn't until I recently developed the capacity to connect to another person that I finally realized this.

Analyzing it further, I'd have to say that I have never participated in anything and have been living like a travel writer who merely comments from the sidelines. No matter how much I struggle (and, truth be told, I haven't struggled much), I haven't managed to be the central player in my own life. For example, when I did things like play soccer, it felt so much like a lie, like a dream in which I'd split into two people, that I'd look at myself making a play as if I were someone else. I didn't fall into a depression if I failed, and if I made a nice play, I didn't high-five myself either. I was there, but it seemed like once I woke up, the me I had been watching would disappear like a fleeting dream. Sometimes you'll find a middle-aged man who says he's "exercising self control" by practicing Zen meditation, fasting, jumping in ice-cold lakes, getting pounded by a raging waterfalls, or the like. As someone who has no self over which I intend to exercise control, I don't understand that sentiment. My self is hollow, substantial only on the surface like papier-mâché, and light and sound are all that's projected into the empty space inside through surface holes like my eyes and ears. I'm a person whose existence is like a movie theater. Or maybe it's better to say I'm the video camera that records that light and sound. That's right; my video camera and I are like two peas in a pod.

Finding my true nature wasn't any easier. I stumbled into my role in life by going to trade school to study film instead of pursuing higher education or hunting for a job. I'm not participating in society by becoming one with a lens or a microphone, but I can achieve a genuine sense of occupying my natural place in society. If I try to articulate it, for me, observing unobtrusively is like being a surveillance camera that my physical self discovered in this present world. The reason for having been found is something the camera itself can't know.

Accompanying the growth of my catalogue of filmed images are occasional moments when I feel very sad at the thought that the substance of my worth, what matters about me, is contained in the volume of a disc. I film what's before my eyes. Whether a sparrow chick is hatched, a kindergartner is stabbed to death, a stupid macho jerk is knocked to the ground when his girlfriend slaps his face, or the petals and stamen of plum flowers are rustled by a gentle breeze, I simply record what I see without getting involved. If I become a factor, it's not as if I could make the egg hatch, the person die, the wind blow, or the lovers kiss. What kind of halfway existence is this? Unsettled, incomplete, suspended in midair, betwixt and between, going nowhere, a living corpse, a dead soul.

When I discussed my ideas with other trade school students and their companions, I was surprised by how much they related. They all understood my ideas so well that I felt like I could rest easy with the assurance that no one was participating in the world. If that's the case, then the world is actually uninhabited, empty. Crowded around that emptiness, non-participants like us observe everything with clear eyes. Taking in the spectacle of it all, we must look like a crowd watching a movie. Conventional wisdom has it that there'd be no life without people. But all that's there is a white or silver cloth that we call a screen and, like idiots, we're transfixed, watching and thinking people are really there doing things like chopping down trees. It's like a bad joke to think that a white cloth with no intrinsic life of its own can satisfy the desires of crowds eager to indulge in watching. It's enough to make you wonder if anything in the world exists.

But those same people who agreed with me when I shared my theories grew serious as graduation approached and let slip statements like, "I want the people who see my films to be moved," "I want to give audiences something to think about," or "I want to change the world." I felt betrayed. These people didn't truly understand what I meant by being powerless, and my face involuntarily contorted into a grimace. Those who fell apart after His **Majesty** died are no different from that bunch.

That's why I wanted to make my graduation project by myself, but the school required that the projects be collaborative, so reluctantly I had to take a partner. That was **Iroha**. Like me, Iroha had intended to make her project independently, and she unhappily surrendered to working with me. She was in a foul mood when we first met, and she made a horrible first impression. Trying to get through it, I asked her what kind of project she wanted to make.

She snapped back, "It doesn't matter even if I tell you because I'd planned to do it alone, so now it's ruined."

"Okay. So, why don't we do our halves separately and present them omnibus?"

"As if that would make things any better."

"Listen, I'm not getting to make what I want either, so can you just get over it?"

"I see. You're the kind of person who can't collaborate."

"You're saying that to me?"

"This sucks."

"Gee, thanks."

"No, I mean this school."

"No shit."

"It's pretty dumb to know school sucks and still keep coming."

"Same goes for you."

From that point on, we had an understanding, and Iroha and I arrived at a project that only could have been made by the two of us. We each filmed the other filming, quietly exchanging barbs, and drawing it out. Then we took our two films, overlaid and rerecorded them as one and called the final product "Mixed Cameras." Iroha and I looked at each other through the cameras, and the footage of our faces was superimposed into a double image, which was, for us, a nightmare that transcended the image. Faces that look ready to break apart speak. It's like a similar alternate world affixed right beneath the surface of the visible world. And while all that talking seems like it should be a conversation, it's actually a strange and awkwardly timed monologue on top of monologue. We each expected to connect to the other, but we really went past each other and remained self-contained; we both just happened to be there. You'd think that aligned in the same space like that we would have merged into a single body, but it was like two totally disconnected people. Iroha and I sealed away the project as if to make sure we'd never have to look at it again.

I worried when I didn't hear from Iroha after His **Majesty** died. She invariably commented whenever I uploaded new footage on my website. Sometimes she'd include ideas for production outlets for my work. But I didn't hear from her during those weeks.

A month had passed since His **Majesty** died when she finally did contact me. Greeting me after I'd rushed to her family home in Yokohama's Motomachi district, she looked as worn out and haggard as driftwood.

"I was feeling blue at the thought that maybe even you had collapsed."

"Glad to know you worried about me. I've had a rough time looking after someone."

"Were you suckered into some kind of film unit expedition or something?"

"Custodial duty for Miko."

"'Custodial duty'?"

"Can you believe it? It's like he completely lost it."

Iroha's lover, Mikoto, was renting the week-to-week apartment where they lived together. He temporarily checked out when His **Majesty** died and wouldn't eat unless fed, she said. I hadn't yet met Mikoto, who started dating Iroha after she finished film school, but based on what I'd heard from Iroha, he was an easygoing guy, not prone to showing off or likely to elicit that behavior in others either, and basically I imagined him to be a pretty regular guy. Fundamentally like me in her eyes-and-ears-only approach to society as a documenter on the sidelines, Iroha for the first time started saying things like images aren't just records, but also a means of expression after she started seeing Mikoto.

"Even if I don't consider it more than a record of what I saw as it was, people who are watching can impose their own interpretations and give the image meaning, so even if it bugs me, my film is still going to end up expressing something. For better or worse, that becomes a source of power. If you don't give this some careful thought, even if you make a point of shooting message-less images, they'll still stick some kind of popular message on them and pull the rug out from under your feet, Shôji Inoue."

I couldn't believe my ears. She was talking just like all the stuck-up, sensible types from trade school.

"You can't affect society from the inside. You can't dismantle the master's house with the master's tools. If you try to move into the nucleus of power to make a difference, you'll end up getting changed yourself. The number of examples of people succeeding at doing it that way is zero. We can only destroy the system from the outside. That's even more of a reason why we've got the power to destroy it with our diary films — by not entering society and acting only as observers."

Iroha said that too. Of course, my sense of being ineffectual wasn't going to be undermined by this pretense of concern. But still, I was won over by Iroha's power of persuasion. I introduced fiber optics, launched my independent, personal broadcasting station, and obsessed over getting stuff on air (well, online really). So that's how I indirectly felt Mikoto's influence. I had a bad feeling about his optimism, but I couldn't help persisting with even that small boost of energy I derived from him by way of Iroha.

That same Mikoto collapsed all too easily.

"He's a wreck inside, and sometimes you can see the suffering in his face, but he won't talk about it. He'd be reading the newspaper or watching TV and understand what I'd say or write, but he wouldn't talk or write on his own. He'd go to the bathroom or drink when he was thirsty, but other than that, he wouldn't do anything or want any meals. So I'd cook some stew and make him eat it, reminding him that he needs to eat if he wants to stay alive. He'd look up at me startled, and the tears would well up. He'd choke on the stew like it was poison. Am I really so cruel? He's so helpless. He'd be right there in front of me, but wouldn't do a thing to stay alive." In one breath, Iroha vented her cumulative frustration.

Without missing a beat, I asked, "Did he say anything about His **Majesty**'s death?"

"Hello! That's what I was trying to explain. He wouldn't talk. No matter how simple my questions were, when he finally got to answering, the only sounds that came out weren't even words. He eventually would start spitting up, so I stopped asking questions."

"Wow. Hey, Iroha, you met Mikoto after His **Majesty**'s Era began, right? Maybe what we thought was Mikoto's own vitality was really just hope he'd invested in His **Majesty**."

"No, that's not it. Miko couldn't care less about His **Majesty**. He even said so, that people could make a big fuss over His **Majesty**'s youth, but they are the ones who are actually putting in their labor, and it's not as if their biological clocks were going to be turned back."

"Now that's straight talk."

"Far from it. His **Majesty** raised society's expectations so much that he had the potential to impact government, a state of affairs that should serve as a serious red flag."

There was a faction of youth calling for a Restoration and advancing a plan to reinstate His **Majesty**'s political rights, and they garnered an unexpectedly large amount of support.

Here's what they said: Politicians today have fallen out of favor because they only work for a handful of vested interests, and those intellectuals and media moguls who could claim some charismatic popularity abused their power until they ended up destroying themselves. No politicians who have since emerged had enough support to take control of the government. At best, we are under crisis conditions in which the "sensibly nonpartisan" NGO-types who move in and out of Parliament's revolving door have exposed their own incompetence. If we extend political rights to His **Majesty** and he's elected, he could attract support that crosses party lines, and, in that case, without any barriers to him taking charge of the government and without harming democracy in the least, our movement could give new life to the shell of this so-called democracy!

It was an impossible proposition, but society was in an uproar, eagerly waiting to see whether or not His **Majesty** could be that much of a political leader.

But for me, their sensational message smacked of mania mixed with a syrupy romance novel and just like the kind of fantasy the mass media love. That could be because no one around me thought it would make a lick of difference whether the prime minister was His **Majesty** or anybody else for that matter. The media denounces political incompetence and corruption, but if the people around me or I were to tell it, the whole political scene is nothing more than groups of statesmen being moved around and played with by some unknown apparatus. Even if there weren't any politicians, society would keep running on autopilot. Or maybe like how the seasons change, governments are one of those things that spin around on their own. That's why even if a really strong leader emerges, that person can't be more than what the machine dictates. We lack the optimistic energy to invest hope in or count on that sort of system. The only people who thought, without any basis, that society would change after His **Majesty**'s era began were relatively older. There probably aren't many people who can so much as imagine feeling connected to a government. That's why the responses of people like Mikoto struck me as a little suspicious and exaggerated.

"Iroha, do you think His **Majesty**'s death wasn't the direct cause of Mikoto's speech loss? That it was nothing more than the trigger that finally sparked an outpouring of accumulated stress?"

"I don't want to think about stupid theories like that anymore. Unless Miko tells me what's going on inside his head, there's no way for me to know no matter how hard I try. Speculating won't do me any good and isn't worth the effort. I stay by his side because he'd literally starve to death if I didn't. But sometimes I wonder if maybe I'm not just another source of stress for him, because he'll wear himself out trying to communicate something he's dying to tell to me because I'm the one who happens to be there. And at night, I have to pry open his mouth to make sure he swallows his sleeping pills. I wish I could be a robot with no feelings."

"But because you're not a robot, Mikoto improved enough to try and say something, right?"

"Who knows? I hope that's the case."

"Has he gone back to work yet?"

"They're really understaffed, so they want him back, but it'll take a little while longer before he's up for that."

I tentatively asked, "Been filming?"

"Oh, I've been filming. Like I can't get enough of it." Iroha answered like she was spewing exhaust. "And I played the film I took right in front of Miko. The image of him muttering nonsense reappeared right before his eyes. That's pretty fucked up, huh?"

Iroha started breathing deeply at that point.

"But I still keep filming him. He stares at his own horrible-looking self without protesting, so I take more films of that to show him. It's gone on and on like that..." Iroha looked up and counted. "Well, it went on like that more times than I can count. At this point, they're pretty much like mirrors. The monitor Miko will be watching shows Mikos watching countless Mikos. To tell you the truth," she took another deep breath, "the one about to go crazy is me."

I could easily imagine those images. You'd see Mikoto from behind and in front of him would be the monitor, and in that monitor there'd be another shot of Mikoto's back, and in front of that a monitor with yet another shot of Mikoto's back with a monitor, and all those countless simulated Mikotos simultaneously moan and groan. You'd get into it and keep going. The person doing the filming, Iroha, isn't visible. Mikoto is a pond toad surrounded by reflections of himself, and Iroha, who is capturing that, simply looks on. There's no exchange between them.

"Was Mikoto okay with that?"

"I'm not sure. It wasn't just images of him. I showed him films I made with you and other stuff too. His face lit up a little when he watched. And it's not like he just watched passively. All of a sudden, he'd scribble something in his notebook and then show it to me. It was stuff like random lines, different versions of the same face, or a sketch of a creepy uninhabited town, and I have no clue what he meant by it all. One day, out of the blue, he said, 'I get it already. I get it, so turn it off.' I asked, 'What do you get?' 'The whole city and this room are full of **Majesties**.' Miko could talk, and all of a sudden I was the one who was dumbstruck. I just smiled."

"So it was like shock therapy?"

"I don't know. I don't know what Miko saw in those films. I can't even figure out how we hooked up in the first place. Miko and I are like two pebbles that rolled close to each other but don't have any authentic connection. Our personalities are totally different."

I didn't say so, but as she talked I thought about how anything you put on film ends up seeming removed, like a stranger's story. Wouldn't Iroha understand why that alone would make her films uncomfortable for Mikoto? It was obvious to me that she had applied concepts from that hideous "Mixed Cameras" to filming him. Knowing how horrible that was, how could she further close in on him by making claustrophobic films while he was in that state? I was exhausted just from imagining how awful it would be. I sighed and thought to myself, "She sure has balls."

"You do the same thing," Iroha said to me in a tired voice. "I wasn't doing it because I like it. I thought I had to do something, and words are so unreliable. Before I knew it, I was filming. I scared myself, because I started filming Miko without taking the time to think about how insensitive I was being to him. That's the kind of people we are, you and me. Even if someone was killed right in front of us, we'd probably keep filming without feeling anything."

Iroha fell silent for a bit, looking me in the eyes, and then she pulled a DVD out of her bag and put it on the table.

"I want you to watch 'Infinite Hell' too."

She gave me a cold stare. I felt like I was being subjected to an elaborate loyalty test. And something inside me warned that I was getting swept up in all her talk. Why was she so insistent about showing me her secrets with Mikoto, whom I hadn't even met? But with a shame I couldn't explain, I took the DVD.

Iroha's mom had prepared an extravagant stone kettle full of crabmeat and insisted I stay, so even though Iroha looked like she wanted me to leave, I stuck around to eat.

"You haven't been by for a while, Shôji," Iroha's mom gently chided.

"No free time for broke folks," I gave as my pat answer. What's more, it was a lie. I don't think about money when I'm filming. And at any rate, I'd given up on earning any. For someone who lives off others, nothing is more depressing than the thought of working in order to eat. Slackers who'd say the same are a dime a dozen, but it's just an excuse. They are nothing more than words for fabricating an "authentic sense of being alive."

Mikoto might be a little different in that regard. He worked in the news department at a TV station. Even though he was young, he quickly was able to buy an apartment in Chiba, where he lived with his parents, whom he'd brought up from Daisen. According to Iroha, Mikoto's parents had no interest in getting by in the world, so the whole family had ended up in dire straits. Mikoto started supporting his family financially when he was still in high school. He rented the week-to-week apartment in the heart of the city after he got together with Iroha, and they shacked up there together off-and-on, on a part-time basis. Mikoto collapsed while he was with her, so his parents had been left to fend for themselves.

"This girl never comes home to visit now that she's moved out. And she acts like a stranger, telling me she doesn't want to trouble anyone when I suggest bringing Miko over here or to his parents' place so that we can all look after him until he gets better."

"Don't talk about Miko like he's a stray cat, Mom."

"If his folks are having a hard time, bring him here. I can be a big help. You can't say that you couldn't use a hand with dark circles under your eyes like that. Honey, you're exhausted." Iroha's mom looked to me for a reply, but I got out of it by trying to change the subject.

"So, has Mikoto been by to visit much?"

Iroha answered in an irate voice, "Only on Mom's birthday and New Year's Eve."

"It'd be nice if he were more eager to come by like you, Shôji."

"Please! He comes here when it suits him. Don't encourage him."

"Hey, I'm not looking for anything."

"Tell me something I don't already know."

"Next time, why don't you bring Miko too, and the four of us can have sukiyaki or something? Or why don't we have a dance party? It'd be perfect — two guys and two women. I'll do some folk dancing. And you can do an old flamenco."

"So, I'll meet him for the first time at a house party?" I blurted it out without thinking.

"What? You two haven't met yet?"

A very exasperated Iroha answered, "Shôji doesn't get along with optimistic people. That's why."

"But Shôji's optimistic, isn't he?"

"I think Iroha is the one who hates optimists. She's projecting."

"You get along well with Miko, so wouldn't he and Shôji be likely to hit it off?" Iroha's mom looked to me for confirmation, and I obliged by saying, "Absolutely."

"I haven't seen past the surface of this guy. I'd be devastated if Shôji copped an attitude and said something negative. And quit humoring me. It's not funny." Iroha raised her voice and looked agitated.

"I'd say you're the one with an attitude. Miko isn't better yet, and doing something fun together might be good for him. Why don't we call him now? It'll be fine, Honey. I'll make sure everything goes well."

"Actually, I can't stay long today." I glanced sideways at Iroha and then asked her mom, "Have you been learning how to use your computer? Can you see my webcast yet?" I made a big effort to shift topics.

"I'm trying. I'm really trying, but it's hard without anyone around enough to teach me."

"You're never going to make it in a tough world like this if you can't take care of things on your own." Again, my heart wasn't in what I said.

"You're so serious, Shôji."

Iroha responded to her mom's absurd impression of me with an incredulous laugh.

"I'm not serious. If left to my own devices, I'd settle like dust in the nooks of a tatami mat. And if you take too long, you'll end up swept aside like dust. That's why you really ought to get going and learn how to use your computer, at least enough to be able to view my webcast."

"Shôji, would you give me a little training course? I'd pay you. You could use the money, right?"

I wanted to ask Iroha's mom if His **Majesty**'s death had affected her, but with Iroha, who was consumed with Miko's condition, right there, I didn't.

Iroha's folks split up when she was nine. Her dad fell in love with another woman, she got pregnant, and he decided to get remarried to her. The relationship with Iroha's mom was already in shambles, so no one objected to the divorce. As part of the settlement, Iroha's mom got some real estate, monthly alimony, and child support, and that enabled her to raise Iroha. She'd worked the register at a grocery store until Iroha finished trade school, but Iroha said her mom never suffered much to speak of and that she fundamentally knew very little about the world. But what "world" was she supposed to know? It's safe to say that, like me, Iroha's mom lives off of others. But the difference is that without questioning, she won't figure that out.

People like Iroha's mom won't be fazed as long as the next **Majesty** succeeds. For them, even if something a little out of the ordinary happens, with time, things will return to normal. They'll feel that way without really thinking about it. The possibility of the world's original nature having been laid bare probably doesn't even occur to them. I'll bet they truly believe that **Majesties** continue on, as does the changing of seasons, and while the nature of the circumstances enabling them to live may change, the essence of everything stays the same.

As to whether or not that itself will change, I can't yet venture a guess, but certain signs have appeared in the mass media. First of all, His **Majesty** died young and single, leaving behind a sister eleven years his junior as his successor. He had two other younger sisters, but each of them had married and was now registered with her partner's family, so the thirty-five year old sister was next in line. This was, of course, reported soon after His **Majesty** died, but it wasn't until about a month later when the shock of His **Majesty**'s death had subsided that they put together close-up stories on the unprecedented nature of this development. Even so, before the State Funeral, in a conservative discussion that swayed public opinion, people divided up into two main camps, those who welcomed the change as the advent of a new era and those saddened at the prospect of losing the last of something.

I don't invest much in society or how a **Majesty** and society are linked, so I didn't relate to either camp. I didn't see how it was going to change anything. What interested me was how the holed-up youth were going to take Her New **Majesty**. When the succession ceremony is held, will they return to lives independent of Her **Majesty** as before and vow never again to be affected by any **Majesty**, nipping the connection in the bud? Or will they paint their cheeks red in wild anticipation and wave the flag? Or will they still stay holed-up like they are now?

I had a strong desire to meet Mikoto and talk to him. What was his take? How would he see all this? People like us aren't supposed to believe in God and all creation. What if we stumbled after His **Majesty**'s death? What does it mean for us to suffer a breakdown like we'd been betrayed?

But I didn't even know Mikoto. I heard about him from Iroha all the time, so I felt as though I knew him, but I didn't have a sense of the real person. I didn't know what he looked like, and I'd never heard his voice. And on top of it all, I felt pretty low about seeing the video footage before meeting him in person for the first time.

As much as I left Iroha's house with a heavy feeling, strangely mixed into that was a sense of hopefulness. I made my way home with the conflicted heart of an old-time soldier having just received his marching orders.

I watched the video as soon as I got home, while I thought I still had the life in me to do it. I kept telling myself that Iroha would be satisfied simply for me to watch it. The images didn't exceed my expectations, but the damage I suffered sure did.

All you could see inside the dreary apartment room was a TV and coffee table. Mikoto was filmed from behind, so I couldn't see his face or tell whether he was in agony or enjoying himself. Iroha was undisplayed on this side of the image, or rather, behind the camera, and faint sounds of her breathing, bones creaking, clothes rustling, and sniffling, along with the noise of camera parts moving to zoom in or adjust the picture, made her mood seem tense. Mikoto was being observed by Iroha, without any exchange of words.

He never turned around. He watched the picture across the coffee table from him. And once in a while, he'd write something down in a notebook on the coffee table. Iroha said they weren't words, but scribbled drawings, but even when she tried to zoom in with a sustained close-up of the notebook, I couldn't tell. Not identifiably singing or chanting, a droning voice reverberated through it all as if thirty Mikotos were all humming a strange tune. At times, he'd point at the screen and cup his lowered head in his hand, but he'd soon lift his head back up again like he'd reconsidered something.

What knocked the wind out of me was the sensation I had as a viewer. The Mikoto on the screen, whom I was feverishly watching, was the Mikoto of a day ago, of the past; he no longer existed. And that Mikoto of a day ago was watching the Mikoto of even a day earlier. The Mikoto of two days ago was watching the Mikoto of three days ago, and the Mikoto of three days ago was watching the Mikoto of four days ago. In short, within the picture, there was a Mikoto for each of the roughly thirty days between His **Majesty**'s death and Mikoto's recovery, and they were all confined there, left as layers taken out of that period of time and placed on public display.

I was seized by the feeling something bad would happen and turned around to look behind me. Sitting there on a tripod and not in use was my camera, its lens pointed directly at me. If a future me was peering at me through the other side of that lens, then my fate was sealed. I felt as though I was being robbed of time.

Those images went on for what must have been about fifteen minutes. Then, from behind the camera Iroha's fatigued voice could be heard saying, "That's it for today," and her figure intruded into the picture. She turned off the film Mikoto was watching, inserted a different disc, and disappeared back behind the camera.

"Here's a new film Shôji Inoue shot. It goes from Shibuya to Shinjuku, but everything seems different from usual, huh? Check it out, hardly anyone is talking." From that point, Iroha moved into a nonstop play-by-play analysis.

Sure enough, that was the film I made and uploaded for my webcast. The Starbucks' customers silently drinking coffee in counter seats facing the six-way pedestrian crossing, the crowds silently crossing the intersection, the quiet car on the Yamanote Line where hardly anyone fiddled with cell phones, and inside the Isetan that was transformed into utter silence.

Mikoto leaned forward over the coffee table and started counting the people shown on the screen. His muttering voice affected me. Finally, the camera arrived in Shinjuku's Chinese-Town and Mikoto turned around to face the camera for the first time and said, "I get it already. I get it, so turn it off!"

"What are you saying you get?" Iroha asked while switching off the DVD power.

"That the whole street and even this room are full of **Majesties**."

Iroha fixated on Mikoto, but was speechless. Mikoto waved his hand and laughed. "I get it. You want to say His Young **Majesty** is dead, don't you? The only people in this room are you and me, right? I'm sane. But since His **Majesty** died, I've had way more than enough of him. Everyone's a **Majesty**. Even though it may not seem like it."

Iroha laughed like she was sucking in air, and she turned off the camera. It went dark. Blue screen.

I was trembling all over. The facial expression of the Mikoto I first saw was relaxed with the enlightened clarity of a happy Buddha. The voice of the Mikoto I first heard was a deep and resonant baritone. And above all was that last line he uttered.

No matter how many times I returned to it, I had no idea what Mikoto was saying. And yet my heart was racing. This nutcase Mikoto was spouting nonsense.

I was agitated and even angry. It was cryptic to show me only those scenes. What will I understand if I don't first get to meet Mikoto and then see the film and ask Mikoto about it? All it's going to do is drive me crazy and make me more anxious. Deal with it on your own, the two of you. Don't drag me into it. You've kept me outside the mosquito curtain until now after all!

That's right. I am outside the mosquito curtain. Not just in relation to this problem. I felt I'd been deceived in many ways and like everything was unfair. But I also had a guilty conscience. In the midst of a breakdown, Mikoto was swimming in the thick of his own role. I wasn't about to understand what that role was. Iroha feeds off of drama in her relationship with Mikoto. She's the one playing a role in their relationship. And yet I'm the one outside the mosquito curtain. I'm not a player. I'm just an observer. As much as I was enraged over this unreasonable manipulation, the shame of me alone being an onlooker ate away at me. By whose fault and for what reason had I fallen into this subterranean mess?

All that aside, I still had to comment on the film for Iroha. I wanted to do so in person, as opposed to over email or the phone. My initial plan was for us to get together tomorrow, the next day, or whenever worked for the three of us to meet at Dormir, the Sleeping Café in Higashi Aoyama. I pulled myself together and wrote an email. I visualized the scene while writing. In the Narcissus Cell, the private yellow room that was a usual base for Iroha and me to take afternoon naps, our films would be running on the plasma display on one of the four walls. We'd doze off, lounging in the reclining seats shaped like red lips. We'd casually wake up and sip herbal tea, and even though the content wouldn't be significant, we'd create an atmosphere thick with tension as we took turns exchanging heated words. Under the indirect yellow lighting, I'd tell a savage little story, Iroha would crack up, and an archaic smile like the Buddha's would spread across Mikoto's face as he looked at Iroha with sleepy eyes.

I had a piercing pain in my chest. I knew I had it wrong. My intuition told me that even though it may have seemed possible, that was only a vision, one that would never materialize. I wanted the three of us to meet innocently like that. But such a moment was lost. Maybe it was because I watched the DVD, maybe it was because His **Majesty** died, or maybe it was because Mikoto changed. Whatever it was, there was no going back. Our relationship had already started evolving into something new.

I wanted to talk with Mikoto. I erased the email message without hitting "send" and went to bed.

Spring appeared suddenly, as if it had chosen that day. A whispering deep chill had lingered to the point that one had wondered, up until then, whether spring was on its way or the earth was headed into an ice age. Even though the frost remained and, to make matters worse, the darkness hadn't lifted from people's hearts, accompanying the edge of night, an almost scalding hot wind began to blow in from the southwest, plaguing people with scary dreams in the wee hours and working them into a tizzy. But once the eastern sky showed signs of light, it vanished back to who knows where. Waking from a light sleep and dragging myself out of bed at the break of dawn, I was surprised that my thin long-sleeved shirt was almost too hot for the weather. When I went out to the veranda to take a look, there were cherry blossoms everywhere, like flesh-colored snow that had fallen and now lay accumulated under the golden morning sun. Fanned by the hot wind, the trees had born buds all over. But the air seemed loaded with yellow sand. Rooftops, street surfaces, and leaves were stained the color of shrimp chips, as if they had been dusted with royal ashes. Bombarded by the humidity, the stench of pollen, the startling pink cherry tree branches, and a lack of sleep, my head felt stuffed up with sand and ready to burst.

This was the day of His **Majesty**'s State Funeral, and I had woken up early to go filming with Iroha. Four days after watching "Infinite Hell," I finally crawled out from under the oppressive feeling and made up my mind to call her. But she didn't give enough of a shit to ask how I'd felt and, instead, asked if I was free to hang out with her on the last day of March when they'd hold the State Funeral. I said I'd be up for going somewhere like Shinjuku Chinese-Town and then nonchalantly suggested that Mikoto join us. Iroha cheerfully replied with an "okay" and said she'd see if he'd come.

When I'd finished getting ready, I started up my camera and walked out the front door. The morning light was saturated with moisture and shining sideways at a sharp angle. The blindingly golden line of light enhanced the pale peach hue of the cherry blossom petals. As if responding to the light, the flowers quivered, spreading out like false eyelashes, stretching out from the stamen to the petals. A white-eye flew down and slipped its head into the thick of the petals, breathing in the nectar. I got as close as I could and zoomed in to shoot that unlikely intimate encounter. The outstretched branches rocked at the slightest gust of hot wind. And a bee, its down dyed yellow by the light, buried itself in a flower to get at the pistil and was covered by petals. I broke into a sudden sweat, so I took off my shirt and tied it around my waist.

The image in my head was the rendezvous at the aquarium scene from the movie *The Lady From Shanghai*. A married Rita Hayworth and not-yet overly fat young Orson Welles for some reason decide to have their secret tryst at an aquarium at night. And even though it's very late, a class of elementary school students is there on a field trip, and the couple's kiss is observed. Behind them, with an eyeball the size of Rita Hayworth's head, an enormous red snapper, moray, or tropical fish swims around gracefully in lieu of mood music. Of course, no fish with an eyeball like that exists, but I was thoroughly enchanted by its lewdness.

With that style in mind, I imagined a cherry blossom as big as someone's head and set out on my mission, chasing down one flower after another with my camera. Perhaps because it was early on a holiday morning, no one was at the station. I passed through the turnstile, walked to the platform, and waited for the first train.

The interior of the train was also sparsely populated. The light cast a diagonal line the color of yellow roses all the way to the far end of the car, and it looked like an evening in the countryside. A passenger aboard was irritated with me, but that didn't deter me. I continued to look through my camera, usually in his direction. He stood up from his seat and moved out of range.

Soon I noticed I was the only one in the car. While dozing off, I'd captured that last old man on film, fuming, "I'm going to get the conductor," but even he didn't return.

A bright cherry blossom hue piercing through the train car was reflected in my eyes. Or should I say it was reflected in my camera-eye? The cherries emitted a florid stuffiness that was suffocating. I was so hot that I wanted to strip off even my t-shirt and underwear.

I pressed my camera lens up against the eastward window, which was shot through with morning sun. The dazzlingly hot mustard-colored fields of greens spread out towards the horizon. A lemon yellow river flowed, trailing the wind. I was about to be sucked into the rhythm of the railway, with which I was in sync.

Well, not really. I hallucinated all that. In a residential district in the heart of the city, the rooftops were covered with waves of yellow sand. That was all. Here and there, reddish cherry blossoms fountained out close to the earth, and a peachy haze of dust stirred skywards. Perhaps reflecting the earthbound cherry trees, the sky was swashed in a yellowish flesh-tone.

The world was empty. The only living things were cherry blossoms. I got off the train alone at Shinjuku, and there wasn't even anyone in the office district where I walked. It was as if all the people had been turned into flesh-colored flower petals on the trees, or the trees had been infected with a cherry blossom disease. Cherry blossoms were stuck on the branches of fat trees, baby trees, and lanky trees springing forth in the gaps between buildings. I documented the accident of it all on film and recorded it inside myself. Then I ducked into an alley to jerk off. The pink semen fell on the yellow sand that had blown in the night before and balled up into the shape of millet dumplings and gave off a sweet smell.

I killed some time by taking a nap under the sun in Central Park. I awoke to find somebody loitering around in a t-shirt. I looked up at the faintly yellow and blurry sky that stretched out. With each increase in people, the cherry blossoms grew fewer. The surroundings filled up with the smell of human beings. I stood up and hurried off to the meeting-spot in Chinese-Town.

Iroha was already randomly filming the surroundings under the Suzaku Gate. She aimed her lens at me when she saw me. I picked up my pace and waved at her with a smile. Iroha smiled too and jibed, "Such shitty acting!"

"Isn't it wonderful? This is fabulous. And all on account of the cherry blossoms."

"It's a little freaky. Like something bad's gonna happen."

I looked around and asked, "Isn't Mikoto coming?"

"He's coming," Iroha turned her camera away from me and pointed it toward the town. "He'll be here. He's meeting up with us later."

"Did he go to the State Funeral?"

Iroha simply cocked her head a bit. I returned the "Infinite Hell" DVD and said, with deep emotion, "That was actually the first time I'd seen Mikoto's face."

"He had no expression, huh?"

"Like a statue of the Buddha."

"He's a character, but he does have a hard face to remember, doesn't he?"

"Does he get mistaken for lots of people?"

"For a statue of the Buddha."

"How about to His **Majesty**?"

"What?" Iroha sounded pissed and looked at me through her camera. "They don't look anything alike. You saw him, so you know, and still you go linking them together like that!"

"Maybe it's His **Majesty** who looks like a lot of people."

"Knock it off. You're gonna drive me nuts. Miko doesn't even understand what he said himself."

"But I don't think what he said was confused or incoherent. Why don't you watch that film again?"

"You must be joking. Why don't you just leave it alone?"

"Okay, but then why did you show it to me?"

"Why did I? Well, I guess I felt like it'd lift the curse. 'Cuz if it was just me, it seemed like I'd stay cursed."

"A curse, huh? You showed me a curse?" I didn't feel good about that. Especially since now that I'd seen it, my intuition told me there was no going back. "What are you going to do now that I'm cursed?"

"I'll just expose someone else to it, and you'll be fine."

"You'll expose someone else to it? A curse isn't something you can treat lightheartedly like somebody else's cold that doesn't affect you."

"You were being weird, so I was just dishing it back."

"You're not funny."

"You neither."

Even while our conversation trickled on like that, each of us stared at our camera monitors like they were compasses and wandered around the Shinjuku Chinese-Town. So our unrelated conversation was recorded along with the neighborhood scenery. When I look back on the rawness and energy in those shots of Iroha and me, I experience a burning self-hatred, shame, and contempt. Tangled up in the lines cast by the saccharine intentions between us, we look hideous. It's painful to watch. But still, my relationship with Iroha continues, and the bond between us now boils down to resisting the pull of self-contempt. Because a camera has usually been running between us, we have always risked creating distance in our relationship and ending up with the lifeless bond of strangers. Just watching how disgusting I am when hanging out with her pushes me to the brink of being an onlooker. But I always manage to clear that hurdle and remain a player, as Iroha's friend. I think that kind of friendship is the real thing.

Seeing as it was a holiday, few people were out and about in the neighborhood. That said, there weren't any significant changes. I spend a lot of time filming around Shinjuku Chinese-Town, so I'd notice any difference. As you'd expect, almost no one was out to view the flowers. We proceeded along with our own mood in tact and at a relaxed pace, pausing, buying things to eat, veering off into alleys, and venturing up to high points where we could look down on the city, which was in a cherry blossom-induced stupor. We ate Taiwan Beef Noodles at a stall, got some take-out peach rolls for dessert, went into a back alley where we climbed the emergency stairway of a lead pipe building, and, from the fifth floor, looked out on the world. The sky covering the rows of houses looked completely yellow and hazy. And once again, with a carefree attitude, we went on and on about what a lovely spring day it was.

We then headed to a porcelain shop, where Iroha bought two scorpion shaped chopstick holders and I bought two cobalt blue noodle bowls. I didn't have a special reason for getting two, but Iroha was uncharacteristically curious and asked, "Why did you get two items, too? Aren't there three people in your house? Are you giving one to someone?"

"What's it matter how many I get?"

"It doesn't really, but if there is someone, I think you're being really secretive about it."

"How come you're asking about that all of a sudden? Have I ever given you the third degree over Mikoto?"

"No. But it has been a while since we went out filming together."

"It may have been a while, but before we were only getting together once every couple of months or so."

"Yeah, but ..."

"Iroha, what's up with you? You're so needy all of a sudden."

"I guess."

"You want me to get a bowl for you too?"

"No, it's okay. Well, actually, that'd be nice."

I added one more, which incidentally had a painted pale blue fish and a matching porcelain soupspoon. Of course, it goes without saying that episode was recorded from start to finish on Iroha's camera.

The woman in the shop warned us, "The yellow sand started blowing outside, so be careful." But we were so high on the thrill from buying the bowls that we weren't prepared. We opened the door to leave the shopping building and were immediately assaulted by a gust of completely yellow wind. My face was pelted with tiny stones, and my eyes were battered. Iroha wears hard contacts and was even more miserable. She cried like she was about to collapse from the barrage of sand in her face and made a speedy retreat back into the building's bathroom. I'd never seen a sand storm that fierce.

A while back, we started getting terrible yellow sand storms that would blow in from the Chinese continent when winter would begin to give way to spring. Forest fires on the continent were strong enough to expand the deserts, and dire predictions abounded about how with no rain to lift the drought, the overflow of sand would be stirred up more and more until it filled in the entire East Chinese Sea and connected these ancient islands to the continent.

Looking semitransparent like a mirage about to vanish, everything in sight would be obscured in yellow on days when the sand blew. Identifiable things were draped in a turmeric veil. Even though everyone called it sand, what crossed the sea was actually dust produced by the forest fires that was fine enough to invade any crevice. And it would hurt like hell when that dust got into your eyes, nose, or mouth, where it would suck the moisture out of mucous membranes where it settled. It would work its way through fabric, even getting into your underwear, causing crotch sores and rashes. Your hair would be as brittle as dried seaweed. You'd be itchy everywhere the yellow sand touched you, and there was a rise in the prevalence of yellow sand-related allergies.

Iroha came back with the capillaries all over her face, not to mention her eyes, puffy and red. I concurred with her suggestion that, while we did have the option of trying to wait out the storm in that building, people were saying it would only get worse, so we should take off now and make our way to the dim sum restaurant where Mikoto would meet us. I covered my nose and mouth with a handkerchief, hunkered down, and flew outside. Because I'd forgotten my glasses, I held onto the hand of Iroha, who was equally blinded, and we did our best to turn our backs to the onslaught of sand and make progress backwards. The dry wind filled with yellow earth was hot enough to make you sweat like you had a fever, like you were standing under an enormous dryer.

Luckily, the dim sum place wasn't far. A server quickly handed us moist towels and said, "You'll have to share a table." Of course, there was no room to be picky. I nodded, and Iroha went straight to the powder room.

"Was this in today's forecast?" Iroha spewed frustration as she returned from the powder room and I was getting up from my seat to go to the bathroom next. Before I could reply, a voice cut in and said, "No, but there were signs, weren't there?" It was the server who'd just given us the moist towels.

"Yeah, actually everything was yellow when we looked out from the building. We should have noticed then," I responded without missing a beat. But the woman didn't even so much as make a move to look at me, and, instead, faced Iroha, saying, "You are pretty slow on the uptake, aren't you? Iroha, you never were the sharpest knife in the drawer." Iroha had looked like she was bewildered in the middle of an oil slick up until that point, but suddenly the strain in her face disappeared, and she said, "Hey, Mokuren! What the hell?"

"Sorry, it's just me."

"What are you doing, working in a place like this?"

"A place like this? That's really nice."

"I didn't mean it like that. Weren't you helping out at your family's shop in Yokohama?"

"You expect me to catch you up on everything that's happened in my life over the past five years while I'm on the job?"

"Okay, so when's good for you?"

"When do you have the free time?"

"I could meet you whenever. Only not today."

"Okay, how about tomorrow night? What's your cell number."

After they exchanged numbers, Mokuren put her work face back on.

The shop wasn't particularly big, so the people pushing inside to seek shelter quickly had the place filled to capacity. The wind shrieked through gaps in the door, and because of the sand mixed in with it, people were sneezing here and there. After washing my face, straightening my hair, gargling, and blowing my nose in the bathroom, I returned to my seat and gave my order for a strong twenty-five year old Pu-erh tea and a lotus seed bun to a server who wasn't Mokuren. Iroha asked for Eastern Beauty Oolong tea and a daikon radish rice cake.

"That's a pretty rude friend you've got there."

"You think so? She's always like that."

"Well, that was quite the lovers' quarrel you two had. Were you close?"

"Who knows? We'd skip school and go to movies together, but I haven't heard from her since graduation."

"It sure didn't seem like it'd been five years."

"Are you interested in her?" Iroha had a gleam in her eyes.

"She definitely didn't seem interested in me."

"That's because she's the type of person who doesn't seem interested in anybody."

"But she did seem interested in you."

"What's that supposed to mean?"

"Nothing. Just that she's a piece of work, too." I said that to change the subject and turned my attention to the TV in front of me. Iroha had to twist her body around to see it.

The live broadcast of the State Funeral meant there was no holiday for the news reporters. The only thing you could make out on the dark screen was a rough yellow wind. If you struggled to look closely, you could almost discern the people in the procession who were enduring the storm. They looked like they were trying with all their might not to be blown over by the sand, and the funeral procession seemed to be backed up in a logjam.

Why couldn't the weather bureaus have predicted a sand storm of this magnitude? At this rate, the funeral procession would be buried underneath the sand like a party of mountain climbers caught in a blizzard. His **Majesty**'s casket would be covered. With time, the entire funeral party would turn to stone like the ruins of a city buried under volcanic ash. Could it be that today these very islands will meet their end only to be discovered in their original form in an excavation thousands of years down the road? Imagining all this, I felt as terrified and helpless as if I'd been ejected from a space ship.

I muttered, "Now that's a real burial."

"There'll probably be an earthquake too."

"Maybe His **Majesty** is calling."

"Not again! You are not funny." Iroha was vexed. As she spoke, an employee called out, "Is there an Iroha here?" Startled, Iroha looked at me.

"I'm over here," she said and waved her hand.

"You have a phone call."

The employee passed the phone to Iroha, who put it up to her ear without saying so much as hello. Then, she said, "Oh, Miko. What's up?" Apparently he'd been trying to call her on his cell, but couldn't get any reception, so he finally called the restaurant from a public pay phone. The sand storm was so bad that he couldn't handle being outdoors, and he was worried he wouldn't be able to meet up with us, so he said he was going to catch a cab to get here.

I was a little surprised. I had assumed that, since the funeral procession was still plugging along, Mikoto would stay to see it through to the end. If he was going to let the likes of a sand storm deter him, he may as well have joined us from the beginning.

Iroha and I waited for Mikoto in silence. For want of an activity to ease the awkward anticipation, we turned to the TV, where all we could see was the earthy yellow wind. Perhaps all the people outside had already sought refuge, but whatever the case, no new customers were coming into the restaurant. Luckily for us, the couple sharing our table suddenly broke into an odd conversation, providing a brief reprieve from our boredom.

The man said, "Motherfuckin' sand storm on the day of His **Majesty**'s funeral! It's gotta be some kind of Chinese plot."

The woman said, "Where do you think you are, you idiot? This is Chinese-Town."

"So what? I can say whatever the fuck I want. It's my country. And I ought to speak my mind. If you just smile while people let themselves into your house, they'll keep coming in and taking as much as they please."

"Give me a break! Who do you think you are? And who do you think is paying for you to be here anyway?"

"It was your idea to come in here."

"But you were the one bitching about not wanting to walk around in the sand."

"Fine. I'm not eating. Go ahead and spend your money on Chinese shit."

The guy left in a huff after that last remark. The woman hissed after him, "Big baby... son of a bitch," and followed him out. That opened up room for Mikoto at our table.

Mokuren sat down in Mikoto's place. The customers were all taken care of, so the staff had a little break.

"My treat," she said as she set down a plate of sesame balls. She looked at me for the first time and asked, "You're the boyfriend?"

I shook my head and replied, "The boyfriend's on his way."

"Whose?"

"Mine," Iroha said.

"Hmmm, so you've got a sweetheart?"

"I guess you've moved on from romance considering how much you used to get around, Mokuren."

"It's not that I've moved on or anything like that. It's just that I can't manage room for a love life right now. What about you?" She asked again of me. "Do you have a special someone?"

I shook my head.

"Right.... Iroha, do you like your boyfriend?"

"Yeah, I guess so."

"Trust him?"

"I suppose."

"It's okay if you don't want to answer. You're a likable nihilist, Iroha. I was always jealous of that."

"That's news to me!"

"It just occurred to me to describe you that way. But it's the truth. You should be careful."

"Other people can say what they like."

Mokuren went back to the kitchen singing, "Someday, I'll find my love...."

"Iroha, don't you get pissed off?"

"Sometimes."

"Hey, you have to introduce me to Mikoto properly."

"Uh, sorry."

"It's okay. Because I'm a likable video camera."

Actually, I was filming that entire episode.

Within seconds of Mikoto's entrance, Mokuren had swiftly glided up to greet him. She brought him to our table and said, "This is him, right?" She handed him a moist towel. Mikoto eyed Mokuren suspiciously, and then looked at us. Having the real Mikoto look at me was a strange sensation. I stood up and introduced myself, "I'm Shôji Inoue." Then, I directed him to the bathroom. It could have been because I had several cups of very strong vintage Pu-erh on an empty stomach, but in any case, I felt dizzy.

"The cherry blossoms are falling because of all that wind. They bloomed in the morning and will be scattered by night. It's such a shame. Or I suppose it's just too hard to live in a restless world like this." As Mikoto was returning, I had started to chatter away about meaningless things like that.

"I said this was like a sign that a big earthquake was coming, didn't I?"

"My theory was that His **Majesty** was calling, but Iroha didn't appreciate that."

"That subject is off-limits!"

"Inoue, do you really think His **Majesty** is calling?" Mikoto spoke slowly. I thought, "Yes! He took the bait." Mikoto followed up with, "It's all a bit too much though, don't you think? That cherry blossoms should suddenly bloom on the day of His **Majesty**'s state funeral and that dirt would fall all over his coffin. With all that, do you truly believe His **Majesty** is calling?"

"Well, no. It was just a thought I had." I was unsteady, and even my speech became more polite. I sipped some Pu-erh. "And how was it? His **Majesty**'s funeral procession?"

"Just like it looked on TV. You could barely stand. And even if you could open your eyes, it was so cloudy with dust that you couldn't see a thing."

"Was there much of a crowd?"

"Maybe. Before the sand started blowing, all the people and cherry blossoms made everything as rosy as a baby's butt."

"Ho ho!"

"What's there to 'ho ho!' about? I swear you two sound like a couple of old men on a porch." Iroha cut in, clearly having lost her patience.

"You're right. I thought it was a little strange too," I said in agreement.

Mikoto forced a smile and said, "I have the bad habit of psyching myself up too much when I first meet someone." I thought, "This bastard's still acting like a stranger."

I looked at Iroha and said, "Well, I'm just happy we managed to pull off this get-together without any mishaps." Iroha nodded.

"Everything's okay now. We're immune from mishaps. When His Departed **Majesty** passed by me, I was able to pray for his happiness in the next world."

"And that's how you'd escaped en route to make it here? I was a little worried that maybe it had gotten too dangerous and you'd slipped away because of that." Iroha's voice was relieved.

"As a matter of fact, I actually feel the same as Inoue, that His **Majesty** is calling out to us. You see, when I was close to him, I actually felt something like a heart flutter. Only this time, I wasn't spirited away and was able to get through it."

We were speechless. I didn't know what to say or how to say it. But Iroha's previously crabby disposition softened into cheerfulness. Even though she'd been hoping the funeral would be a kind of conclusion for Mikoto, maybe she was relieved he hadn't changed that much.

"So, you call that being spirited away?" I broke the silence.

"Seems that way. That's what they called me when I went back to work."

"I wonder if all the people who were spirited away turned out for the State Funeral?"

"I got the sense a lot did. There were people who seemed like they'd come by themselves, showing up here and there, milling around without talking."

"You were one of them."

"Well, not really. Even in the midst of the comeback crowd at work, I was more lighthearted. For every person who was spirited away, there was a specific reason why. Before today's State Funeral began, all the people I saw in His **Majesty**'s woods were opening up their hearts and praying so sincerely that I thought His **Majesty** wouldn't be able to rest in peace."

We fell silent again for a bit.

"I don't really see how His **Majesty** would have trouble resting in peace simply because lots of people were praying for him," I posed.

Mikoto glanced at Iroha. Her exhaustion showed, and she said, "If you want to talk about it, go ahead and talk about it."

"I've been through this with Iroha a lot, so she's sick of hearing about it, but since you asked ...It's also hard for me to talk about, because I don't remember what it was like to be spirited away all that well. And, at any rate, all the words that were in my head at the time are gone. I learned that memory pretty much relies on words."

As someone who records light and sound, I wanted to object and say, "not necessarily," but I didn't say anything.

"You do understand that not everyone who was spirited away was so because they were sad over His **Majesty**'s death, right?"

I nodded.

"The breakdown caught me unawares, like a sneak attack. I don't remember clearly, but I thought something to the effect of this is nothing more than one person's death, and when one person dies, somewhere another is born, and it doesn't change anything. Then, I suddenly lost the will to do anything."

"Because the same thing goes on for eternity?"

"Up until that point, I'd been amazed by the concept of eternity. But this was different. What I felt was, first of all, what I'd just thought had been a lie. The end of one life wasn't going to be replaced by the beginning of another. Because, at least in this Island Country, more people are dying than are being born. I can count the number of friends or superiors in my life who have kids. Inoue, I'll bet you've never even touched a child."

"Now that you mention it, no, I never have."

"See? Children are a rarity these days."

Leaving behind her camera, Iroha got up from her seat. I thought maybe she was going to the bathroom, but she disappeared back into the kitchen. Mikoto sealed his lips in seeming agony. In an effort to end the conversation, I said, "I'm sorry. I shouldn't pry in other people's business. I'll go get her." I started to stand, but Mikoto stopped me.

"It's a misunderstanding. I'm a man saying this, and it might sound like I'm criticizing Iroha, the woman, and I acknowledge that, but if I can't say it honestly, I'm not going to be able to express what I'm feeling. And with every word I say, I hurt Iroha more, so I can't get past my reluctance."

"Do you want kids, Mikoto?" I aimed my camera at him. He didn't flinch.

"I know it sounds that way, but that's not what I'm saying." He sighed. "Honestly, I don't know the answer to that question. Iroha and I never make it through this discussion without stumbling. Ever since we started living together, I thought to make the world real, you had to contribute to future generations, so I'd ask things like whether she wanted kids or what she'd do if she got pregnant, which could happen no matter how careful we are, but that was all theoretical for me, and I don't know how I personally feel about having kids. Of course, no one really knows until they become a parent, but that's not what I want to say. What interests me is whether parents are necessary, whether it matters if I have kids and become a parent. That's what I'm trying to get at. Because, you see, can kids even be a possibility if I don't feel like I'm really living? It's hard to believe the future will go on after me. When I say that, Iroha goes ballistic, demanding that I come to some sort of decision and then say whether it would make the world real to me if I wound up with a baby I had to raise on my own. And when she puts it that way, I can't sort it out myself."

I was extremely uncomfortable. I couldn't believe he could speak so frankly about subtle relationship problems to someone he'd barely met. Iroha is who she is, so she forced me to watch "Infinite Hell." Why did someone outside the mosquito curtain like me have to be privy to all this? Was he telling me all this precisely because I was on the outside, uninvolved, and thus couldn't be hurt?

Regardless of whether or not he was oblivious to my revulsion, Mikoto kept talking.

"If everyone felt like I do, nobody would have kids. When His Young **Majesty** died, you see, this world was actually dying. It felt like a world of the dead to me. The notion that the human race will continue on for eternity has been drilled into us, so we believe it; that's all. At first, this realization immobilized me. But I also thought we have to find a way to change the things that allow us to keep believing our society is alive. But then if the communities of the living are shrinking anyway, it doesn't really matter, does it?"

"But the overall global population is rising."

"That's another point. Do you think all those people are satisfied with their lives? Don't you think the reason babies aren't being born in this Island Country might have something to do with the fact that the people who could become parents feel like life has no value? Now, let's suppose people in those overpopulated places start feeling the same way. Then the population there would suddenly drop too. For the majority of the planet where the population is rising, the reasons why life has no meaning are different than here. It's a question of time. You don't come to this awareness on your own. It's the will of the world."

Mikoto stopped, looked at me, saw that I wasn't responding, and nodded his head to himself. His eyes were welling up with tears. I was shocked. What he'd been saying didn't amount to much more than simple, hypothetical trash-talk, but he was emotionally invested in it nonetheless.

"Even though it's something you can't see yet, I really do believe the world wants to die. When His **Majesty** pointed this out through his death, it clicked for me. Why

His **Majesty** died is beyond explanation. He would have had the very best doctors giving him regular checkups, and still his heart just stopped. I'm convinced that was His **Majesty**'s intention. When I was in the grip of despair and had lost my ability to speak, Iroha showed me the film of countless Mikotos watching the monitor, right?"

"Yeah, I saw that too. Iroha called it 'Infinite Hell'."

"Right, that's it. 'Infinite Hell.' Every day, another me was watching the screen and we multiplied one at a time, and nothing changed. The same thing repeated over and over again, and nobody was trying to get away and escape that repetition. It's a horrible film."

Memories reeled through my skull. I had a hard time breathing. I wanted Iroha to hurry back. All the better if she came back with Mokuren. But neither of them appeared, so I was stuck having to listen to Mikoto talk. There I was, sipping Pu-erh without a clue as to what to do with myself.

"And then, while I was watching something like three hundred of me trapped in the screen, I came to my senses. I knew we had to escape, that we had to break out of this endless cycle. His **Majesty** died in order to say that."

Mikoto's face lit up for a moment, and he said, "You're thinking I'm full of it, right?" He sighed. "I don't have the facts about His **Majesty**'s death. Like I just said, it's truly beyond me. But some of your footage runs at the tail end of 'Infinite Hell', right? Not a soul was speaking on those quiet, busy streets. Every person you filmed looked like a **Majesty** to me, and I don't mean that allegorically. Of course, I don't mean they were actually **Majesties**. Just that they looked that way to me. But that's what's important, that I saw them like that. It got to where I wanted to count and see how many of them there were. Actually, . . ." Mikoto paused to pull a college notebook out of his backpack and flipped through the pages. It was the same notebook in which he'd scribbled in "Infinite Hell." "Four hundred and eighty-three people. Not that there's any significance to that number, but I wanted to count them to verify my perception that there were four hundred and eighty-three **Majesties**. I felt like if I could quantify them like that in numbers, they'd all be the same. It's like when you're counting beans. There's no meaning in the individual bean. In the same way with those four hundred and eight-three people, there's no meaning in the individual person. Each one of them was just another **Majesty**. You could even say they were copies. It'd be like all those three hundred of me in "Infinite Hell' each existed with a difference face. But in reality, it's just one person. And that person is The **Majesty**."

"You mean there are millions of **Majesties**?"

"I mean there's no difference between a **Majesty** and us. Check this out, no matter how hard a **Majesty** works, no matter how seriously he takes his role, he's not going to change society. At most, he'll die and that'll make some people feel sad or whatever. Basically, you could say that, like us, a **Majesty** isn't a part of society. The environment he finds himself in isn't something we don't know. Or maybe we've put ourselves in that kind of environment to be like a **Majesty**. All I'm saying is that a **Majesty** isn't a part of society, so we don't have to be a part of it either."

Mikoto handed the notebook to me. On one page were a bunch of similarly shaped giraffes that didn't differ a bit even though they were clearly drawn freehand. On other pages, there were things like fava beans, turtles, strawberries, somebody's nose, and a freakishly realistic-looking hand, all multiplied until they filled up the pages. As the pages went on, there was a portrait-like sketch of Iroha, one that was maybe what he imagined I looked like, and while it didn't look at all like him, one apparently of His **Majesty**, all drawn on the same page like they'd been stamped there. None of those copies exceeded their bounds and trespassed onto another page. And on the last page was a cityscape without people. It was probably the neighborhoods in Shinjuku I filmed. There wasn't a single person in the geometric late afternoon city that was shaded in contrasting light and shadows. The weird part was that the sky was completely filled in and totally black.

"What are these broken lines?" I pointed at a page that wasn't like the ones with illustrations. This one had disconnected zig zag lines stretching horizontally like a graph.

"That's music. I don't know how to read or write music, so I tried writing lines that reflected the relative highs, lows, and lengths of the notes in my head. I can still sing it." Mikoto showed me by humming some random notes without a melody. It was that chant-like humming. It was excruciating. I was feeling the agony Iroha must have felt all that time.

"You were practically on a fast at that point, weren't you?"

"You can say I was confused or describe it however you'd like. Whatever works for you."

"Did you show these drawings to Iroha and explain them to her, too? Did she get it?"

"She does her best to understand the perceptions and images of the world that course through my body. But we end up talking about different things. She'll get angry and say something like, 'Okay, so you're saying that I can save the world from dying if I increase the population?' Or she'll get sad and say that even if the world does have a will of its own, can't we still have our own different will? And all I was trying to do was communicate something." Mikoto sipped his Blue Oolong tea. I gulped the watered-down dregs of my Pu-erh.

"The number four hundred and eighty-three includes Iroha. And you and me, of course. We are also **Majesties**. And if we can't find a way out of the recurring cycle of **Majesties**, there won't be any of ourselves left. That's what His **Majesty** showed us with his body. He said that we should cut ourselves loose and run away. Those words flashed before me when I watched the footage you filmed, and I could speak again."

"Just like with the Ten Commandments. The light of heaven carved the words in stone."

"I can see why you'd want to make fun of me. I could have been hallucinating, but I am sure that the message I took away was something his **Majesty** literally bet his life on. It's intuitive, not logical."

"Sounds like a divine revelation to me."

"You're wrong. There wasn't anything divine about it. That message came from a human being we call His **Majesty**."

"All those spirited away people were caught up in that message." I started to stew. Something wasn't sitting right with me.

"I already told you it was different for me than the others who were spirited away. I was more lighthearted. I understood the extent of that difference when I talked to the others who came back to work. They said so themselves, that they'd had to realize how up until then, they hadn't ever had to think about who they were, because His **Majesty** had carried that burden.

Even though I'm actually a member of this Island Country, I'd taken the stance that I was nobody and that life didn't matter, so I hadn't invested any personal effort in living my life here. His **Majesty** had been quietly supporting me. The only person carrying the weight of one hundred million slackers was His **Majesty**. It's such a luxury for us to say we don't feel like we're alive. Because when His **Majesty** died, there we were, frightened that we could die too. I realized that the essence of life was being alive even when you don't feel like you are. It was the first time I'd felt grateful for not having died. The reason we could get by without any hope or despair was because His **Majesty** had taken on the despair for us. He'd turned it into a world in which it wasn't necessary to have hopes.

They were sick at the thought they'd killed his **Majesty**, that the tremendous responsibility had worn him down. And they were even more distraught over losing the person who'd connected them to this land. Now they'd have to withstand the despair of being a person of this Island Country on their own. They collapsed because they felt like His **Majesty**'s load had suddenly been placed on their shoulders. They'd been living their lives unconsciously dependent on His **Majesty**. And they were shocked to see how apathetic they'd been, because, to them, that unconscious reliance had been natural, like air."

"You'd been aware of it?"

"Oh, I was aware ... that I wasn't depending on His **Majesty**. That's why I didn't misinterpret his message. Everyone talks about being spirited away, but we were the ones hiding away His **Majesty**. We pretended not to see the kind of world he was trying to show us, and we concealed his true meaning. I wondered why we hid him and why we were spirited away. And I concluded we were copies of His **Majesty**, and he was telling us to escape that. I took his appeal to heart. But if we're imitating him when we run away, we'll still be copies, right? We all have to decide for ourselves what precise course of action to follow in order to meet with His **Majesty**'s approval. I'm thinking that instead of being spirited away, this time I'll try to hide from myself."

"Is that some kind of new spin on playing tag?"

"You've been twisting my words around from the beginning. Are you afraid of hearing the most important parts?"

"I don't know whose most important parts they are, but I suppose I got the gist of being spirited away. What matters most to me is that I wasn't even in the market to get spirited away."

"Well, there's always the question of timing. And you were already hidden behind your camera. When a person who is already hidden wants to hide, there's really no need to be spirited away, is there?"

"I watched 'Infinite Hell' and I didn't get even a hint of the kind of coded message you're describing. There was no invisible ink secret message or anything missing. Things that can't be recorded as sound or light simply don't exist. I don't believe in anything except sound and light."

"That's fine if that's the case. I'm not looking for other people to believe what I'm saying. I only want to convey the information I got as accurately as I can and let someone know that I plan to follow His **Majesty**'s lead.

"Do you think you're The One? Isn't your religious background a little different from His **Majesty**'s?"

"You're the one who's been using sacrilegious metaphors, Mr. Inoue, not me."

"Quit being so pretentious. You're older than me, aren't you?"

"Sorry. But age doesn't matter, does it?"

"No, but were you trying to be condescending?"

"Why do I feel like you're trying to pick a fight with me?"

"All I'm saying is drop the attitude. It's pissing me off."

Mikoto clammed up and glanced towards the kitchen. I felt something like vertigo swirl through my head. I started to get woozy, and it felt a little good.

"Sorry, but if you'll let me finish...." While Mikoto's mouth was still open, a power surge rushed through my body. I stood up, grabbed him by the collar with both hands, told him to "say it outside" and pushed him all the way up to the front door.

The automatic door opened, and a sandy gust of yellow wind pelted my eyes. I muttered, "Don't preach to me, fuckin' sand" and pushed Mikoto down onto the ground. When he tried to get up, I shoved him back down, spit, and turned on my heels to follow my steps back inside. He let out an intense and high-pitched wail at my cruel back: "His **Majesty**'s message was that this world is the otherworld, so you all should die too! Stop trying to use force to run away from it like a coward. Face the truth head-on. If you can be brave enough to do that, I'll still be your friend."

Looking back, I used muscles I'd never before used in my life to wield power over Mikoto like a demon. I couldn't believe myself when I let loose a war cry and, with all my might, kicked over a huge motorcycle parked nearby.

Inside, Iroha and Mokuren had heard the ruckus and returned to our table. Iroha filmed me as I drew closer. Unable to open my eyes, which had filled up with sand, I quietly packed up my camera and things. "Fuck," she said. "Stupid… embarrassing."

I felt horribly sad through and through. I was sure I'd break down if I tried to answer.

Iroha closed in on me with her camera lens and said, "I feel betrayed."

"Don't look at me through the camera, damn it. It's sleazy. If you want to see, look with your own eyes," I protested. Instantaneously, tears and my nose started running. But that was because of the sand.

"But isn't this exactly what we always do, Inoue? We were doing it just now. What's wrong? Did you suddenly become a fundamentalist? Did Mikoto get to you? Where did Shôji Inoue, the camera, go? Who are you?"

Iroha hit me where it hurt with those accusations, which she fired off at me without letting up her gaze. I couldn't answer any of her questions. For the first time, I felt the perils of being alive. It upset me to think that if I kept getting played like that, I'd have to keep living. I thought about what to do like my life depended on it.

What I needed to do required Mikoto.

I wanted to hear that last thing Mikoto said again. I was determined to become a central figure in his life. I picked up my stuff and the bill. I could only manage to say, "I haven't taken care of this yet" and then went up to the register and paid Mokuren. I paid with my dirty money. Sucking down the rotten juice of what this country stashed away was what enabled me to get by, and I paid with that unclean, fake money. The parting words I tried on Mokuren were, "You and Iroha are pretty tight, huh? You gave me quite a show." She answered with a coy smirk. It looked like I was getting the silent treatment again.

Not that I didn't expect it, but there wasn't a soul to be found on the streets when I went out into the gusty sand storm. With only the exception of an occasional car passing by, everyone was holed up inside. Of course, it wasn't like Mikoto was going to be waiting for me. But I wondered where he'd gone. I regretted not at least getting his phone number, so I tried calling Iroha on her cell, but because of all the sand interference, the call wouldn't go through.

Still, I didn't feel like going back. Even though I was used to seeing the empty streets, it drove me crazy to walk through them. I busted out my camera, which was protected by a handkerchief and plastic bag. Flowers had fallen from the cherry trees that were as brutalized as if they'd been riddled with bullets. The fallen flowers were covered with sand and would soon be completely buried. The city would be entombed.

I was full of sand, as though I'd been dragged through dunes, and had no idea which way to go. In a city with no people, it doesn't matter which way you go. No matter where I looked, all I recorded was a city shrouded in air that was thick with yellow sand. Because of that, it wasn't long before I couldn't open my eyes. Little by little, my eyes were coated in a hard lacquer of sand that even dried up my tears. And it wasn't just my eyes. Sand filled my ears to the point where noises were muffled. My nose was so stuffed that I had to try breathing out of my mouth, which felt chock full of gravel. I'd want to swallow saliva, but my mouth was so dry that it hurt when I tried. I was wrapped in an armor of sand, separated from the outside world, barely surviving the grains of sand that hit the skin on my face and hands and felt like shotgun fire. Once I was numbed to even that sensation, I would be completely closed in with no way out. It was not a good situation. At that rate, I would spend eternity with His **Majesty** like an ancient slave buried alive in an enormous sarcophagus along with the deceased ruler.

Every ten minutes or so, I'd force myself to open my eyes if only for just a second like a shutter. In a flash, a picture of a world with only light and shadows and no clear outlines was burned into my retina. My eyes froze shut. All I could see was the afterimage of the lemon yellow light and the jet-black shadows. The glare of the blazing sun was so blinding that it had the opposite effect of appearing black. The street surfaces and corners and glass of building clusters were illuminated by the sunlight, and everything that shot through my eyes looked overwhelmingly lemon yellow. The air looked like it was struggling to breathe because of all the yellow grains of sand dancing around in it. Everything was flipped around. The backlit silhouettes of buildings and telephone polls were cut off from the sunny spots and looked like caves.

As strange as it was, I felt an intimate attachment to this new world I'd met, a world that was only harsh light, shadow, sand, and heat. Then I remembered the sketch of the cityscape at the end of Mikoto's notebook. This looked just like it. The scenery was divided into light and shadow, the sky was smeared in darkness, and there were no people.

Even though I'd never been to the moon, I felt certain that Mikoto had drawn the lunar surface. That's what my heart was telling me even though I didn't have any reason to feel that way. Mikoto foresaw that this earth would gradually turn into the surface of the moon. And at that very moment, I myself was seeing raw lunar landscapes. I'd flown to a life-less lunar desert. I hadn't been spirited away, but I had just taken a trip to the moon. I stopped, stood still in the middle of the sand storm with my eyes shut, and laughed at myself. What the hell?

I thought about His **Majesty**, about how he was a thing and not a person anymore. This lunar landscape is the fresh world he showed us through his death: a simple world in which everything is objectified. If His **Majesty** is an object, then I am an object too. The same object takes in light, casts a shadow, absorbs heat, and then gives off that heat.

In that lunar world where I'd become indistinguishable from an object, I figured out the meaning of my life. I was fully alive in a world without other people. I transcended naive worries about whether or not I was participating. I was there.

This is the real nature of the world. Regular people are like screens shrouding the reality first made manifest in His **Majesty**'s funeral. The illusion is projected onto human skin. My camera ingested that illusion and exposed the deal.

Even though my camera records the illusion, it doesn't record the truly real. I arrived home covered in sand, looking like I'd barely escaped a swarming anthill. As I showered, I tried to recapture the true essence of the world I'd just been shown. I turned off the light in my room and savored the thrill of the moment in the growing evening darkness while staring at the light of the LCD monitor.

Displayed there were images more or less like what I'd seen on the TV in the dim sum restaurant. Specs of dirt like flying ants danced in rhythm with the whistling wind inside a yellow light that was a bit brighter than before. The sparkling silver sun, lemon-colored halation, and cavern-like black sky weren't visible.

But I wasn't discouraged. Mikoto was right. These images showed the true nature of reality as it was. It wasn't as if a lunar world would show up on earth. That was nothing more than an illusion. I had been hopped up on strong, vintage Pu-erh tea and jittery at the time. And on top of that, I had sand in my eyes and ears and was in no shape to get a handle on my surroundings. I'd seen it all because I was under the influence of the tea and impaired vision and hearing. I realized all that.

And yet, I couldn't deny the tangible intimacy with which I'd experienced the spectacle I'd witnessed with my own eyes. Whether or not it was a hallucination, what mattered was the fact that I saw it. All that's recorded through my camera lens is, after all, the world of people, and even if I could capture the illusion, the essence it veiled couldn't be shown clearly. In that sense, I'd seen images that couldn't be reflected through a lens, so I wasn't really a camera anymore. The one who peeled away the illusion of the world of people was His **Majesty**. To borrow Mikoto's way of saying it, I'd come face to face with the naked world through the cracks that His **Majesty** bravely ripped open by volunteering up his body. I had to revive the lemon yellow light and heat of that world and convert it into a camera recording. That was the purpose of me seeing the illusion. This was being spirited away for me!

So, what Mikoto said wasn't enough. If the raw, scorched world illuminated by the glittering sun had been laid bare, couldn't you say that His **Majesty** had been the phantom concealing it? And if so, was the world burning under the brilliant sun a world without a **Majesty**?

That's it! By removing His Very Self, which had been hiding the true nature of the world, His **Majesty** had stripped the world completely naked. We had already been released into a world with no **Majesty**. It wasn't just the individual Young **Majesty**, but **Majesty** itself that died. **Majesty** was dead. There would be no more!

I was thrilled at my discovery. I arrived at the truth without being led there by Mikoto. The duty to show people what a world without **Majesty** was like was mine. I wasn't a camera, so I had to convey the naked world I'd known in words. I'd have to explain my central role in relation to it in a message. If I didn't, I'd still be nothing more than a bystander.

With that, I put some writing up on my website. Tapping away at the keyboard, I tried putting what Mikoto said into my own words. I typed so much faster than I could think that it seemed I might flood the monitor with words. I felt like I was taking notes on someone's lecture. There, all the contradictions melted away as I plunged ever deeper into the world.

As if possessed, I finished writing the short piece in no time at all and then set about processing the film. I only had the hazy lemon yellow and black colors to work with in the digital processing, so I pushed the contrast to the limit and managed to recreate the shadows of the lunar surface. Then I tacked on footage of the blossoming cherry trees and ended up with about fifteen minutes of film.

It was already quite late when I uploaded the following text with the footage. I arrived at these truths with all of my body and soul. I have no doubts.

"I never thought I was alive until now. I always wondered whether it mattered if I died if I didn't feel like I was living. But before I could come to a conclusion, I'd be overwhelmed with shame, and since it was too hard to continue thinking beyond that, I'd try to repress the feeling.

But today, I figured out that it would be good for me to die. Or rather, without a trace of guilt and in good spirits, I wanted to die and accepted this revelation as if it were the most regular of things for anyone.

I saw it for myself on the day of His **Majesty**'s funeral. This world was already dying. I understood it, that this is a post-mortem world, that this place is like the surface of the moon and we are all just residents of the Sea of Tranquility or Sea of Fecundity caught in a recurring afterimage of once upon a time when life was normal. I saw that raw heat and light mercilessly bake everything exposed under a platinum sun and that, as the temperature is changed by rising waves of heat, we are all but fleeting illusions.

Because this is a post-mortem world, it's natural for those who are still living to desire death. But even though this is a post-mortem world, it's not the afterworld. It's this world itself that is post-mortem.

My wish is that I might achieve a state befitting this world. I want all those dead people who are still living to die, to really die, to rest in peace in a quiet desert. I want the post-mortem world to be seen for what it truly is. Because that is the homeland where I belong."

A few moments later, I got an email from Mikoto.

Subject: Beautiful

Text: Well said! I had a feeling you'd get it. It's a little on the extreme side, but I can feel His **Majesty**'s message alive in your words. And maybe you can't communicate the real sense of it all without exaggerating some like that.

It's the same with those images. Beautiful! They gave me shivers. I really was moved.

Actually, I'd seen a scene like that before. Not on the day of the sand storm, but at dusk when a typhoon was building. Even though the sky was filled with black clouds, the sun was beating down on the western horizon. I watched that orange ball of a sun suddenly turn silver just like the color changes when you flip an Othello piece. Just then, the colors everywhere faded, and the sky, the mountains, the cape, the river, and the houses all reflected the shining silver in monotones. Places where the sunlight didn't hit looked as black as bottomless pits. I was overcome with emotion at the time and felt like I was viewing someone's residence. No doubt, that's the "homeland" for all of us, including His **Majesty**. We'll have to repaint the flag, huh? :)

We have to return there. I mean really return.

Of course, each in his own way. After you "punished" me, I took a taxi back to the funeral procession and stayed to watch until the end. My eyes were mostly shut, so I suppose I should just say I "stayed." :)

What I felt at the time, and I don't mean this is in a spiritual way, was that everything from dead people to animals, grass, and trees had a soul. And those souls didn't go to the afterworld. They were staying here in the world in which we live. Corpses rot and decompose, and souls become the energy that propels future life. You can't see that develop with your eyes, but we live our lives framed by those souls, saved by them, and empowered by them. You can call it the Law of Soul Conservation if you want, but the amount of life on the planet is limited. Let's say the sum of that life shapes our world and dead bodies and spirits occupy a proportional amount of space above ground. We can't just go about our lives ignoring that. Or maybe we grow uneasy because we do disregard it, act as if it didn't exist, and relegate the "afterworld" to the place of myths, where we forget all about it. The living and the dead are unrelated inorganic matter, and even though we are barely able to relate to anything, we only see one piece of the puzzle, so we feel like some great unknown enables us to live as opposed to anything of our own doing, and we start to feel like we are worthless and fake. We think the world wants to die because we are caught up in our own feelings of powerlessness. But of course we're powerless. We don't even try to tap into the strength of the spirits. That's why I first thought that this world is the afterworld, the world of the dead, and that I wanted to be able to see the existence and power I'd never tried to see before. I want to escape from the illusion of a world inhabited only by living beings.

That's what I was thinking while seeing off His Young **Majesty**, every inch of my body like eyes. But I'm not so sure about your manifesto. Our interpretations seem a little different.

But it's okay if they are. Or rather, they have to be different. You'll have your own way of doing it. His **Majesty**'s message was for each of us to start by finding our own way. It'll be no good if we all fall in line. If that happens, the true form of these islands will be taken back. Either way, we have to start with honest explanations, right?

Not to change the subject, but do you want to grab dinner or something tomorrow night? Iroha made plans with that woman Mokuren from the dim sum place, so I'm free. I probably won't get done with work until after seven, and if it works for you, how does Dormir, the Sleeping Café in Higashi Aoyama sound? If you don't know where it is, call me on my cell. Even if you can't make it, I'm going to relax for a while there, so please come if you feel like it.

I read that email four or five times. The first thing that welled up inside me was the satisfaction over having connected with Mikoto. I'd waited to meet him for so long, and to think that this person, who mattered more than anything to Iroha, now mattered more than anything to me made me feel like I'd been accepted by this couple as a life partner. It wasn't exactly what I'd fantasized about, but I was excited that this marked the beginning of a new relationship for the three of us.

I was also thankful for having been guided into experiencing the essence of the world. I didn't understand it at the time, but when His **Majesty** died, I felt a lot of anxiety and guilt because I wasn't spirited away or emotionally affected by his death even though so many of my peers were. The door was open, but I was still lost and looking for a chance to get in when, thanks to Mikoto, I made it right in the nick of time. Moreover, I resorted to violence with Mikoto while he was still weak, but he didn't abandon me.

What worries me is Iroha. Am I going to be able to persuade someone who didn't even try to understand Mikoto's explanation? It would probably take considerable patience and time. I trust Iroha, but I'm not confident enough to say that she'll get it. The foundation for the new relationship involving the three of us was the world with the shining silver sun. If we don't get there (or, more accurately, here), we'll be separated. Will Iroha appreciate what this means?

I thought it wouldn't be a bad idea for me to have a *tête à tête* with Mikoto the next day. And at any rate, there were so many things I wanted to talk about with him. I sent a reply email, accepting his invitation for dinner and letting him know I'd make reservations for the Narcissus Cell.

As soon as I sent that, I received a message from Iroha.

Subject: I saw it

Text: Who the fuck do you think you are?

Do you think dying is going to make you all high and mighty?

Please! I'm the one who wants to die. For more than a month, I gave my all to keep Miko from dying, and now you? And I thought you knew how heartbreaking Miko's "custodial duty" was for me. I shared my loneliness with you and thought you'd at least lighten the load a bit for me. You even watched the video. What? None of it registered with you at all? I thought if we got together, you could help me bring Miko back from the brink, but no, you went his way instead.

You are acting like someone else. I have no idea who you are anymore. The only Shôji Inoue I knew was a skeptical observer, an autotoxic guy caught in his own weirdness and sensitive to the goings-on in his own head. I don't know where the fuck he went, but he's gone. I've learned how much I trusted and needed you the hard way. Miko's gone, and so are you. You've left me out in the cold. Why did you have to be so heartless?

I'll be the first to admit that I have some responsibility in all of this too. I should have just skipped all the bullshit worries and introduced you to Miko back when we first hooked up. I created an awkward moment for you both when I turned to you all of a sudden when Miko was in dire shape. And you are a total reactionary, so it's entirely consistent of you to roll that way when given the chance.

The only one crushed by this is me. You two are inside your little dead zone world. But, whoever you are now, can you understand how devastating this is for me? What's going to happen to me if you two go off and commit love suicide? What am I? Just some kind of supporting character?

The most painful part is that I'm not trusted. You and Miko wouldn't think dying was okay if you trusted me. Didn't our friendship begin back when we made "Mixed Cameras"? We didn't succeed at merging into a single body and soul and ended up totally separate, like we were there by accident. We agreed on that plan and knew it would be kind of half-assed, and we started to build a bond between us. Was that bond fake? Is half-assed not good enough for you anymore? Do you need to be united in a 100% pure and completely lofty death? Is everything we felt back then just null and void now?

If you mean it, then I mean it too. If you read this mail and still want to die, go ahead and fucking die then. I'll survive and completely ruin your plan.

It was just as I'd feared. But I winced at the actual sight of those cruel words and fell into a depression. I regretted not having kept quiet and waited until after all three of us could have met at the Sleeping Café instead of writing over the net and arranging to meet alone with Mikoto first. It could have been more like what I'd hoped and not how it has played out. We could have been sleepily lazing around in the kitschy and cheap interior of the Narcissus Cell, the three of us getting along and transforming the space into a fallout shelter where we could find refuge from the world of lies and watch the projections until we were bored. Then, we could have started to watch our own films instead, sipping herbal tea when we woke up from catnaps in the red lip-shaped reclining seats, spending our day engrossed in heated conversations about nothing of consequence.

There were all sorts of real possibilities, but now **there was no going back**. Iroha hadn't tried to bring us together during those years since she first started dating Mikoto. She was building up trust without any interference from either of us. The thought of that never occurred to me, but now I can really see why. It was Iroha herself who never truly trusted me. She positioned herself at the pivot of a folding fan, making sure her relationships with the two of us were stable by trying to control everything. Now that His **Majesty** is dead, Mikoto is deserting, and the folding fan connections are crumbling, she still won't recognize Mikoto's transformation.

I don't want to go so far as it say such-and-such was the deciding factor. Only that it's too late now. From this point onward, we have no choice but to rebuild our relationships anew. For that to happen ... I've written it so many times that I'm not rehashing it yet again.

If I tried to reply and explain things at this point, it would only have the opposite effect. The written word will only lead to misunderstanding. For now, all I can do is meet Mikoto and then later get together with Iroha in person and invest a whole lot of time and patience. I erased Iroha's message without reading it a second time.

After that, I got in bed, but one line from Iroha's message kept swirling around in my head and keeping me awake. She accused Mikoto and me of planning to commit love suicide. Where the hell did that idea come from? It sure wasn't me. That was the only accusation I hadn't already run through my head. I was restless and dizzy.

And then I embraced it as my conclusion. I finally truly knew exactly what I should do. I'd found what Mikoto called "my way." The last hesitation vanished from my body. It wasn't a question of persuading Iroha to get to this point. Ironically, Iroha had convinced me.

I scrupulously spelled out the particulars that brought me to this point, including that plan of action, and my notes expanded to become the text you all are reading right now. It's ended up much longer than I'd expected.

It's currently five o'clock in the morning and starting to get light outside. I can hardly believe that only twenty-four hours ago, I sighed at the sight of unruly cherry blossoms. Now that I've "participated" in society's raw form, it seems like the world is something entirely different from what it was yesterday. I have a sense of belonging.

I'm going to finish these notes. I'll sleep until evening. And then I'll never have to clear my head again.

If I wake up and feel like the previous twenty-four hours have been a lie, I'll contact Iroha. But the chances of that are roughly less than zero.

On the other hand, if my understanding of reality remains what it is now, I'll head out to Dormir. And from there, I'll upload these notes.

I have one request.

If I die, my website, films, and notes will probably be shut down quickly. Those of you who sympathize with what I've written, please download this page and, if you can, the film files too, and save them. And, if possible, please mirror it all or post excerpts on other websites. It doesn't matter where. If the film files are too complicated, these notes alone will be fine. If as many allies as possible spread the words of Mikoto and me, and the images, we'll get that much closer to a world without **Majesty**. If I put this record out over the net and lots of people circulate copies, it can continue to multiply even after I reach the afterworld.

At this stage, I can't know whether or not my wish will be fulfilled. But I've had more than enough of the idea that the so-called competition for survival will lead to a world like the fountain of youth – vibrant and passionate. What begins today is not the survival of the fittest, but the demise of the fittest. There are no winners and losers, only a quiet procession. At least that's what I believe.

I'm heading off to die now. But my death alone won't stop the world from dying and writhing in agony. I need someone else, another person with whom I can return to death. My passionate desire to disappear all the people, animals, and plants left behind as illusions from the past will not be enough. My own strength is insufficient. I need to enlist the cooperation of another. Any attempt to change the world solo in one fell swoop is, generally speaking, a mistake.

I can do only what is within my range of ability, and hopefully that will be enough to disappear us. I'm sure I could probably bring along three or four people, but if one person can find just one accomplice, I think that's plenty. If a million of the living dead who remain in this world take the journey with a companion, that will make two million dead. And if two million people become dead, then perhaps the number of sympathizers will increase to four million and even eight million. There's no way to save the world from suffering over its own duplicity other than by steadily expanding the pool of sympathizers.

I will lead the vanguard and sacrifice myself. If enough of you identify with my dream, we can really bring this world back to what it is truly meant to be. We can extinguish the phony world and return to the real, natural, and authentic world of the dead.

But it's too soon to say. If there are more people with lingering attachments to this fake world than the like-minded, I'll probably be labeled a murderer and relegated to the dustbins of obscurity. That's up to fate.

May my prayers somehow be answered.

This world is the other world, and you should die too, together with someone else.

Shôji Inoue

slight chill works its way through the still hot and humid wind like a single gray strand mixed into a head of black hair, and it's full speed ahead into winter. This year, that cool air began to blow today, on September 27. I had gone out to Yellow Hell Spring for a bit to gaze at my reflection in the mirror-like surface. The floating reflection of my face on the water quivered as gusts of wind called up waves. It crumbled into bits that spread out across the pond. Shivers ran up and down my spine, and not just because of the touch of winter in the wind. Somewhere in my body I could still hear a voice that wasn't Miko's or Inoue's calling out to me.

That happens every time I go to the spring. I'm not saying I channel spirits there. I don't get anything useful like an inspiration out of the experience, and nothing impressive enough to make me a believer. I've spent a lot of time out there by the water, trying to resurrect memories of Inoue and Miko, so much so that those memories now live in the water. Whenever I look at the color of the water and smell the water and grass, I feel the presence of Inoue and Miko, like a conditioned response. The real Miko and Inoue didn't even know about this place, so this series of associations is a product of my own imagination. If at times their presence is comforting to me, there are also times when I'm overwhelmed by a bitter sense of fate. To honor these moments, which have taken on a special meaning for me, I make the fifteen-minute walk from the mountain lodge to the spring almost every day, regardless of what might await me there.

We had so much rain this summer that we might make it until next summer without suffering a drought. There's also been more water bubbling out of the spring than usual this year, enough to overflow the banks of the mountain stream that continues up to the lodge. Waste not, want not, so we carved out a makeshift tributary to guide the water into an open well for storage. The series of heavy downpours led to more flood damage in the Kantô Desert.

Whose idea was it for water to become such a precious commodity anyway? The abundant freshwater on these islands, which are surrounded by sea and filled with mountains, has all but disappeared in the span of only five years — like rats fleeing a sinking ship. They say that the amount of water reserves has dropped a third of what it was five years ago.

Luckily, our mountain retreat has a number of wells and the spring. So even though our "reservation" on Ascension Pass is isolated, we get by just fine. Of course, it would be a different story if someone poisoned our water. That would pollute the land too, and we'd have a real mess on our hands. I started making my daily pilgrimage to the spring out of a personal desire, but now it involves the added serious purpose of double-checking on the water source. I can't feel at ease unless I visit the spring at least once a day, no matter what the weather is, and if I have the time to do more than that, I also keep watch on the surroundings through images transmitted from the surveillance cameras. I set the cameras up myself, originally to record minute changes in the water, light, and sound from moment to moment. The equipment is ultra-small like the kind a spy would use, so I doubt anyone will find them.

I've spent the past five years peering into Yellow Hell Spring, which glitters like a golden mirror because of all the yellow sand that's settled at the bottom. I'm reflected on the surface of the water now instead of in Inoue's camera lens, which once took in light and served as an extension of Inoue himself. When I admire myself like that, or rather when me and I look longingly at each other, I can't help but remember the unrelenting images of "Mixed Cameras."

Narcissus fell in love gazing at his own reflection in the water, and he kept staring at himself after he'd been turned into the flower that bears his name. For me, there's no escape from the images of what happened at the Narcissus Cell in Dormir, the Sleeping Café. What Inoue did to himself and Miko was shot on film from start to finish and left addressed to me. I only watched that film once. It's recorded and archived inside me, and whenever I look at the Yellow Hell Spring, the images are displayed there before me, as if I were a projector. And like a bewitched Narcissus unable to look away, I'm compelled to keep watching Inoue slide his knife into Miko's heart and liver and then, while Miko's blood is spilling, stab himself in the throat, cutting deep through and bursting his carotid artery.

It's as if I've lost track of the passage of time, and the incident is always happening in the moment. Memories have a mind of their own. I've probably undergone some significant changes over these past five years, but, for me, each and every second of the present always starts back at square one. Inoue's document, which you all have just read, is not merely an artifact from the past.

I also sometimes feel as though I was born and raised in this mountain retreat and that people named Inoue and Miko are my imaginary friends and that the incident is also make-believe. Back then, just as it says in Inoue's document, I thought we were all born clinging to the sense that we were alive. That's why I thought my heart couldn't break. I still haven't changed my mind. However, over the past five years, I've been forced to accept a different way of living. And it's only made me stronger and able to endure more. To borrow Mokuren's words, maybe I am something of a good-natured and friendly nihilist, but even so, the unleashing of Inoue's posts over the internet and the anticipation of my own arrest have really taken their toll on me.

As I'm sure you're aware, it's against the law to expose others to Inoue's files. I may already have been arrested by the time you are reading this. Yet once those files are copied onto millions of hard drives all over the world, there will be no way to erase and destroy them. When people start to forget, I wander out into cyberspace to release them once again.

Why would I do something so heroic at this stage? And what's more, why am I writing a document of my own and linking Inoue's up to the present like this?

Is it because I want to give new life to Inoue's final request? Please! There's no way in hell. If Inoue came back to life and started talking that same shit again, I'd kill him myself.

Do I want to rewrite the curse Inoue put on society in my own words? Maybe I do. But then what use would I have for that long-since forgotten document of his? Wouldn't the rambling document I'm writing now be more than enough?

Am I sick and tired of having to keep a watchful eye out on the "reservation"? If anything, I've been sick and tired of life since I was born. And the actual circumstances here aren't what you'd call particularly tiring anyway. Visitors to the "reservation" have to go through a strict security check, and we lodgers are few and far between. We're supposedly psychologically isolated, but those of us who live here are free to come and go as we please. Mokuren and some others are always traveling overseas, we get along well enough with the cops here, and once you're used to it, every day is nice and quiet. Looking over my shoulder while uploading these files to get the public's attention takes a lot more out of me.

To be honest, I don't really know myself. Let's just say I want to take advantage of the times and leave it at that.

Unlike Inoue, I'm not asking for these files to be circulated and multiplied, or any other kind of chain mail crap. Those who don't want to read can stop here. If you are irritated, then please close it. And it's okay with me if you mark the content as harmful and enable a filter. I half-expect browsers themselves will be outlawed.

But for those of you sympathetic readers, I recommend you print and bind it. You can read different things between the lines that way. Reading it out loud on a street corner might be good too. If you are shocked that you'd never heard any of this before, go ahead and ask your history teacher or someone about it. Then you can be a threat to security too. Presto! Doesn't that make you feel alive? Or else you can keep these secret truths close to your heart and start to feel like you are someone who matters.

The waters of Yellow Hell Spring are still, so the yellow sand settled deep in the bottom looks like it's pushing up to the surface, which has turned into a golden plate reflecting the atmospheric light. In my eyes, the yellow-hued Narcissus Cell naturally materializes in that golden surface. The underwater room is awash in the yellow rays of indirect light bouncing off the floors and walls and floating like fog. Buried beneath the surface are the three red lip-shaped recliners, the grass eyelashes placed oh so carefully along the edges of the oversized table modeled after an eyeball, the wall-unit laptop and AV panel, and the huge plasma monitors.

Inoue and I got a kick out of that kitschy and artificial interior, and we often met there to nap and chill out after a day of filming. Inoue always said, "When we get together with Mikoto, you have to bring him here. I'll already be asleep anyway, so all three of us can sleep together. Wouldn't it be just like us for the first time to start with a nap?" We really did sleep well. We could sense that we existed while we were asleep. I think a lot of other people must have felt the same way, because with the momentum of a single cell organism dividing and reproducing, Sleeping Cafés suddenly started to pop up everywhere in the capital.

But now, the only people asleep inside the Narcissus Cell I see reflected on the yellow screen are Miko and Inoue. I'm not there.

The two of them are arguing, every day a repetition of that day. The document Inoue had worked on until dawn to finish is projected large on the wall monitor. Before uploading it, Inoue wanted Miko to read it and give his consent, but Miko's response is harsh.

"Don't let me get in your way. I won't stop you. But I don't know about this. I'm just letting it be known that I have reservations." The only figure visible on film is Miko's, and he looks directly at the camera while speaking. He wears a light-colored t-shirt, but little else is distinct under the yellow lighting.

"But I learned all this from you. I digested your teachings and just paraphrased. Don't tell me *you're* not sure. You have to fucking get it." You can't see Inoue protesting on film, but his deep voice resonates more loudly and clearly than Miko's, which lets you know he's close to the mic.

"I just think there's been some misunderstanding."

"Didn't you send me an email last night to say you felt the same way?"

"Actually, I was trying to tell you I felt a disconnect. I think you're turning His Young Majesty's intentions upside-down."

"Fuck His Majesty. I worked hard to understand what you were saying. But you come here and take back everything you said. That's pretty cowardly, man. What, you just can't handle the responsibility anymore?"

"No, I'm just not going to take responsibility for something you thought up." Miko smiles sweetly and moves outside the camera's line of view.

"Read it! I didn't twist around your words and dream this up on my own." Inoue stands up, and the camera appropriately bears down on Miko.

"Okay, maybe you got the spelling right, but you distorted the meaning. Look, up to here, you've got the meaning exactly backwards."

They go back and forth with that inane bickering.

The intensity of their dispute only grows more heated with the buildup of abuse they hurl at each other, and it seems the next logical step would be for them to come to blows. I imagine Inoue felt incredibly wronged right before he lost it.

But he didn't rush into a love suicide because he'd lost it. For one thing, in spite of the severe content and as hot as the discussion was, Inoue's voice was blissed-out. He seemed almost slap-happy. As long as he could keep up that abstract and philosophical tug-of-war with Miko, he would have continued to put off the love suicide plan even if he had been moved to violence again. The feedback from battling wits and standing his ground in an engagement with Miko must have made Inoue feel alive, more so than the actual content of their conversation. That extreme talk and even those subversive notes were nothing more than attempts to stage a fight, to provoke Miko.

But Miko sabotaged what was supposed to have been Inoue's beloved game with an unexpected announcement. Namely, he said that I would be there soon.

I actually was on my way to Dormir at that very moment. Mokuren and I had moved up our plans and hung out the night before, so I ended up with free time. The day before, the day of the State Funeral, Miko and Inoue both took off without me after their fight, so I figured what the hell and went out drinking with Mokuren.

We were out until after two in the morning, getting hammered. While Mokuren was downing shot after shot of seven year-old Havana Club like it was green tea, she gave me a hard time about still being in love, poking fun of my tragic abandonment.

When it comes right down to it, romance is a simple game of pretending to be lovers. Jealousy, affection, and lust included, it's all just play-acting, and how we play our roles is established at the beginning. It gets to be pretty fucking ridiculous after you walk through it over and over again. It's no big deal if you know you're acting out a story and are having fun with it. Sure there can be a certain amount of variation. But no normal adult is going to enjoy playing the same role all the time. And when you gradually do step outside your role, the battle begins. There's a power struggle between you and your partner, and nobody wins. I don't know how you feel about it, Iroha, but from what I saw earlier, you all hit the dead-end of a triangular relationship. I'm not talking about the kind of triangle where everyone's vying for a lover. No, there's an unnatural power relationship with you three, and it seems like each of you thinks it's not worth it. If the endgame of your romance is that sense that it's not worth it, you might as well call it off. If you want to get things straightened out, why don't the three of you come out to our place in the country? My family just bought a lodge up in the mountains. We still have a lot of repairs to do and could use a few extra hands. Count me in too, and we all can work on rebuilding relationships one at a time. Wouldn't that be nice? All together, there are six ways it could go, what with four of us. Sounds good, huh?

That hit me where it hurts, but I also had the good feeling that comes after a well-needed overhaul. I was still feeling the effects of Mokuren's words when I got home and, as was my routine, checked Inoue's site, which was why I wrote that email message you read in his manifesto.

I woke up the next evening and called Miko to see if he wanted to have dinner with me. Miko said, "Perfect timing. I'm about to head out to meet Inoue at Café Dormir. It'd be great if you'd join us." I felt the blood rush to my head and hesitated for a moment, but I got a hold of myself and answered, "It'll take me a little while, but I'll meet up with you there later."

I brought along the cobalt blue bowl and porcelain spoon Inoue had left behind at the dim sum restaurant. When I arrived, blockades were set up on all the streets around Café Dormir. On the other side of a pile of squad cars and ambulances, a steady stream of cops filed in and out. Police tape adhered to the surroundings like moss. I called Miko's cell phone. A voice I didn't recognize answered. Before long, the owner of that voice appeared and took me away in a squad car. The owner of that voice also officiously explained that what I'd already predicted had indeed taken place. Maybe he thought I'd faint or lose it, because he held me tightly by the shoulders and didn't let go.

When Miko announces that I am on my way, Inoue forgets his lines and clams up for a bit. It was probably like what happens when you're engrossed in a movie and the film starts to burn up right at the climax. The world into which you'd been drawn suddenly disappears, and all you see is an empty white screen.

"Well then, we'll just have to finish this before she gets here. Otherwise, it wouldn't be fair to her." Inoue's voice is unnaturally cheerful. The camera moves away from Miko's face and zooms in on the wall monitor. You can hear Inoue's finger click the mouse, and his documents are uploaded.

Unless you're exceedingly stupid, I'm sure you can imagine what happens next. But Miko didn't try to run away from the Narcissus Cell. He didn't call out for help. He didn't even try to contact me. He sat back quietly in the red lip-shaped reclining chair and watched intently as Inoue set up his camera in the corner of the room. Miko betrayed me in the end. He made the choice to become Inoue's partner in crime.

Inoue separates from his lens and moves diagonally to the opposite corner, the first time his own image had ever been filmed by his camera. He is wearing a whitish shirt. He pulls an army knife out of his backpack and asks, "Is that spot okay?" Miko replies back vacantly, "Yeah, sure." Inoue returns to the central table and drinks the rest of his herbal tea, then moves further away from the camera again, turns his back to the lens, and stands next to Miko.

A muffled voice says, "All right, hold your breath for a sec." Inoue's arm works furiously. Miko makes coughing noises. A soothing voice says, "Hold on. Just a little more." Inoue's arm quickly moves back and forth many times. Meanwhile, Miko's coughs and groans reverberate.

Before long, Inoue lies down alongside Miko. For a brief moment, his red-stained arms and shirt cuffs, as well as his splattered chest are recorded, but once he lies down beneath the camera level, he's no longer visible – just moans, coughs, and violent breathing like Miko's sewn together by a red arm and red knife that rise and fall from view several times. Finally, the arm rises even higher and falls with greater force, and after that nothing stirs in the room. A short time later, the disc is full, and the recording stops.

Even after the camera dies, Inoue waits for the world to change in the darkness between scenes. But since for him the real world itself is the world of the dead, he doesn't have anywhere to go after death and has to remain in this world. The moment of death is drawn out for countless hours and days and years of everyday dying, and the cathartic transition to eternity never comes. I gaze at the surface of the spring and see the knife thrust into their flesh thousands and millions of times, veins punctured, blood that never stops flowing, faint breathing that never lets up, and four eyes holding onto the last flicker of life that look up at me with unrequited passion. But I refuse their passion and don't try to understand it, instead taking it all in as if only light and sound, just another overblown film by Shôji Inoue. He was a camera until the end.

To me, that film is a joke. It's not a nightmare anymore. What worse joke could there be than for Inoue to think his camera-self watches and keeps recording the image of him killing and dying just like it was "Mixed Cameras" or "Infinite Hell."

Why did Inoue and Miko act out such a B comedy? They surely would have been happy enough to get some thrills out of a heated argument and exchange of blows or something, so why did Miko have to set it off? He had to have known how Inoue would respond to the announcement I was on my way. Did Miko want to die at Inoue's hand? Inoue had become a slave to his own crazy theory and simply backed himself into a corner where the conclusion meant dying even without wanting to die. But Miko must have really wanted to die. And if so, what the fuck was I? Was he letting me take care of him for no reason? I was always dogged by the sense that life was phony and it didn't matter when we died. But the desire that led those two to die seems fundamentally different. They had faith that I'd understand and sympathize with their desire, but I flat-out will not. The death they advocated feels more like a lie than any death I feel. They were so sweet. Why did they have to reject all my ideas like that?

My thoughts on not forgiving them and the torment I feel are exactly like what I wrote in that final email I sent to Inoue. They haven't changed since then, and they can't be replaced. And, if I can just add one thing, he wrote that he erased my message without reading it a second time. That is a load of crap, because the whole thing is included verbatim in his document.

If I'd been driven to despair and tried to follow them in death, it would have looked like I'd put his theory into practice, and maybe that would have gone a long way towards satisfying public curiosity. The incident was widely reported as a love suicide following His Young Majesty in death. The media learned of the existence of Inoue's document the next day and began training the spotlight on me, as the person who held the key. Was I supposed to laugh at the big joke? Was I supposed to be enraged? Was I supposed to be consumed with grief? My feelings were stuck somewhere between all three, and I was at a loss. But I am certain that I called Mokuren a bunch of times to say, "Fucking kill me already!" Mokuren wasn't about to cut off contact with me at a time like that, but she grew irritated, which was obvious in her attitude and forced comments about how I didn't die, so all I could do is keep on living. I nodded appropriately.

The incident was Inoue's demented brainchild, and it took each step on its own without paying me any mind. The next day, a twenty-two year old man and twenty-four year old woman committed suicide by poison in a members-only private room in "Roppongi Hills," a reading lounge.

Initially, people thought it was merely a lovers' suicide pact carried out in Roppongi. However, evidence that they'd accessed Inoue's site was discovered on the computer that came with the private room, and speculations that they'd killed themselves in response to Inoue's call abounded, so the event took on a different meaning than what would have been the case had it just been seen as the individual actions of a particular pessimistic couple. Because they didn't leave behind any suicide notes or other writings of their own that might have explained their reasons, public interest immediately turned to Inoue's work on the internet.

Just as he'd planned, Inoue's document multiplied by leaps and bounds over the net and was even picked up and mauled by the rabid mass media, which went crazy with sensationalized interpretations of the shocking contents. People even made their own compilations of earlier films Inoue had sold or aired on his webcast, and viewers could tack on their own bone-chilling commentaries, which were replayed on TV. I was appalled to watch a TV anchor at a broadcast subsidiary of Miko's company look anguished while recounting the ins and outs of Miko's past with the attitude of someone who had a special right to do so. I thought about ways to assassinate whoever was responsible at the TV station at the time. They went through his "spirited away" period after His Young Majesty's death and the days I took care of him. They even aired footage from "Infinite Hell." I'm not sure if it was for a cash payoff, but Miko's parents let themselves get used and handed over his personal effects.

Whether or not it was true, all sorts of bullshit was reported about the person of the moment who piqued everyone's curiosity, me. When they found out that the couple who'd poisoned themselves were both "spirited away" after His Young Majesty's death, they featured exposé close-ups on the "spirited away" connection. They said we were seeing the early stages of a cult that believed people who had been spirited away were the "chosen ones," and their proof was Inoue's own written admission that he had been converted by the revelations Miko had while "spirited away." They labeled me the lover shared between the two sect founders who would take over the reins in accordance with their wishes and make them saints. Of course, my real name was circulating freely over the net, and my mom's house was surrounded by the mass media, so it wasn't as if my name was really withheld. If Mokuren hadn't helped my mom and me escape up to her mountain lodge to hide out, I was so close to the deep end that I might have started talking in curses just to satisfy the general public's expectations.

Thankfully, I didn't have to go to Miko and Inoue's funeral, but after seeing the ridiculous images, I wondered how much a corpse matters. At most, they were wax figures, and I couldn't stop smiling at the idea of the two of them at the crematorium, like two identical burning candles. Probably the best they could spin out of that would be stories like "the lover of the cult founders finally goes mad."

Ascension Pass is located in the small Peaks of Many Gods mountain range that connects the boundaries of Okuchichibu and Jôshû-Shinshû in a place where the ridge dips a bit into a small canyon. Apparently there used to be a road that crossed over the pass, but now the main access is through a tunnel, and since the forests of cedars on the mountains grew so thick, people stopped coming up here to hike or climb. The lodge was basically deserted when it caught the eye of Mokuren, who was entrusted with the task of house-hunting.

Mokuren's folks, who kept shop in Yokohama's Chinese-Town, went in on a vacation home purchase with some colleagues who shared roots back on the continent. They were charged with locating the property and negotiating everything, and the lion's share of that responsibility fell to Mokuren. She made use of her vast network of connections to find the mountain lodge and decided on her own to make a bid on it. She negotiated a real bargain of a price and managed to raise enough money to finance it. She parlayed that success into claiming the biggest voice in how the property was managed.

Mokuren had told me that the place was a fixer-upper and that she and the friends whose help she'd enlisted were in the middle of some home improvement projects, so I'd imagined a dilapidated and moldy, old house. But to my surprise, it was a fabulously renovated log cabin. We arrived at the crack of dawn, and it looked like a big, gentle living creature that had emerged from the sea and was lingering playfully on the shore.

Nobody inside the body of that living thing was awake yet, and as soon as Mokuren showed me to the bedroom, I collapsed and fell fast asleep. I slept straight through for two days. When I woke up on the morning of the third day and got my bearings, I felt like the last twenty-five years of my life had been a bad dream.

The day I woke up, Mokuren, her dad, and a bunch of her friends were there working on the lodge. They said I didn't need to do anything until I'd recovered from the fatigue, so my mom and I helped out with the cooking and cleaning, and the rest of the time, I just loafed around, filming everyone while they made tables, chairs, shelves, and things. The following day, some people left and others arrived, with yet another rotation a few days later, and then Mokuren's dad headed back down the mountain a week later. With all the comings and goings, I couldn't remember the names of the only two people remaining, a couple, a man and a woman. They introduced themselves as Udzuki and Kisaragi, probably not their real names. According to them, as long as you did your part to help out, you had the right to use the lodge free of charge. They said all the people coming and going were Mokuren's friends. They were a curious pair whose only common thread may very well have been their shared connection to Mokuren. No one had a grasp on the big picture of what all those relationships were.

I'd had a taste of this sort of scenario with Mokuren before. In high school, she had networks of friends I didn't know outside of school and a slew of flashy romances. She gave me a hard time over my relationship, but back in the day, she earned the nickname "the anaconda of love" because her relationships were anything but normal. You'd see her with a new guy or girl on an almost daily basis. No one could tell if a particular person was in the running for something more serious, if she was dating lots of them at the same time, or if she was just going through one lover after another. She hooked up with a lot of people, but it never seemed to make a dent in her personal pace. She was never in a hurry and was somehow laid back about it all, detached and positive at the same time like she knew she had to flirt a little to get some loving or that she wouldn't get fireworks without first advertising a bit. But whatever the reason, her capacity was so large that she never reached the saturation point. At the time, I felt like a mere blip on the corner of the screen in the movie of Mokuren's life. She saw me as more than that, but the fear of betrayal kept me from getting too close to her.

She got older, and her relationships matured, which might account for the range in ages and types of people who gather here. Intellectually, I understood, but still I was as cautious as before and didn't want to get too closely acquainted with any of them. Mokuren said it was okay to trust everyone, but how was I to know who would disappear with such a high turnover? Luckily, we can live as we please here. Those who want to get involved in intense conversations can do so (which is how Udzuki and Kisaragi met and got together here), and no one bothers those who prefer to be left alone. So, all I did was hide behind my camera and take walks.

When I left the lodge and ventured out onto the mountain ridge, I was immediately surrounded by a different kind of stillness. All I heard were birdsongs and rustling leaves. I slowly hiked along the edge of the mountain while filming. Along the way, I walked down a side road on the western slope, where all I could see were cedars, a novel sight for someone like me who lived in Yokohama. The landscape is starker now. However, rows and rows of different kinds of trees peppered the eastern slope back then. That part of the forest was manmade. Somebody apparently planted a variety of trees over there as an alternative to the cedars in the days when people freaked out about allergies. They didn't just plant seedlings, but actually brought fully grown trees all the way over from deep in the heart of Shinshû's mountains. The woods were thick with curvy trees and fat trees, hollow trees with lots of holes and big trees with a gazillion leaves. I was met with one fascinating surprise after another when I first explored that environment, which was inhabited by strong and sturdy wild animals like bears and wild boars, as well as poisonous bugs, snakes, and plants. (Were they also transplants from Shinshû?)

I was nervous, because it seemed a little dangerous. But I'm someone who lives behind the camera, tucked away from the world of lights and sounds in a small, dark, and totally empty pocket. Nothing can harm me, because I don't brush up against anything in the world, and nothing in the world can touch me. Telling myself that allowed me to relax and walk out into the woods with confidence.

Once there, I was immediately bathed in the fresh green smell wafting down from the trees that spoke in inaudible whispers, words, and sighs. Those sighs were filled with oxygen, so when I breathed deeply, it felt like each cell in my body was rejuvenated and the parched thin outer layers of old skin disappeared.

I burned. That old skin had been like reels of film that shielded my little pocket from the world outside. Without those reels, I thought a poisonous bug or lizard would bite me before long. And sure enough, a wasp or hornet was hanging around in the sunlight, and a winged bug I didn't recognize grazed my ear, leaving behind a whirring sound in its wake. Billows of dark mist were skirting over the horizon right at me, and I thought they were probably mosquito-infested. A single white spot jutting out of the red earth was a mushroom. I had to worry about whether a fat mountain leech the size of a penis would fall on me from overhead. And the scariest part was when I stepped on dry leaves and it sounded like someone was following and steadily gaining on me.

I made a speedy and desperate getaway to the interior.

My feet fell into something soft and cool. I let out a cry. When I looked down, I saw that my feet were covered in mud. For a moment, I thought, "Shit, I'm standing in a swampy sink hole," but it was only a puddle where some water dripping off the crags had collected. The mossy crags were moist and very green. It was almost like green water oozed out of the rocks themselves. I made my way up to the top of the crags to investigate. The water was bubbling out of a crevice in the ground that was surrounded by trees and sending a thin stream out over the crags to keep them moist. I was thirsty, but the water wasn't deep enough to scoop up in my hands. So, I went back down below the crags, where I could finally cup my hands to catch a trickle and quench my thirst. The cool freshness of the water revived me. Water that bubbles up through tree roots must carry tree essences, so I think there was probably as much oxygen in the water as there was in the trees' sighs.

I shed several layers of old skin and was revived many times over. I returned to the lodge in good spirits. Of course, film reels aren't soft or supple, so they don't vanish so easily. I was like an onion wrapped in layer upon layer. No matter how many layers you peeled off me, no inner form would be revealed, just more layers and then nothing. That's because I'm like the blank space where whatever is caught on a reel of film is recorded and imprinted. Fresh water in the palm of my hand, the sigh after I licked the water off my lips, the shining green moss, the green day, the sunlight, the sunbathing wasp, the sound of the bug's wings, birds' chirping, my yelp, the stirring of the wind, and everything else is stored on a disc. That recording came in handy later.

It was back when the search for water became an issue. Electricity made its way up to the mountain lodge, but we had to rely on our own nearby well for water. There were signs that the old well might be running dry, so we had to ferret out another water source.

I told everyone about the water I'd found bubbling out from the crags and showed them the footage. I took Mokuren and an expert there so they could survey the location and water quality. The expert held a rod, which looked like a slick crape myrtle branch, against the ground and then gave us the go-ahead. Apparently that rod was somehow a listening device, and the expert heard water running.

First we had to dig a hole at the base of the crag to serve as a reservoir. After plenty of water had collected, we released some goldfish to keep bugs from breeding and carved out a path for a stream to carry water away from one part of the pool. That little channel runs up to the lodge, where we built another little well in the garden for storing the water that gets pumped up through a purification system. We also made a back-channel for when we get a lot of rain.

In those days, we just called the reservoir "the spring," and it was still protected by a thick grove of trees. But year in and year out, the number of days when the hot yellow sand-filled winds blew increased, battering down the trees until it looked like a forest fire had cleared the woods, and yellow sand settled into the loamy red soil, changing it into a desert. The old trees by the spring didn't have the strength to resist either, and they, too, were destroyed. The only thing standing guard by the spring now is a lifeless old trunk. To keep the water flow from evaporating quickly, we ran it along the sides of the crags. That killed the moss, which was left standing as earthy yellow fuzz. The water used to be resplendent in obsidian underneath the shade of trees, but now the yellow sand at the bottom interacts with sunlight, and the surface glistens in gold.

The water has continued to flow from the spring, so the lives of everyone on Ascension Pass have been granted an extension. With precious little protective cover from the hot yellow sand storms, the flora died though, and the area was transformed into a wide-open field devoid of life. And still, so much of these islands' population clings to dusty plains of concrete and sand. The introduction of drought-tolerant plant life played a role in mitigating the water shortage. But whenever the short rainy period comes, there is no escape from the floods produced by the onslaught of consecutive days of heavy rain and run-off from the surrounding mountains. Each year, the damage gets more extensive, but the residents don't move, because those floodwaters are also their lifeline. The special characteristics of each of the four seasons became as indistinct as if they'd donned a Noh mask. All we have now are a cold dry season, a hot dry season, and a brief rainy season. We've lost the cyclical sense that a year with four seasons might come again, and instead it feels like we are progressing along a single desolate path, where sometimes it's hot, sometimes it's cold, and sometimes a squall hits.

I later asked Mokuren if she had checked into water sources when she first bought the lodge because she had a premonition of what would happen. Without so much as cracking a smile or pausing from pulling up clumps of weeds, she asked, "Are you implying it was my idea for us to be confined to this reservation?" That shut me up. "It just worked out like this by chance. That's all. Actually, it's a freak of chance that we are alive at all."

From her lips to the world below, where it was all the rage to say "the self-reliant who have survived are the chosen ones." According to those who have taken this motto for our times to heart, we are all corralled here.

But I'm getting ahead of myself. It was already summer by the time we finished making the reservoir. We dug down about two meters, and water started spurting out all over the place, which is how we learned there really were several underground water veins in our area. We sealed the base with a sturdy layer of clay, covered that with pebbles, and then inlayed large rocks along the walls. The water level rose steadily, which meant the lodgers had to work quickly and ably. I devoted all my time to the project for days on end. It was so hot that people made dumb jokes about how our sweat alone would fill the reservoir.

It turned out to be an astonishingly large reservoir, and it must have taken about two weeks for the whole thing to fill up with water. During that time, we started construction on the channel stream beds. We were small in number and proceeded with the work carefully. I paced myself, taking time off for walks and to check out the mountains.

As I got increasingly used to the eco-system's variety of bugs, birds, and lizards, I grew fascinated with the subtlest of changes in the woods. Through a change in the smell of the dampness or a bird's call, I could sense that it would rain even if there wasn't a cloud in the sky, and I could tell autumn had arrived even if it was still hot. If the wind blew a certain way, the sound of the whole forest would change. And there were all sorts of rhythms and sounds: the ruffling of the leaves, the chafing and creaking of tree limbs, the fierce whistling through the gaps between trees, the warbles and cries of birds, the bugle calls of the cicadas, the bell tones of the evening bugs, the pattering of raindrops on leaves from pianissimo to a thundering forte. One could never get tired of listening to this soft and eternal recital. If I could have absorbed sustenance through my fingernails and skin the way leaves and branches do, I would have stayed there forever. I was so enchanted, and I caught what I could on film. I'm reminded of something Miko said. "Your films are all about you. They're completely personal diaries and too private. It's like you'll end up losing yourself. If you get to that point, you'll be reborn somewhere where your films can start representing something."

I feel like now I can understand what he meant by that. While filming, I'm like a slightly funky tree planted in the forest. It's a little different from the anonymity I experienced while becoming one with my camera in the city. Back then I lost myself. But I didn't disappear in the forest. I became a part of it. The forest also accepted me and was changed ever so slightly by my presence. Under the awning of trees, fish darted around the overflowing waters of the new obsidian spring faster than ever. I also felt tempted by the desire to melt into the spring – like I'd wanted to become just another tree in the forest.

I suppose I've always wanted to be something else. I was my skin, a reflective cocoa powder-colored screen. Maybe that's why I adopted Miko's ideas as my own so easily.

Miko wasn't like Inoue. Inoue was like me, nothing without something to reflect, just an empty screen. A blank sheet of paper until someone writes something on it. We took our cameras into every nook and cranny of these islands because we enjoyed being able to capture detailed bits of light and sound. However, we didn't express interest in one another. If we had, we would've confronted the awkwardness of having to look at the reality we tried to avoid, the reality you can see in "Mixed Cameras," the reality that there was nothing between us.

While sharing my sense of being a broadcast receiver, Miko was, at the same time, trying to be our projector. When he tried to face the screen and release light and sound, he struggled.

For example, we went out filming, and he would not stop trying to get me to talk about myself while I ran the camera. He wouldn't let up, questioning me about memories of my dad and what I thought of my mom, giving me the third degree to try and expose something authentic about me while I was seeing myself as the camera. I couldn't keep filming the way I liked, and he wouldn't let me stay hidden behind the camera. The result was footage with major discrepancies between the words and images. The images took on a strangely painful meaning because of my speech. Actually, the truth is the footage itself had no meaning. The story of my life just made it seem like it did.

That was a terrible experience. Why? Because if you dress up something that is only light and sound in meaning and stories, there's bound to be a lie in there somewhere.

"Iroha, you're always saying that anything you get on film is all sound and light, that there's no difference between people and things, and you're right about that. But that sound and light take on new meaning when they're transmitted through the camera. Saying you feel like you'll disappear if you're captured fully on film is a cop-out. After all, if you are holding the camera, your presence gets recorded too, even if only in the slightest noise or shadow. To break it down further, let's say your body temperature makes the area warmer. That's going to trigger a change in the color of the surroundings. Or what if you were filming in a rural village somewhere in Africa? It's not like the people there could be oblivious to you or your camera."

"We've already been through this. Whether it's a building in Shinjuku, a giraffe in Africa, or a meadow, once it's filmed, it's digitally transformed into a recording signal."

"Okay, so even if you think you yourself and a building are just recording signals, that doesn't mean you don't have feelings. The indifference you feel when you think you disappear and are merely a recording signal is still a kind of feeling, and your films will never ring true until you take responsibility for that as a part of this world. I couldn't care less when it comes to myself. And that's why I really want to really live and say. 'Hey, this is how I'm living'."

The real Miko was very reserved and didn't stand out in a crowd. The average person wouldn't even notice he was there.

You could have said the same about Inoue and me. However, we were also the kind of people who'd show some concern for our own survival by hanging on for our dear lives if we were spared in a great flood that swept away everyone else.

I didn't pretend to proselytize my ideas even to myself. What patted, licked, and nibbled at the emptiness, or "apathy" even, of my melancholic depression was the recognition that I wasn't simply projecting light. I was touched by the smells, shapes, and substance bound up in living things. The temperature, air, moisture, and weight of their breath, as well as the palpable presence of Miko filled me with feelings other than "apathy." Maybe Miko's ideas were just starting to resonate with me.

So you can imagine how hard it was for me when even Miko was spirited away after the great flood, His Young Majesty's death, hit, and why I couldn't help but think Inoue was full of shit when he acted like he was trying to bring about the end of the world with all his talk about disappearing. And I can only describe Miko as having been destined to betray me, and nothing I could do was going to change that.

I was fairly dark and sullen when surrounded by the lodgers, but dyed in shades of green when I entered the woods. There, my substance melted away and I could think about Miko and Inoue like this, and my treks to the spring became a daily ritual.

My afternoons were spent working on the water channel and other projects and hiking in the woods during my free time, and my evenings were devoted to editing work in my room. Therefore, I didn't get too involved in relationships with other people in the lodge. Mokuren said the policy on Ascension Pass was that people who wanted to live that way could, so I always approached people other than Kisaragi and Udzuki as casual acquaintances. These escapees, evacuees, and refugees enjoyed a relatively relaxed lifestyle here. Of course, that's the way Mokuren arranged everything.

But not my mom. You couldn't tell her from the others when they were working, but she felt like she didn't belong. Her constant refrain was, "No matter how much you try to convince yourself this is only crisis management, the way of life here is simply not normal." She said that a "proper life" meant working hard and, at the end of the day, "spending private time in a private place."

She complained like that and wanted to return to the life she'd had before as soon as possible, but public interest in Inoue only escalated. I worried that the media might zero in on her, and she'd run off at the mouth and end up saying something weird. I also smelled some kind of impending violence in the air. So while it took a little effort, we detained her. She couldn't adapt to life at the mountain lodge, and what we'd done depressed her so much that it seemed like an act of cruelty to do so.

A chronic helplessness ate away at her. Since she didn't have anywhere to go when even we weren't getting along, she soon became a radio junkie. (I'm glad we didn't have a TV in the small room.) She'd listen over the kind of comp headphones they hand out to old guys at the race tracks and give me the play-by-play on the latest news as soon as she heard it, especially if the news involved a love suicide related to Inoue's document. She'd wrinkle up her forehead and recount the details as if she were telling me current news about Inoue himself. I definitely did not want to hear it. It was hard to stomach the mentality that reproductions of an unparalleled masterpiece were diminishing in quality. But my mom seriously thought it would somehow console me for her to validate Inoue's influential powers, and she'd say things like, "What Shôji said really struck a chord. You might even say he had the gift of foresight. That is, if you allowed yourself to think about it positively." And that's not all. She made that comment after recounting the following story of a mother-daughter love suicide without batting an eye.

I think it was the third love suicide, and it happened right before the beginning of the rainy season. A thirty year-old who worked as a temp at a local bank and still lived at home strangled her mother to death and then hung herself. It happened in a residential Sendai suburb.

Of course, they discovered Inoue's document down-loaded on the woman's computer. Furthermore, she agreed with Inoue and advocated his ideas in an anonymous online journal.

"My sentiments are exactly the same as Shôji Inoue's. I want to quietly libertate [original spelling as is] tired and confined living beings. That is what I am too after all. Without people like us, this world would surely have grown stronger and more meaningful. We are the kind who lead a futile existence together with the increasing herd of other useless people. Soon, and it won't be long now, am I to become another sacrificial lamb?" Yada, yada, yada.

This person's goal was to get all the useless people out of this world by turning this world into the otherworld. Well, that would mean that once this world is the otherworld, where ever she is would be filled with the same useless people.

That's not to say that a part of me doesn't sympathize. I am keenly aware that dipshit parents raise dipshit kids. I even felt faint while listening to none other than my own mom tell me the outline of this love suicide story.

You also saw the opposite pattern. A twenty-six year-old clutched her newborn baby and jumped into the sea on a stormy early summer day. The note she left nearby read, "After I gave birth I realized that to bring a child into the world at this time is like planting summer grass seeds at the end of autumn. What can become of one fated to die so soon? It's a pity. I want to take the blame for that. I'm sorry, baby. I'm taking you away to be born again in a better world." Thus went her sicko-lullaby. The outraged public's hardcore back-lash against this woman was particularly vicious. "What kind of bitch could expect to be forgiven when she apologized first so that she could die with peace of mind?"

Before that mother-child love suicide, at the peak of the rainy season, the corpses of two men were discovered inside a parked car in Aokigahara. Exhaust was running in through a hose. They were students at the same university in the city, where they apparently hung out quite a bit. They were holding hands, their wrists bound together by rope, and, in what appeared to be painful homemade tattoos, each had the name of the other etched into his arm with these words: "Chung-chi, Blood for Life" and "Kôsuke, Blood for Life." All the more horrifying, each had a couple hundred cc's of the other's blood, which was of a different type, injected into his own body. There was also evidence they'd taken narcotics. It must have been some kind of weird sexual union for them. I was devastated again and privately sentenced those assholes to death. The method of punishment would be draining their blood until they died of blood loss.

In the shadow of each incident like that were the stagnant and stale frustrations of the unseen concerned parties, people in positions like mine who were surely fuming. But the news accounts couldn't touch more than the tiniest piece of the surface, and most of what they did cover was distorted anyway. Even with Inoue, they started out with taglines like "pure-hearted youth of today follow His Young Majesty in death," but once they learned of the existence of the document, reporters started describing a fanatical cult before you could say boo. That's why I know I'm probably being too reckless by relaying these stories with news reports as my only sources and without knowing the individual circumstances.

Even so, I can still be certain that there were some threads connecting the various incidents to Inoue's document. The media also reported subsequent love suicides as related to Inoue's words, which, in turn, shaped the public's understanding. Internet service providers were asked to delete uploads of Inoue's document voluntarily. Most providers complied, but the request wasn't legally binding, and there were more than a few individual servers that went under the radar. And if you factor in how it could be circulated via email too, it was virtually impossible to obliterate the document altogether.

An exasperated Tokyo Special Prosecutor must have thought a message still needed to be sent even though the document couldn't be destroyed, so more than three months after he died, Inoue was charged with felonious homicide. (Years later, he was found guilty, but it didn't make the news.)

It was all so ludicrous I couldn't stand it. If you're part of a love suicide, you'll get sentenced to death for murder? How the hell is that supposed to deter anyone from dying? The craziest part was the overwhelming public support for these measures.

Inoue was hated that much. There were even vitriolic rants on various newspaper's online message boards – with choice comments like "mother fucking grim reaper." While I was in a place where I knew I was safe and definitely wouldn't be killed, suicide instructions appeared one after the other, preying on the weaknesses of earnest people who were precariously teetering on the edge. Someone would whisper into the ear of a person who was really trying to make it and say, "We're just letting you live. That's why it's so painful. If you die, you truly can be yourself." That's the kind of malicious crime that should be outlawed! Even if only for show, they could say a law was powerful enough to eliminate that kind of behavior, and maybe that would deter such cruelty.

From my perspective, society was hoping to manufacture a sense of security by hating Inoue. Including my mom. She would express indignation over the way the media and courts dealt with Inoue, but without even noticing it herself, she also had her own way of putting down Inoue and Miko. She'd tell me, "The type to get spirited away was too serious, or maybe you'd say too pure." I learned this later after I'd found it on the net, but she'd ripped that comment off from a psychiatrist who was quoted widely in the national papers. The fact that lots of people were "spirited away" notwithstanding, after Inoue's document circulated, they were portrayed as fragile innocents who didn't have the strength to resist, and with that, the climate of bitterness spread. I wasn't "spirited away" myself, which I didn't think was cause to feel either proud or ashamed. It just didn't happen. That's all. People who scorn me for that must want to avoid looking at how they are really the ones ruled by their own weaknesses and dependencies. But Inoue's existence offends them the most because he talked about not having been "spirited away" like it was a dishonor.

I feel compelled to defend Inoue, so I've had to put aside my problems with what he wrote and did. I have to suffer living with him.

My mom reached her limit in the dog days of summer. Her daily routine had grown unnatural and disrupted. She listened to the radio until daybreak and slept until the afternoon. She was sick of feeling like a pest who didn't belong in the mountain lodge and lost the will to do anything. I wasn't in great shape either, caught in the straitjacket of my guilty conscience and irritability.

We were rescued from this stalemate around the end of July, when Kisaragi scored a job at a variety store in Jiyûgaoka. She decided to go back down the mountain and start a new life with Udzuki. They could fit another two people in the car and asked if we'd like to join them. I declined, but my mom jumped at the chance. I was secretly relieved.

The night before the three of them left, we had a cozy going-away party just for us. Even then, my mom was incorrigible with her news anchor-esque rundown of the latest headlines. I couldn't get over her inability to forget about current events for just one night, especially since she was about to leave, but the spirit of the evening had me feeling generous, so I complimented her, "You've gotten pretty good at talking while listening to the radio. Simultaneous interpretation is a real talent."

"According to the latest survey, twenty-three percent of the population feels hopeful about Her New Majesty, eighteen percent does not, and fifty-six percent doesn't feel one way or the other." Mom relayed what she heard, and, with that, the good mood I'd managed to muster abruptly soured.

"What kind of survey is that? Who cares how much support there is for Her Majesty? What's the point?"

Kisaragi was similarly disturbed and grumbled, "Yeah. It's not a celebrity popularity poll after all. When the mourning period ends, I suppose Her New Majesty will get to work."

That didn't jibe with what I was thinking, but Udzuki was even more annoyed and said, "When Her Majesty gets to work, you'll be getting to work too, Kisaragi. And with everyone getting busy like that, we'll go all narcoleptic again when Her New Majesty dies. I don't give a rip if Her Majesty is still in the dumps. I want to be gettin' busy either way."

"I know what you mean by 'getting busy' – don't be such a jerk."

I teased the two of them, saying, "So you and Kisaragi would fall into the twenty-three percent who feel hopeful about Her Majesty?"

"Hardly," Udzuki replied, facing Kisaragi instead of me. "I'm narrow-minded. So, I don't give a damn about anything that's not right in front of me."

Kisaragi explained to Mokuren and me, "That's where I screwed up. I found a job, but he didn't yet, so he gets mad at the idea that everything will get brighter after the succession ceremony and that more people will hit the job market."

"Hell yeah. Is Her Majesty gonna hire me? Is she planning to run an Imperial Employment Bureau or some kind of human resources outfit? She doesn't have the power or authority to create jobs. You're talking out your ass."

"Kisaragi, are you holding out hope for Her New Majesty?"

"I don't know. I wasn't really thinking in terms of Her Majesty so much as what I've got to deal with, with this guy. But maybe some kind of change will come. You know how when one thing starts, another thing ends."

"They said the same thing about His Young Majesty." I could sense the sarcasm and exasperation in my own voice, but I couldn't help myself.

"Well, stories start with beginnings, right? Like you can't have hopes without something bad happening first to open up room for better expectations?"

Udzuki looked mortified and spewed, "What's your deal, Kisaragi? Are you so bored that you actually care about Her Majesty?"

"Oh, I entertain myself just fine. But we are regressing

back to the days before His Young Majesty."

"Seems so," I nodded in agreement.

Maybe it had it something to do with the fact that she was still observing the period of mourning, but compared to His Young Majesty, Her New Majesty came across as formal and stiff like Their Previous Majesties. She was truly an exceptional case, so during the initial phase of succession, hopes, or fears depending on one's outlook, ran high that she might say something bold and audacious, but she dodged all such expectations. Even so, people still hoped her conventional demeanor would only last until the official period of mourning ended the following March and that then she'd let her true colors show.

Udzuki said, "I get the sense Her Majesty wanted to be able to go on with her life unnoticed. So, I think we ought to stop paying attention to her. There's nothing rude about ignoring someone who wants to be ignored. I'm more concerned that what Kisaragi keeps yapping about is boring."

"I have high hopes for Her Majesty too," my mom entered the conversation. "Like Kisaragi was saying, there's something radical about her. Like she'll make a difference that affects us all." My mom was doing the hustle by herself, looking like a fool, and working my last nerve.

Exasperated, I snapped, "Why is everyone so hung up on Majesties?"

"Because Her Majesty is single and a middle-aged woman. Honey, think about what that means. A single woman at that age is assuming such an important position. She's going to serve as an inspiration for other single women her age not to give up and to believe that it won't be long before their day comes too."

There was an element of bragging to that comment coming from my mom, who'd worked on her own to raise me when I was a teenager. I'm not trying to say she never suffered in the process, but she didn't have it that bad. She got alimony, real estate income, and child support payments, and she only worked at the register four half-days a week for about ten years. I'd be lying if I described her as a woman who did it all on her own. And anyway, I was the one who had to listen to all her bitching and moaning back then. It was like who was looking after whom? Who was the parent? At least that's how I see it.

"If that's the case, Mom, why don't you get started on your own new project?"

"My computer? I will. I'm definitely going to start learning how to use it when I get back home. It'll be a way to honor Shôji's last request. I wonder if Her Majesty uses a computer? She probably does. Nowadays, you can't work unless you know how to use a computer, I guess."

"Can you imagine real-time live chats with Her Majesty? That'd be sweet," Udzuki said.

Kisaragi barked, "See! Even you think Her Majesty matters! You can't ignore her either."

"Speaking of jobs, what is Her Majesty's job? Mom, do you know? Does it involve inspiring middle-aged women?"

"Well, I'd say just being a female leader, a woman in charge, the lady who runs the show, who keeps shop. That already counts for something."

"What, so she runs a restaurant too?"

Udzuki's question seemed serious, which ticked me off. "What, are you brain-dead? My mom was just trying to say that her work entails hosting foreign diplomats and stuff."

Mokuren cooly added, "Oh, so she's a restaurant hostess because she's a woman, huh?"

"Her Majesty's a hostess? Isn't that a little nasty?" Who knows what Udzuki was imagining?

Mokuren wasn't going to let the issue go and said, "Hostesses are employees, so I suppose you'd rather call her mama-san?"

Udzuki still didn't get it. "Her Majesty is a downtown mama-san!"

Mokuren pushed back, "Not downtown. More like in a palace surrounded by a moat!"

Udzuki belted out a tragic "a mama-san trapped behind a moat!" He pretended to swoon. "Doesn't 'mama' mean mother in English?"

"What on earth is this child talking about?" I feigned a pensive glance at Kisaragi, laughed, and continued, "Haven't you yourself called my mom 'Iroha's mama'?"

"No, seriously. Check this out. You can call a single middle-aged woman a mama, but that doesn't mean she's a mother."

"A mama's job isn't necessarily mothering." What the hell was I saying?

"I have no freaking clue what you're talking about," Udzuki protested in a loud voice. "Her New Majesty is a Majesty, and she's nothing else, right? So why are you going on and on about all this? Can't you just leave it alone? Gimme a break already!"

"Udzuki is right. It's best to stop." I wanted the conversation to end too.

But my mom was too engrossed and said, "Times have changed. Before His Young Majesty came on the scene, no one gave Majesties a second thought." She was really bothering me. She went right back to the same subject even after I tried to shift gears.

"Yeah, I didn't even know who all those little old men were. I knew the word Majesty, but had no idea what one did, nor did I care to know." Even Mokuren got caught up in the conversation.

Udzuki concurred, "I still don't know. What *do* they do anyway?"

"Weren't you the one who wanted this conversation to stop?"

"Well yeah. I don't have a problem with not knowing. It's not like knowing will solve my personal problems."

My mom couldn't stop though and said, "There's so much they do, like the important task of praying for everyone in this Island Nation and other things I learned as a child."

I ignored her and asked Udzuki, "What personal problems do you mean?"

"Well, number one is a job. But that's not all. It's possible for me to get by without a job right now. That problem is really more a question of time. Number two is Kisaragi. I'm worried about her. What's our life together going to be like considering the current climate, what might happen with Her Majesty, and all the other external factors around us?"

"Udzuki, that is so typical! Only you would be able to say something that embarrassing right in front of me. But you're so thick-skinned that it doesn't bother you to blurt stuff out without thinking about what you're saying. You're insensitive like that, so insensitive that I end up having to deal with my weaknesses all on my own."

"You're saying that I'm thickheaded, cold, and insensitive?"

"You're not listening to what ..."

"What are your weaknesses, Kisaragi?" I asked in the interest of fairness.

"Udzuki might be special, but I'm normal, so they're the same as anyone else's." Kisaragi's tone suddenly took on a touch of irony. "I feel pretty low saying this to you, Iroha, but I'll go ahead and say it. I've been reading that document. It was a total shock. I felt like parts of myself were being explained right there in the words I was reading. Some parts were too hard to understand, but I still more or less got the gist. It freaked me out."

She caught me off guard with that, and I lit into her with a cross-examination. "So, I guess that means you understand what happened next?" I immediately felt ashamed and, without waiting for a reply, said, "I'm sorry. You don't have to answer that."

But Kisaragi did answer, with sincerity. "I don't think anyone can understand those actions. Even if a lot of people claim to sympathize, they're doing so based on their individual misinterpretations. In my case, I was a little envious that someone could still feel the freedom to die even when he talked about being powerless and meaningless. And to feel the freedom to write a document like that and have people read it. I mean, I could write a suicide note, but it wouldn't be the same. If I wrote one and died, people would ignore or quickly forget about it. It would be a waste. I couldn't die believing that my death would even matter."

Udzuki drew a deep breath like he wanted to say something, but no words came out.

It was heart-rending for me to hear Kisaragi describe with such clarity feelings I'd had too. But, at the same time, that damned document had turned Inoue into the root of all evil. Still, I couldn't simply condemn him for being so popular.

"Why are you really leaving? Is it just because you got the job? Wouldn't you be happier staying here, Kisaragi?"

"Because it's a bad idea to get too cozy. I don't go for that sort of thing. And Mokuren and Udzuki hate it too, right?"

"That's right. But even though we might have made the decision to be more independent, I'm worried we're handing our futures over to Her Majesty." It seemed like Udzuki was talking to himself.

I thoroughly identified with Kisaragi's uncertainty despite the fact that our personalities were nothing alike.

"You two have to come back. You'll always be welcome here. And hurry back right away if you're on the verge of being 'spirited away' or something."

"Oh, Iroha! Are you the owner now?" Kisaragi glanced at Mokuren.

Mokuren teased me. "Seriously. You plan on staying for the rest of your life? Not that I'd mind, of course, but ..."

"I want to see what it's like to live independently too."

Udzuki then asked the big question, "Do you think this sort of setup is living independently?"

My mom whispered to me, "Honey, will you be okay money-wise?"

I was too irate to speak, but Mokuren, whose keen ears picked up my mom's voice, answered for me, "There'll be no problem there. Iroha's going to work for me as the live-in manager, and I'll be paying her."

"Really? Well, as long as she can support herself. Honey, I won't have the extra to send you an allowance, so if it gets tight, please come home."

"You mean if I get fired, you'll take care of me? Gee, thanks, Mom. It's nice to know I have comprehensive unemployment insurance."

"You're getting a little too old for that kind of sarcasm. You're not going to be able to get away with irresponsibly picking fights like that anymore. You could learn a thing or two from Her New Majesty about taking work seriously and acting responsibly. But you're probably thinking about how much you'd like me to shut up right about now."

"I was just thinking at least this is better than listening to you tell me I should get married."

Mokuren stepped in with words to snap me out of it, "Iroha, you can't pout and be stubborn and childish forever. Try to behave."

"Okay, let's drink and make up. Let's start the party over again. Kisaragi, you and Udzuki haven't climbed the holy mountain yet, have you? Let's go up to the top and drink a toast." That invitation was also my bitchy way of spiting my mom.

Just as I'd planned, my mom put on a smile and said, "I'll pass. I'm not as in shape as the rest of you, and I need to get my rest for tomorrow." She looked at Udzuki and Kisaragi and said, "I'll see you two in the morning. Thanks again for the ride. Have a good time. Goodnight." With that, she headed upstairs.

Without missing a beat, Mokuren calmly announced, albeit with a defiant attitude, "No one wants to get in an accident because they're hungover, so let's call it a night."

Mom paused to give Mokuren a big smile and release the tension with words of praise before reaching the second floor, "Thank you. I am so grateful to you."

Kisaragi and Udzuki agreed that "the party mood" was over and excused themselves.

I took my lousy and self-critical self up to my room, where, for the first time since coming to the mountain lodge, I gave Inoue's films new life on my computer. Before when I used to feel that bad, I'd call Miko or look at Inoue's webcast, and I must have been trying to compensate.

The file I randomly opened was the two of us walking around the center of Shibuya. You could hear us talking about truly silly things like, "one of these days, let's use the water in a pool as a screen" and "after you meet Miko, why don't the three of us make a comedy version of 'Mixed Cameras'?" What vulnerable voices, vulnerable words, vulnerable gestures. Sometimes Inoue would respond to something I said by turning his camera away from whatever scenery he was filming and point it at me, so my face showed up in some frames. It was back when I wore my hair straight and long, to my shoulders. The toasty late-summer sunlight glittered on my short-sleeved blouse with the blue-green flower print and the younger arms that stretched out of it. There we were, shining and going along as if every day was even-keeled with no mountains or valleys of hope in our way, talking to each other with such openness. We thought we were so cynical and sophisticated, but we were just powerless, vulnerable, and innocent kids.

The unbearable yearning to have that moment back made me want to cry while watching those images, and I also wanted to deny the poisonous grip nostalgia had on me. But then again, misery suits me.

Leaving me only the sadness of knowing I can never get those days back, Inoue and Miko went and died. The two of them, my mom, who is indifferent to my loneliness, Miko's parents, who were wholly dependent on him, Inoue's parents, who had such minimal interior lives … they're all like kids who let other people clean up their messes. No sooner had I thought that than I realized I could add myself to the list for leaning on Mokuren.

Inoue said that we were "being kept alive" and that we couldn't just "starve to death," but of course children who always have someone caring for them aren't going to die so easily. It's also natural that they can't participate in society in the real sense.

I wonder just how many mature, independent, self-sufficient, and responsible adults there are. Maybe those of us on these protruding islands are just a bunch of kids playing games like make-believe grown-ups and make-believe lovers, pretending to want to die and pretending to die. It's an island of children, where children just produce more children, and in a place like that, there can be no society in the true sense. Even though there are some kids passing as parents, there are no actual adult parents. In that sense, each and every one of us is an orphan. Where are our real adult parents? If they exist, who and where are they?

I made myself sick with such restless doubts. I was up half the night because grotesque images of "real adult parents" in my dreams made it hard to sleep. I woke up completely exhausted with the sunrise. Two hours later, still early in the morning, Kisaragi, Udzuki, and my mom left by car. As of the present, that was the last time I saw my mom in the flesh.

After those three made their get-away, a steady trickle of Mokuren's friends came and went, and I held down the fort. For every familiar face from the earlier construction work days, there was someone I'd never seen before. Not only were they new to me, some of them were even people Mokuren didn't know personally either. But each occupied a position in Mokuren's intricate network.

They didn't all necessarily come to enjoy a vacation. Many came with work to do. One would be focused on writing while others hauled in materials to craft huge art pieces. A person who ran laps around the mountain as part of a training regimen, a person who diligently processed documents filled with calculations on the computer, a person who spent hours on the balcony hashing out never-ending arrangements over the cell phone, a person who literally read constantly, a person trying out experimental recipes who got on everyone's nerves, a nerdy person glued to the computer monitor morning, noon, and night, a person chilling out in the garden hammock ... a good-natured, but high-strung corporate-type, a low-key commercially unsuccessful musician, an actor who kept to himself, and an overly serious student who'd corner whomever he could in a philosophical debate... and so on. As long as they didn't bother anyone else, they were free to gather in the salon to relax after dinner, debate, wander around the mountain in the middle of the night, have sex in their rooms or the woods, or do whatever else they liked. And I'd like to take this opportunity to thank Mokuren's folks and their hometown friends who sometimes came and cooked up the most fabulous Chinese-Food for us.

My job entailed the general management and upkeep of the little lodge, as well as handling guest affairs and room arrangements, purchasing groceries, and giving troublemakers a warning or asking them to leave. Mokuren assigned guests to water management, home repair, cooking, cleaning, or security-surveillance squads in order to encourage fresh relationships on Ascension Pass. I didn't want to get caught up in her spider web network though, so I made sure to maintain my distance from lodgers. Truthfully, I was repelled by the stench of the world below they brought with them. Mokuren's the kind of person who could swallow poison and transform it into a cure, but in my case, that same poison would just circulate until it killed me.

I couldn't stand it when Mokuren called me down to film a weekend fiesta, a task I greatly resented. (They apparently wanted the feel of a lively Latin dance party, so everyone was busting a move to Latin music.) I was trapped in the middle of a herd of crazy, dancing fools, and it wasn't long before I put down my camera and started twirling around with someone too. As intimate as that act was, I felt pleasantly detached. While this was a welcome change in me from Mokuren's perspective, she still expressed concern and said, "Don't overdo it, okay? Iroha, you should pace yourself. If you're trying to keep up with everyone else, I'd rather you took it easy and just watched through your camera."

"Is that what it looks like?"

"I don't know. It just doesn't seem in keeping with the low-impact pace you've set for yourself."

Mokuren was completely right in her observation. You see, I was still following the news from the world below even after my mom left.

She called incessantly with her usual rundowns of the news mixed together with stories about whatever was going on with her. I'd always worried about my mom not having a close friend. I'd never imagined it would get to this point, but I did suspect my eventual independence would be a source of anxiety for her, so I figured I'd have to continue being there for her. Sure enough, that's what happened. It was a pain, but I kept her company by phone.

I can't really blame my mom for my having become a news junkie. In one sense, I was cut off from the world below. I tried to forget about everything and walk the mountain, halfway feeling like I'd become a little creature that belonged here, sheltered beneath the shade of trees. You'd think that would have been enough, but I grew restless in a matter of days. At night, I'd go online and pour through news sites like I was opening up maps to get a bearing on where I was. I also listened to the radio my mom left behind. When she called, I'd pretend it was the first time I'd heard about a particular story, but I was already well versed in whatever news she related. I devoured as much information as I could, and it became harder and harder to separate myself from the world below.

The rate of love suicides escalated with each passing day. During the summer months one similar death followed another, and most people had had enough. With looks of disdain they said, "Anybody that hell bent on dying ought to go ahead and die already!" Even so, those same people who had been fed up with it all suddenly responded to the following incident with worries that they too might be ensnared in the trend. The level of uncertainty rose and fear ran rampant when the grasses were withering and tree leaves were beginning to fall in the cool, dry autumn breeze.

It happened in the middle of October, when they announce the results of who passed the bar exams. A thirty-three year-old who failed eleven times in a row, counting that year, stabbed the Minister of Justice and then killed himself. That was the first of what they called the "assassination suicides." Right before he did the deed, he mailed a statement of intent to the mass media, so the next day, the text of that statement was all over the place.

"For over a decade now, while I've continued to fail the bar, the legal world has fallen into a sorry state of affairs. Prosecutors, who were once the guardians of the Law, are now the pitbulls of government officials. Judges are grave keepers who only follow precedent. And the so-called human rights attorneys are that only in name, their actual role being nothing more than playing bodyguard for the masterminds who rake in the big bucks through the corrupt system. That is what the legal profession has become in a nutshell.

I won't go so far as to suggest that things are this bad because I haven't passed and thus can't work to make a difference in the legal world. Nonetheless, I truly want to combat the corruption, but for ten years have been forced to stand outside the mosquito curtain, where all I can do is gawk and stare — a profound humiliation. The bitterest pill of all and what galls me to no end is how immoral stooges who accept things as they are and who don't even see the corruption for what it is are permitted entrance into the legal profession.

I would have given up if it were simply a matter of my own failings, of me not being up to the task. However, they routinely fail me by a hair. They announce they reached their quota as soon as my number comes up, and with that, the door slams shut. Each time it's my turn, I am cast out by such a slim margin. There has to be something seriously flawed in a rank-based decision-making process like that. Is the legal community trying to protect itself by preventing any flexibility when it comes to qualifying applicants? Is it their way of upholding the status quo?

Just as Shôji Inoue indicated in the incomparable indictment he left behind, my parents put my future down as collateral, and I have eaten off their advance payment. The net result of all this being that now that my future prospects are merchandise beyond their expiration date and starting to spoil, my shares in my own future are as worthless as wastepaper. Without any ties to this world or even the permission to work towards change, I have no value at all anymore.

But is that really the case? Am I really not worth anything? I salute Mr. Inoue. He has my respect for having been unfettered by the laws of this world in his actions. Looking from the outside at "this world" as it is displayed on-screen, I wonder if perhaps I, too, might have a hint of value left in me.

They are trying to prosecute Mr. Inoue according to the laws of a land that are far beneath him. I remain outside the mosquito curtain where I have no means of thwarting them, nor can I hope to replicate the achievements of Mr. Inoue. Yet I am rising up to the challenge to correct society. According to Mr. Inoue's teachings, we will not realize our worth and will remain unable to participate in a society where people simply follow the old traditions until we write them off for good and create a meaningful system in a world made newly tranquil without certain people in it. We must break away and take the leap. We must reclaim society. Following Mr. Inoue's doctrine, I intend to die and take with me a symbol of corruption, the person responsible for the bar.

This is human kind's final combat. Here's to the soldiers who will follow, that they may stand firm."

It was obvious, more so in form than in substance, that this statement was a take-off on Inoue's document. This guy humiliated himself to prove Inoue's point about worthlessness, and, all I could think was that he really wanted to settle the score for Inoue, but since that was beyond his power, he lashed out in a crazy direction.

The Minister of Justice pulled through and, without wasting a second, filed charges against the dead suspect. I suppose they wanted to treat him the same way they did Inoue. Meanwhile, the Chief Secretary of Cabinet called the attack "an act of terrorism." On the basis that Inoue's document and films incited terrorism and couldn't be left uncontrolled in the public domain, he proposed amendments to the Communications Monitoring and Prevention of Subversive

Activities Acts. Parliament passed the amendments quickly after a forty-three year old temp worker took up the pathetic would-be lawyer's call early in the following November. He poisoned to death a high-level Trade Ministry representative of the party in power who was on the campaign trail and then killed himself by drinking poison. The new amendment made it illegal, retroactively from Inoue's document onward, to author and/or participate in the dissemination of materials inciting others to commit crimes. And on top of that, Parliament seriously deliberated over the preposterous recommendation that in cases involving someone who commits suicide soon after taking the life of another, it might serve as a deterrent to record the disgraced perpetrator as having been executed for a capital offense in the official history, thereby robbing that person of the reality of suicide.

Yet it wasn't the government or any committee that had me feeling really helpless. As Inoue pointed out, it might look like politicians run the show, but that's not real. They are moved by a power we understand even less. One example of that unknown power was how the electorate or society actually embraced the government's swift revision of the laws with popular support. That's why, to me, it sure seemed like whatever that greater power was, it could manipulate the electorate too. Inoue said that hardly anyone was able to participate in society, and maybe that unknown power was like a geyser spouting out of the emptiness of a society without people.

Okay, so then that brings us to why none of us can participate in society, which I think is related to the idea of this place being islands of children. The fact that we remain in a state of childhood creates the vacuum, and out of that vacuum emerges the geyser, and the geyser, in turn, moves us around. To put it simply, we are made to move by a force we unwittingly created.

Everyone living on these islands, from the electorate all the way to the politicians and even Her Majesty, develops the way they do because that kind of power keeps them alive. So, what the hell kind of person is Mokuren to look at us as if we are really living?

Criminalizing Inoue's document as "prohibited text" was like disabling people's impulse control. Declaring the document a capital offense won't keep people from absorbing the message. All I'm trying to say is that treating people like freaks and criminals is enough to make them not need a reason to die or give a shit about who they take with them. It was only a matter of time before we made the leap from "assassination suicides" to "indiscriminate love suicides."

The first indiscriminate love suicide occurred after Christmas near the end of December when the Communications Monitoring and Prevention of Subversive Activities Acts were revised.

It was the afternoon rush hour on the Yamanote Line at Shibuya Station, and passengers on a crowded train were waiting for the door to close. The passengers up front had their hands pressed up above the door like they were trying to avoid being pushed out of the train when one man hauled ass to squeeze in at the last minute, barreling into the stomach of a man up front and practically tackling him. But the guy who tried to get onboard was repelled back onto the platform by the middle-aged paunch on the man up front. So the guy gave up then and ran toward the far end of the platform. The doors closed, and the train left.

A few seconds passed before the passengers onboard realized something was wrong. The man who'd just been tackled was coughing and spitting up blood. Blood was dripping down his legs. The woman next to him turned pale, screamed, and reeled back, struggling to get away, which pissed off the man behind her, who snarled, "What the fuck's your problem?" People with cell phones simultaneously started dialing for cops and ambulances. The train was already pulling into Ebisu, the next station, by the time the news reached the conductor.

Around that time, the next train was approaching Shibuya Station. Looking like a doll turning somersaults, a human figure jumped from the end of the platform onto the tracks in front of the oncoming train. The conductor covered his face with his arm and lowered his head. Bloodcurdling screams and roars filled the platform along with the faint sound of friction as the train car ran over foreign matter. He was decapitated by the wheel and died instantly.

The man inside the train had been stabbed with a long blade during the tackle. The paramedics waiting at Ebisu Station stopped the bleeding and transported the man to the hospital, but his heart couldn't withstand the shock, and he died.

At first this incident was reported as another crime influenced by Inoue's document. But the police department released information related to the suspect, a language arts teacher in a public middle school. They said he was driven to the breaking point after losing control of his unruly homeroom class. They found no indication whatsoever of any connection to Inoue and chalked it up to a single, isolated freak occurrence.

Still the Chief Secretary of Cabinet proclaimed, "This is indiscriminate murder and a new breed of suicide terrorism. It differs from crimes of a personal nature such as love suicides." His rejection of the term "love suicide," over which Inoue's shadow loomed, struck me as a way to rush to bury Inoue and, at the same time, to maintain people's outrage over the murder-suicide.

Inoue's name disappeared from both the print and TV news media, as if were in lockstep. Rumors spread over the net, like the one about how just when a very influential weekly magazine had prepared an article linking the suspect to Inoue, they received a threatening message from Homeland Security officials who had hacked their way into reviewing the text before it went to press. The publisher buckled under the pressure, and the piece never saw the light of day. It supposedly revealed evidence that the suspect had actually printed out copies of Inoue's document at an internet cafe he sometimes used and explained he wasn't on leave due to anxieties over his class, but was instead unable to return to the workplace after having been "spirited away." There actually was the possibility that reporting links between the incident and Inoue without incontrovertible and hard proof could be seen as the dissemination of material inciting crime and thus could be interpreted as illegal under the revised laws, and in all likelihood that's exactly the chilling effect the government had in mind.

The mass media didn't delve into the particulars of any case, but instead started to fill the airwaves with special features on how to avoid "personal terrorism." They offered friendly advice on avoiding rush hour trains, busy streets on weekends, and crowded places from which it could be hard to flee, and created stereotypical profiles of "dangerous types" to watch out for. There were also segments on how to use martial arts techniques and legal weapons to fend off attacks from suspicious characters. Every channel and every magazine tried to attract attention with more or less the same kinds of baseless predictions about how the economy looked better for next year and how that meant fewer people would want to die. And the commentators who enjoyed the most popularity were hawkish right-wingers who accused the government of "sitting around and doing nothing while the people's security and safety were in jeopardy."

Along with deep chills, the dead of winter saw an increase in incidents branded with unfortunate labels like indiscriminate love suicide, random street killing-suicide, personal terrorism, and suicide-terrorism. There were seven more incidents in January and an even sharper rise in February, when there were eleven in the first two weeks alone and not a single day in the second half of the month without an incident. By that point, society was pretty much in a state of panic. The police increased their street presence all over the country to little effect, because it's simply not possible to prevent crimes when you don't know when and where they'll occur.

For that reason, police guards were stationed in conspicuous places. Their highest priority was the forest where Her Majesty lived. Cops stood guard like trees lined up alongside the roads all along the perimeter in a singular show of pomp. They worried that the approaching anniversary of His Young Majesty's death might push some likely perpetrators over the edge, and they warned that someone might be devising a terrible plan. Intending to put the kibosh on the rumors and whisper campaigns, the government announced that it would allow TV broadcasts of a news conference with the unprecedented successor on the first anniversary of His Young Majesty's death, February 30th.

It was a very snowy year, and the temperature dropped enough to freeze the hearts of all living creatures. You would have thought the rainy season had come in winter, because every day thick clouds covered the sky, and even when the snow stopped, there were only brief glimpses of blue sky or the sun every now and then. Ice kept everyone confined indoors, and it felt like there was no way to run away from fate.

The level of alcohol consumption skyrocketed nation-wide, and fixing stew at home became the thing to do. As the restaurant industry suffered a marked decline in customers, more and more businesses went under.

Incidents occurred in every type of location. It didn't matter if you were in a busy urban downtown neighborhood, a provincial train station, an apartment complex in the sub-urbs, a village in the boonies, a path between rice paddies, or a quiet and empty trail in the woods. No place was safe. Most incidents involved men approaching women, old people, or children and stabbing them, strangling them, bashing their heads open with rocks, lynching them, or taking them by force to the top of a building and pushing them off. But there were exceptions, like the patrolman who gunned down a middle school kid who had come to the police box asking for directions or something and then put his revolver to his own head and shot himself. Or the female bartender who, when only one customer was left, laced cocktails with arsenic, drank one herself too, and they both died. And then there was the female taxi driver who drove herself and her passenger, an elderly woman, straight into the sea and the eleven year old boy who smothered a younger kid to death, got drunk, stuck his head in a plastic bag, fastened it tight around his neck, and then fell asleep before dying.

The vague and uncertain news coverage only exacer-bated the climate of fear. The ins and outs of how a crime was committed would get covered in lurid detail, but it seemed like a suspect's inner life or any information that might point to a motivation were strictly off-limits and the real questions were being suppressed. Meanwhile, even if they thought of it, no one would dare mention Inoue's document, and that only made its murky presence loom larger in the background.

Like I've said before, the real horror of each incident lies somewhere that can't be seen from the outside. You can run down the list of any incident's surface details, but that's nothing more than rattling off statistics. Every case is bound to have its own individual circumstances along with any similarities it shares with others. The cause-and-effect stories that get attached to incidents are usually distorted. They change to suit whatever works for the storytellers. I can only know the horror of my case and all its nitty-gritty specifics. When it comes to another incident, all I can do is imagine based on my own experience. And everything I imagined gnawed away at me, without me even being aware of it.

You don't know who'll be targeted or where. You don't know what kind of person will be seized with the impulse to kill or when. If it could happen to anyone, what's to say you won't be next? Somewhere along the way, I internalized those paranoid suspicions that held so many others in their grip.

One day I phoned my usual distributor to place the weekly grocery order. They said they would stay closed past the New Year while things still looked dangerous. What could I do? So, I asked them to refer me to another store. They said it wasn't likely other shopkeepers, who didn't know me, would sell to me, but they gave me a name anyway. As it turned out, that store did agree to supply us, so I struggled along the icy path down the mountain to pick up the order. The earthy old guy at the shop had a warped sense of humor, and he was on a roll.

"You kids are lucky, livin' up there, not havin' to listen to the news. Don't even need to think about society. Yup. Up there, in a little cabin. No neighbors. Pretty safe like that, aren't ya? I reckon ya never knew what it's like to feel all alone with nothin' but strangers everywhere."

"Strangers? But don't you pretty much know who everyone is in a small town like this?"

"Knowing who someone is don't make 'em your friend. It's on account of you kids not knowing about what's going on in the world that I don't mind having you here. And hell, it beats closing shop and having to go somewhere. City people are always on edge. All that stress wears 'em down. Yup. They up and drop dead from overwork."

The old guy saw us off, warning that we should be careful about going to stores we didn't know, because if we looked a little strange or said something even slightly out of the ordinary, we'd get reported.

Having my vulnerability pointed out like that left me feeling as if I was always being watched, and I couldn't shake the idea that someone was looking over my shoulder or spying on me. Life on the mountain didn't change. We still lived apart from society and enjoyed a tranquil existence. But the arrival of each new guest rattled my nerves with suspicion and paranoia. Even if a person who just arrived from below appeared cool, I'd assume they were a nervous wreck inside and somehow using all that nervous energy to overcompensate. For me, that feeling in and of itself is proof that insecurity in the world below is contagious.

The snowfall didn't let up, and when there was a pause every now and then, it would freeze in a flash. It was like we lived in an ice castle. I went to the spring many times, but there were no reflections because it was frozen over and covered in snow. The stream froze too, and the only secure water source we had was what had collected in the dried up old well. We were faced with bona fide Snow Country tasks – running water to prevent freezing and shoveling snow that fell off the roof in front of the door. And the whole lot of us had way too much time on our hands. Gaps of free time were more openings where uneasiness could breed.

After we finished shoveling, four guys in their early twenties who'd been working with me asked, "We're warming up some wine. How's about a cup?" Even though I was uncomfortable, I was won over enough to stick around. Then one of them started talking about how another had a brush with indiscriminate love suicide. Seeing how shocked I was, they tried to downplay the topic as if it wasn't a big deal, explaining, "Well, if five people get together, usually at least one of them will have been through that sort of thing."

"So you're saying one in every five people is targeted?" I couldn't keep from trembling.

"On average, yeah, that's about it."

"It could happen to anyone. If you're alive today, your chances are pretty much the same as the next person's," said the guy who'd been through one.

"But you must have run away. You ran away because you didn't want to die, right?"

"It wasn't really a question of will so much as my competitive instincts. I play rugby, see, and once I knew what was up, I made a move, and the other guy fumbled. He could have picked himself up, pulled it together, and come after me, but he gave me a quick once-over, looked away, and then charged after someone else. It didn't take him long to learn that he was messing with the wrong guy."

"Weren't you scared?"

"I just didn't want to get hurt. If it wasn't going to be painful, I might have gone along with it even knowing I'd die."

Another guy agreed, "I know what you mean."

"So, you really do want to die?"

"No, it's not like that. I just think it would feel awesome to give into that kind of rush, if I looked at my destiny and was all like, 'Bring it on!'"

"For real. That would be total ecstasy. Better than drugs or sex."

"Death is an extreme high?"

"It doesn't have to be death. Any extreme game of fate. Like say for instance you'll get shot if you don't shoot your girlfriend. So, you give into it and pull the trigger."

"Not me, man, I'd rather take the bullet and die right there in front of her."

I told myself these kids were at the mountain retreat because they were connected to Mokuren, so they weren't typical people from below and were just letting loose a little and talking trash, but I couldn't shake how disruptive all this was. I wondered about the figure of one in five. And I'd been close enough to share air with someone who escaped an indiscriminate love suicide, and we'd had a conversation. I felt like I'd been tainted by something that wouldn't go away. The incident had caught up to me. But it hadn't arrived with a big ground-shaking entrance. It came naturally, like an everyday strand of new hair.

With the burden of this new awareness that even the reservation wasn't safe, I said to Mokuren, "At a time like this, maybe we should be a little more careful about who we let stay here."

"Didn't the old guy down the mountain say we were safe in our 'little cabin' up here?"

"Sure, but the new people come from below. Everyone down there is more or less freaked out by the indiscriminate love suicides. I think some people caught up in it all end up perpetrating. Just because someone might normally be calm and collected doesn't mean they won't do it."

"If you want to think something bad is going to happen, I can't stop you from imagining whatever you imagine. But there's no reason to think anything like that will happen here. Everyone here is either a friend I trust or one of their trusted companions, so there's nothing to worry about."

"But there are people I don't know."

"Hell, there are people *I* don't know, but I trust them."

"Have you talked with all of them? When I talked to some new young guys the other day, they seemed pretty sketchy."

"I don't know who you mean, but when I say nothing bad will happen, nothing bad is going to happen. This isn't a matter of logic. It's about people sense."

"Are you saying my people sensors are out of order? That I felt those guys were dangerous because I'm the one who's messed up?"

"Sometimes, my little likable nihilist, you are a supreme pain in the ass. You are the most vulnerable and well-meaning, but also the most suspicious. We still have to figure out a way for you to stop that behavior. Incident, schmincident, you were already worrying back in your news-phase. Don't blame that on my friends. If anyone is going to start an incident, it'll be you."

That one sentence really hit home. I felt like my whole body was made of sand, and all my confidence just spilled out of me. Still, Mokuren was merciless.

"It was the same in your relationship with Mikoto and in that whole triangle with Inoue, wasn't it? You are still caught in the same spot, Iroha. You think you can take in a few ideas from society, one at a time, and just observe them. But no one is more chained by those ideas than you. You think you aren't though, and so you move deeper, step by baby step, without realizing that you are drowning in the process. I suppose some people could leap headlong into the thick of it without hesitating and somehow inoculate themselves. But people like you aren't so good at being decisive, so when you do jump in, your timing is off, and that could be why you are so easily suckered. Well, my primary concern is making sure you are safe, so why don't you just give it a rest?"

Maybe strong people have always been clear-headed and determined, while the weak have always had to battle their fears. But what Mokuren said was wrong: case in point being Miko, who seemed ready to stand by my side, steady and cool, but who was all too easily "spirited away," who encouraged Inoue's love suicide, and who died. So, at some level, I can't bring myself to trust in Mokuren's strength either. For the time being, I turned my way of life over to this mountain retreat and my friendship with Mokuren, but only for the time being, a temporary risk. I was surrounded from every direction by a vast and deep surface where nothing was clear, and as it spread, there was no way to tell top from bottom or left from right.

The mourning period for His Young Majesty came to an end in those uncertain times.

After the government announced Her New Majesty would grant an audience on the anniversary of His Young

Majesty's death, the level of anticipation rose quickly. Her New Majesty had never been one to show her face in public much. She was plain and didn't stand out, so TV stations and magazines ran special features to introduce her to the public. People were led to believe she'd always been close to them through interviews with her classmates, who told stories about what she was like as a student, and programs on her work in the conservation movement before she became Her Majesty. People started calling her by a name they hadn't even known before then.

The public was hoping to relive their memories of His Young Majesty's succession ceremony of four years earlier. Back then, His Young Majesty related to us on our own level and swept away what had been until then a gloomy mood. It seemed as if he'd beamed an optimistic energy straight into the hearts of those who listened. In the same way, people hoped maybe Her New Majesty, who was wounded by His Young Majesty's death, might feel our pain and bring us comfort. Maybe she could quell the evil intentions of those in the grip of violence and make this nightmare end.

Of course, those were the selfish hopes of people looking to a higher power for salvation. The believers in Her New Majesty's ability to fulfill that soothing role were members of her generation, in their mid-to-late thirties. Most were women, but even men who were initially put off accepted this image of Her New Majesty.

There was a group arguing that it was pointless to place such hopes in Her Majesty. They were even more visible than in his Young Majesty's days. They said that we were the ones who'd determine the course of society, that we can't forget the lessons we learned in His Young Majesty's days, and that if Her New Majesty words were heartfelt and revived the people's spirits, the effort involved in making that happen would still be ours. To lose sight of all that would mean we were rehearsing for a reenactment of the tragedy following His Young Majesty's passing. Her New Majesty can only voice her individual desires. She doesn't have the power to stop a world careening out of control.

I was no stranger to words like that, because Miko practically beat me over the head with them. That alone was enough for me to feel uneasy, to anticipate a big backlash.

On the other hand were the eerie rumors that the public would hit an all-time low after Her Majesty's interview. Some people said we might see the biggest and baddest murder- suicide in this Island Country's history on the day itself.

According to the policy makers' spin, a specific public safety plan was already in place, and they were on top of everything, but it all sounded fishy. Etched in everyone's heart was the idea that the love suicides up to that point would seem laughable once things really started to escalate, almost as if to ensure the creepy rumors would become reality.

They didn't want the live broadcast of Her New Majesty's press conference to be as big a deal as His Young Majesty's succession ceremony, but the audience share was still substantial. I watched the TV station's live coverage streaming on the net. First, Her New Majesty read a prepared statement:

"Over the past year since His Departed Majesty left us, I have prayed for his eternal happiness. Citizens, I know your profound sadness over His Departed Majesty's premature passage to ancestor. The sadness may not end with today's official close to the mourning period. Let us not forget His Departed Majesty's bequest nor our own grief as we step out and face the construction of a new society. For this will make His Departed Majesty's wishes possible."

I kept a recording, which is why I could transcribe it like this. When I heard it live, I couldn't get over how weak, pointless, stereotypical, and completely uninspiring her words were, like they melted away in the surroundings and disappeared. I couldn't even understand what she was saying.

Her answers to questions were also vague. When asked about her memories of His Young Majesty, she said, "While he was very noble, he also had the heart of the common people. When we were children, he was the ideal big brother."

—— How will you approach your new role?

"I want to protect the values that have been handed down by a long line of Majesties, and I hope a life-size society will be built."

——The situation for our society has been unbearable since His Young Majesty's death. What are your feelings about this?

"It pains me greatly. My prayers go out to the people so that we may all soon live healthy and safe lives."

——Do you have any ideas for what might help that happen?

"If we renew his call and all the citizens band together, I think His Departed Majesty's bequest can be realized even in his absence."

——What do you think His Departed Majesty's bequest is in concrete terms?

"For each and every person to think of this Island Nation as their own and to foster a society where people can live with a sense of security."

The interview went on like that for more than thirty minutes, with her flip-flopping all the way, until it just trailed off at the end like a video feedout.

My mom called as soon as it was over, and she was livid. "That's not going to stop the killing!" She rambled on in a one-sided conversation about how her hopes had been dashed. She tossed aside a final confession, "I'm not investing any more hope in this Majesty. I was stupid," before hanging up the phone.

My mom's negative reaction was consistent with the general public response. There weren't many people who criticized Her New Majesty in public, but a deep and angry undercurrent was evident behind closed doors, where people railed against her and privately lamented how betrayed they felt. The desire to forget about her quickly led to indifference, and less and less attention was paid to her presence. In actuality, her health deteriorated after the interview, and for months she disappeared from public view.

I wasn't surprised in the least. That's the true nature of Majesties. Udzuki was right. There's no problem as long as Their Majesties and the people don't interfere with each other. No matter how big a negative reaction such apathy might provoke, the end result is still getting "spirited away." The wild love suicide maelstrom occurred during a prolonged reactionary period. The emptiness of apathy gave rise to the tempestuous extreme. Even the increased hopes placed in Her New Majesty might have stemmed from an insatiable desire to connect to another, to be cared for and to care. When Her Majesty didn't satisfy those yearnings, it became clear that nothing could be done about the climate of violence. The "anyone will do as long as someone dies with me" mindset was bound to blow up into a singular and absolute obsession.

The temperature suddenly rose in March, and who knows whether the prior owner planted them, but in the woods surrounding the lodge, red and white blossoms burst into full bloom along outstretched plum tree branches, greeting and asphyxiating people with their perfume. *Mokuren*-variety lily magnolias lit up branches like enormous candles giving off white flames. The rough currents that had kept me on edge until that point no longer needed calming, because the sudden warmth was a sign that the yellow sand would soon follow. The idea of heat and great sprays of sand called to mind the cherry blossoms that bloomed overnight, and the sensations of that day of the State Funeral were rekindled on my skin. My eyes were battered by the sand pellets, and for days and days the pain and tears wouldn't stop. Even though I was blinded, Inoue took my hand. I can still feel his palm against mine. I still cherish and use the cobalt blue bowl and aqua spoon with the fish design. Miko and Inoue were beaming with joy even while they were so flustered and embarrassed when they first met. I was so stupid to watch them like that, feeling so pleased with myself. After they left the restaurant, the regrets and guilt kicked in. I drank with Mokuren that night and innocently thought I could ask for a do-over, that we could go back to square one and make a fresh start. And when I saw Inoue's document, I was angry enough to explode.

At what point did I seal my fate? I must have known that I was fanning the flames of a fire that would burn me.

I don't know. I just can't bring myself to think of it all as some history I've moved past. That incident isn't over yet. Even now, Inoue and Miko haven't finished dying. The murder is still happening. And the hand that keeps killing them is groping for me, trying to drag me in too.

Unlike the New Majesty boom that hit shortly before the anniversary of His Young Majesty's death, no one says a word about Inoue and Miko when their death anniversary draws near, and not even on the day itself. That goes not only for the mass media, but for the general public too.

The indiscriminate love suicides were still raging. The pace dropped off some, but that was because people were too scared to leave home much. Ever since the let-down after Her New Majesty's interview, it was is if the world was waiting for the sky to fall.

Honestly, it was like living through a war. "Evacuated" households were sent to remote locations, and rich people sought refuge overseas. In order to be more self-sufficient, people started vegetable gardens on rooftops, in backyards, or anywhere else they could find space. It was around that time when the phrase "self-reliant living" became popular and growing your own food took on a powerful, new meaning. I wonder why the soil became the "real deal." Everyone went on about how it was the "true origin of human life," so a lot of people were carried away by the half-assed, pseudo-return-to-the-land craze.

Meanwhile, government officials looked into legal options for sending in the Self Defense Forces to keep the peace or instituting martial law, because only the police were charged with maintaining order, and sometimes a cop would commit an indiscriminate love suicide. Those fiercely opposing such measures argued that if a member of the Self Defense Forces were to commit an indiscriminate love suicide, the attendant shock would be severe, and Self Defense

Force members threatened to resign if ordered to treat their own countrymen as the enemy, so the matter was dropped.

It's arrogant to lose sight of how it all started and act as if these unusual circumstances had been around for ages as just another aspect of everyday life. I don't think there were many who actually forgot about Inoue and Miko altogether, but based on what I could gather from the occasional internet message board entry, the two of them were being purged from society's memory and records, as though people only wanted to remember it as the incident that made the lack of interpersonal connection seem trivial. There was no sign of the Inoue-hating that had given everyone their motivation at one time, as if all that had been a lie.

Even if people have some semblance of memory, maybe what they don't have is a sense of history. For me, that one day was drawn out for a year (and another five years since then), but they must remember it like a high-impact Hollywood blockbuster. Everyone is caught up in it for a time, but maybe only the terror right in front of them seems real.

Of course, I'm hardly one to talk. I responded just like anyone else when it came to a love suicide involving someone other than Inoue and Miko. I trembled in fear.

On the first of April, I went out to the spring just before dawn. The moments before sunrise were freezing, but the cold also revived me. It was as if all the excessive poisons and regrets were being wrung out of my body, and I could breathe easy again. At that hour, the birds were stirring in preparation for the morning. The sequence started with the chattering of the little birds and ended with the crows. The sun began to rise in the eastern sky, which was the color of Kôshû grapes. Even with the sun out though, the spring was still well under the forest's protection, so I'd gaze at the transparent rays of light that made their way through the spaces between leaves and branches, sometimes just basking in the golden glow piercing through into openings in the woods. Like a spotlight, the light began to shine down upon the glassy surface of the spring and illuminate the carpets of moss covering the rocks. I ate the toasted cod roe rice balls I'd prepared the night before, sipped the sweet green tea I'd steeped at 160 degrees for a few minutes, and savored the caramel-colored light. With my camera rolling right beside me, it was better than words can describe.

I didn't want to see anyone or say any words that day. That's why I'd planned to stay there through the middle of the night. A cool wind blew almost all the whitish petals off the mountain cherry trees onto the surface of the water. The mountainside was bursting everywhere with white flowers. Lulled by the warm air produced as the sun rose higher in the sky, I stretched out on a rock and napped off and on.

After waking up from one of many, I went to the spring to wash my face and thought I saw someone other than myself reflected in the mirrored surface. I looked closely, but not much light made it to the black water, so I couldn't tell if maybe it was a shadow or something underneath the surface. I looked up and scanned the area all around me, but there was no one besides me there.

I looked back at the mirror-like water. This time I saw two figures, not counting myself. Before long, one of them brought his right hand up against the side of his head and waved his five fingers like he was playing the piano.

"Miko!" I couldn't help calling out his name. That was Miko's way of greeting me. And that meant the other person was…

Yes, it was Inoue. He held out his beloved handheld camera. Caught in the dream, I grabbed my camera too and tried filming around over my head. The two of them were nodding. It seemed like they were outdoors, sitting on some kind of rock or stump. Scattered clouds drifted behind them, and sometimes their hair would be blown by the wind.

I remained gazing at the water in that position for a while. Just seeing Miko and Inoue breathing, their shoulders going up and down, was more than enough. They'd look at each other too.

"It doesn't matter whether or not you are really here. The important thing is that I'm seeing you two now." When

I remembered what Miko and Inoue said in Inoue's document, reality came crashing down on me.

"Maybe that's what you want to think, Iroha, but I'm really here." Miko's voice called out to me, not coming from anywhere in particular. It was probably just a voice in my head. It was a conversation I constructed. That's how I know the details. Even so, what really mattered the most was the fact that I was hearing Miko's living voice.

Miko said, "We got this chance for a reunion, so please say something. Let me hear your voice."

I asked him, "How long will you be here?"

"How long? How long, indeed?" Miko looked at Inoue.

Maybe my eyes had grown used to the dark water, but whatever the reason, I could now discern the subtle details in their expressions.

Inoue replied, "Forever, right?"

Miko agreed, "That's right. Forever and ever."

"You know, you were right, Iroha. The two of us aren't done dying. We've been here like this the whole time."

"Well, it's not like we really want to die. We're waiting here."

In a joking voice, Inoue asked, "And what is it we're waiting for?" Then he pretended to pass a mic to Miko.

"Isn't that your area of expertise, Mr. Inoue?"

"Well, it looks like I'll have to answer then. We are waiting ... for the Majesty-free world to become a reality."

"A Majesty-free world? But Professor, is that really possible?"

"Please, now pay attention. The Majesties are doing their best. Therefore, we should take responsibility for how we live and not create any further trouble."

"You don't say! A world without Majesty."

"Hm! You two sure got friendly," I said, even while knowing I was creating the entire conversation in my head.

"That's the way it goes. We're really close."

"And you got pretty close to Mokuren, huh, Iroha?"

That irritated me, so I answered, "You know full well why that happened."

"Iroha, are you filming right now?"

I was overcome with a desire to throw a rock into the spring.

"Iroha, what you saw wasn't good or bad. It was just a film. Miko and I aren't going to die. We're stuck in a not quite dead place, in a botched in-between. Once your world over there becomes a world without Majesty, then we will naturally remorphize."

Miko cheerfully said, "We are still 'spirited away' in other words." That left me with a painful heartachy yearning, and all I could say was, "oh." I silently looked at the two of them. We had this amazing chance to communicate, but how much more retreading of the same circular path was I supposed to handle? But still. I wanted to take it all in until it hurt and everything was absorbed into part of the forest along with the wind, the temperature, the green, and the aromas. All of it. Miko's voice, Inoue's gaze, both of their sighs, and feeling their presence so close to me. And I wanted the two of them to feel the same way about me. Every piece of that was part of an illusion I created. The sensation probably resulted from constantly thinking too much and rehearsing scenarios. Even so, what really matters is that I experienced it. It was tangible to me.

Red-tipped clouds swept away the remains of the day. The claret sky reflected on the mirror-like water, and the sharp silhouettes of Miko and Inoue stood up.

Inoue is purposeful, never looking at me, and says, "We should be going." He walks away and vanishes from view in the mirror pool. All I hear is his voice asking, "Is that spot okay?"

Miko sluggishly replies, "Yeah, sure," and he is lying down in that very spot.

Inoue reappears. In a muffled voice, he says, "All right, hold your breath for a sec." Then the coughing that never leaves my ears begins. And finally there's just me, who doesn't die.

When it was all over and only silence remained, the area surrounding the spring was veiled in darkness, and there was no way to distinguish the outlines of Miko and Inoue from those of the fish. Without fail, this vision is never more than its beginning.

Several days later, I received a letter from my mom out of the blue. She still can't use her computer and, of course, never sends email, so she relies on phone calls. She did send me a postcard once, but she couldn't wait until it arrived and called me up to tell me everything she'd written before I'd had the chance to read it. Other than that, she hadn't used the mail.

Enclosed in the envelope was a clipping from the opinion section of the April 2 morning edition of *Sun Rising*, this Island Country's leading newspaper for "all the news that's fit to print." Under the heading "I, who might kill," was a piece contributed by "Sara Ogawa, Free Time Worker." I'd somehow missed this one when checking the net. I looked at the byline picture, and damned if it wasn't Kisaragi.

"I can relate to the despair Kisaragi describes in this essay. Everything about the feeling she describes and why she had to write about it go back to February 30. If Her New Majesty had said just one thing, made just one statement at that press conference about how she abhors murder, things never would have deteriorated to this point. If you were thinking about killing another person and heard Her Majesty condemn murder, somewhere you'd start to feel a little guilty. It's like with children who are scolded by their parents from a young age. Somewhere along the way the guilt kicks in and children learn to distinguish between right and wrong.

We talked about this by phone too, but I have really lost heart and was even on the verge of being spirited away (forgive me for the inconsiderate word choice). But it seems Her Majesty had already lost heart first. At this point in my life, I finally appreciate just how weak a person I am. I've lived my life by keeping it together as best I can, and I guess I simply ignored my weaknesses.

I wonder what Kisaragi is up to these days. Please tell me if you know how to get a hold of her. Honey, you should try to cheer her up too."

I was starting to feel queasy at that point. I got a grip on myself and read Kisaragi's essay.

We are now terrorized in two ways. First, as you know, we live in terror that someone will suddenly kill us. The other is the terror that someday we ourselves might kill another person, that we might want to kill, or that we might inadvertently cause the death of another. I cannot say for certain that I will never end up in the killer's shoes.

The reason is that I don't want to be killed. However, I am not confident I can prevent that from happening. Since I don't believe I can prevent it, I'm always preparing for the eventuality of an attack, and I'm thinking ahead to anticipate every possible scenario twenty-four hours a day. And no matter what I prepare as a countermeasure or exit strategy, I give up in the end, thinking that when someone wants to kill me, I'm going to die, and there's nothing I can do about it. It's as if I'm already dead in a way. It's not just me though. Isn't it the same for all of us? And I'm not talking about the natural course of things or how every human being dies someday.

Is there any difference between your own murder and the murder of another if your death is set in stone? "I don't care if I die" becomes "I don't care if I'm killed," and "I don't care if I'm killed" becomes "I don't care if I kill," so "I want to die" equals "I want to be killed" equals "I want to kill." They are all just variations on the same theme. My reality is that death is not taboo, negative, evil, or dark regardless of if I'm killed or I kill myself. Rather, death is as usual an occurrence as breathing or going to the bathroom, and no matter how important a person might be, no one has the authority to stop or challenge that. It all depends on how you see it.

It seems like even though we really do *not* want to die, we are making a mad dash straight at death anyway.

How has this happened?

I don't have the answer. A lot of people are saying different things, but none of it rings true. Or at least that is how I feel. We have to find the brakes to stop this breakneck speed race, because the stakes are life and death.

As I said at the outset, I cannot say for certain that I will not end up a killer. I am scared of myself, and I do not trust myself. And I definitely do not trust other people either. I recently broke up with my boyfriend. I was crazy about him and trusted him. But it takes an incredible amount of energy and work, not to mention patience and creativity, in order not to die together, but to live together with another person. I am too tired to muster up the will to try anymore. I doubt I'll ever want to try building a life with another person again. It's like I may as well die, and that's okay. You could easily call this a cop-out, and surely there are plenty of people who can criticize me.

In this depleted state, I am too tired to try not to be killed.

This is reality as I see it. I want you all to take a cold, hard look at this reality and resist the urge to look away. I don't want all our energy to be invested in not being killed. That's why I wrote this.

I had a hunch that Kisaragi wrote this piece to coincide with the anniversary of Miko and Inoue's deaths. I quickly called her cell phone, but the number was no longer in service. And when I sent her an email message, it bounced back to me.

Then I tried calling Udzuki, who sounded really angry.

"She was alive at least up til she wrote that crap."

"She was really that close to dying?"

"Fuck if I know. All of a sudden I had no clue what was going on inside her. Well, she was full of shit I didn't understand before, but even what I did understand disintegrated until I couldn't even recognize it anymore."

"Was it always that way after you came down from the mountain?"

"What's with the fucking inquisition? What's done is done."

"I'm sorry. But I really need to find Kisaragi."

"We broke up at the beginning of the year. She said she wanted to be by herself since she couldn't be sure she wouldn't end up in a love suicide with me. I tried to say that was okay and that we could work together to make sure that never happened, but she was like, no, it's useless for me to try and live with someone else until I fix what's wrong with myself. Or something like that. Then she left. And that's why I don't know where the hell she is, okay? Even if I did, I have nothing to say to her. You wanna tell me how I'm supposed to communicate with someone who closes herself off and shuts me out like that?"

"Are you living by yourself in the same house?"

"No. I have a part-time job and lodging at an inn in Bôsô."

"If that's the case, why don't you come back here?"

"I'll think about it after I save up some cash."

I couldn't say he didn't need *any* money. Mokuren's policy was that everyone who stayed here had to pay the pro-rated amount for one month's actual upkeep costs for the lodge plus board. Udzuki used to be able to contribute his share in work though, and he could stay on for a while without any significant savings, so that really couldn't have been the problem for him.

Next I showed the clipping to Mokuren and asked whether she thought we should contact the newspaper. Her initial response was, "That's not like her to send a letter to the editor." After she thought about it for a while, she simply said "leave it to me" and took the clipping.

Rather than thinking through a plan with me, Mokuren preferred to go it alone, in keeping with her self-righteous personality. As much as she got around in high school, I still couldn't stop trusting her. Even now I still trust her for all the reasons I've described before.

I was unnerved by what Mokuren correctly pointed out as Kisaragi's uncharacteristic behavior in sending that piece to the newspaper. Even more than the actual contents, the act itself seemed to have meaning, but when I tried to analyze that meaning, I felt sick, as if my body was infected and putrefying. Starting with Inoue's document, there have been online diaries or manifestos, claims of responsibility for crimes sent to the media, and all sorts of other unilateral bombardments of personal beliefs on the public. None of this is followed by an interest in audience responses or critiques, but instead by straightaway actions to match the words, which makes the unidirectional feeling even stronger. Kisaragi sent her opinion to a national newspaper, so you can't help but wonder what she wanted to achieve. Maybe Mokuren had a firm handle on that and was thinking of ways to respond. If so, what more could I do than leave things to her? With that in mind, I tried my best not to worry.

But my bad feelings were dead-on. In mid-April, around one week after Kisaragi's essay appeared, a homicide that was not part of a love suicide occurred. In a Nagoya college neighborhood, a student saw his friend walking up ahead and ran to catch up with him. When he made it, he patted his friend on the shoulder, at which point his friend turned around and stabbed him to death.

There were signs before that something like that might happen. People were overreacting if someone just brushed up against their shoulder or arm on the train. They would shove or even brandish a weapon at whoever had inadvertently done the touching, and the number of such cases resulting in bloody brawls had increased. And sometimes simply walking in the same direction as another person even in a residential neighborhood would end in trouble. The upshot of all this was a widespread aversion to other people and rampant paranoid hostility in crowded places.

In court, the student who stabbed his friend claimed he was acting in self-defense.

"Of course, I am beside myself with grief over having killed my friend with my own hands. The reality of that is more than I can bear. The profound regret and sadness I feel will never go away, nor will the voice that reminds me that I am to blame for all of this. No matter how sad I am though, I am nothing more than a traitor.

The reason why I am entering a plea of justifiable self-defense even while acknowledging all that is because this incident isn't merely about me or my personal situation. I was at the mercy of powers greater than myself, the circumstances that have made it possible to kill one's own friend. I speak to you as a traitor so that we can face the bitter contradiction and make sure nothing like this ever happens again.

Frankly, I cannot say whether or not my friend had it in for me. Maybe he did, and maybe he didn't. Given the way things are today, how could anyone know for sure? He once let slip that he sometimes wanted to disappear. Perhaps anyone who has ever been depressed, including myself, has had such thoughts, but I can't say that didn't raise my suspicions.

If someone like that suddenly runs up on your from behind, there's no way to judge whether or not they are going to kill you. The present social conditions make things hard enough, and it's only natural to want to protect oneself and stay alert to avoid harm. At the same time, if you don't want to die, wouldn't you also want to avoid any actions that might be misinterpreted? Trying not to appear suspicious is one means we have of protecting ourselves after all. At a time when everyone's nerves are rattled, making others nervous is asking for trouble.

The need for us to protect our own bodies from harm is greater now more than ever. The times demand that we expand the range of what we consider justifiable self-defense. I wasn't killed, but is it really so crazy to think that later on someone else might have been? And then wouldn't that other person have been killed instead of me? And were that the case, could I really feel relieved that I was spared and go on with my life? Wouldn't I look back with a different kind of regret from the one I feel today? In that sense, don't the times call for a broader understanding of collective self-defense?"

That passage comes from the diary he kept while in detention, which was later released as a book.

A heated debate erupted in response to his argument, because you can't draw the line when it comes to matters of bodily danger. However, an incident that occurred during the course of his trial affected the outcome. In that case, an unarmed person was called from behind and then stabbed to death as he turned around. The court took this into consideration along with the man's statement and handed down a not guilty verdict. That took place during an almost rainless mid-June. From sentencing to verdict was only a month and a half.

Qualifying his response to this decision as a personal opinion and not a government perspective, the Prime Minister said that in circumstances where anyone could be a possible terrorist and there were limits to the police's ability to prevent such crimes, it was incumbent upon the people to prepare to defend themselves. He further suggested there might be concrete means of supporting such preparedness through official agencies and, at the same time, a need for amending justifiable self-defense law to include the prevention of murder.

Surprisingly, the prosecution didn't appeal the not guilty verdict. And that's not all. Barely a month after that case concluded, *The Value of Survival*, the memoirs of this same student (although by that point he'd dropped out and was an ex-student), was released by a major publishing house and became an instant bestseller. He became a household name and an over-exposed darling of the media.

Even more astounding was the fact I read his book, which my mom sent me, knowing that, once again, the writing would be completely unidirectional and the contents would have me seething.

Assuming readers would relate, he wrote the following "Preface: Dedicated to my Buddy."

I grieve over having driven my buddy to an early death, but that grief itself is proof I am alive. The pain I carry with me connects the extreme terror of that moment when my buddy ran up on me and placed his hand on my shoulder to the awful moment when he met my blade. Without a doubt, my life was in peril then. Not in terms of whether or not my buddy might have been trying to kill me, but because I had to choose whether to live or surrender my body to the danger. It was possible I could be lucky if I risked physical danger. But it was equally possible I would die a horrible death. I stood at the edge of that cliff for a brief instant. Then I broke away from fate or chance and made up my mind to defend myself with my own hands.

My sense of being alive is stronger now because I survived that brush with fate. My newfound power and vitality make my former life seem empty. My existence is enhanced, and I feel grateful to be alive each and every day.

Surviving extreme danger might be the ultimate experience of life's essence for human beings. The world that is truly alive is the one in which life matters. Survivors survive because we have the strength and ability it takes to survive. To put it simply, we merit being alive.

All of us are now being tested to see if we are worthy of life. Perhaps it is arrogant to think a long-neglected natural order has returned and is selecting us. I could very well die the very next minute. But all the same, I embrace life, and that is how I am able to feel the value of my own existence.

This is the meaning of having driven my buddy to his death. You might even say my buddy laid down his life to show this society crippled by fear how to live and be courageous. He wagered his body so that we could dare to stand down our fears. Of course, I know this is a self-serving explanation. My buddy's death was senseless. And yet, I yield from it the optimism that our society might strive to be valuable, so his death will not have been in vain.

If Inoue's document was deemed illegal, surely this text would spell legal trouble and be banned, or so I thought. But it was not seen as inciting murder in the least. Could people really not see how even if they eliminated Inoue's document, the curse was still being passed down steadily and surely? This ex-student's appeal for a competition for survival went beyond Inoue's "demise of the fittest." I can't help feeling that this world is already turning into the other world.

Aside from deciding to increase the number of police officers a little bit and provide tax relief for self-defense, all the government did was beef up the round-the-clock police escorts for members of the executive and judicial branches, cabinet ministers, and legislators. You had to have advance clearance and still carry a picture ID to enter government offices or Parliament. The slogan "your body is yours to protect" was, in effect, a proclamation that "public institutions won't protect you," and the sense that "no one will protect you" only grew worse. There was a colossal self-defense boom.

The so-called petit bourgeoisie, who believed they were socially weak, broken, and losers in the struggle for survival and were being jettisoned out by the oligarchs, joined with old-guard liberal activists in angry protest against the government. The government's blatant disregard for the protests sparked more violent forms of direct action. Lawmakers' hometown relatives were assaulted, and police stations were burned down. The Prime Minister quickly retaliated by directing the concerned government parties to consider what was authorized under the scope of legitimate self-defense. However, it would be three years before indiscriminate love suicide and its counterpoint, random justifiable self-defense, were bundled together in the legal codes.

The rainy season came and went with several overcast days, and by early July, summer was in full swing. The heat wave that brought several days of nearly 100-degree temperatures might have played a part, but after what critics called "random justifiable self-defense" had been decriminalized, those incidents began to occur at the same rate as the indiscriminate love suicides. People avoided going out and interacting with others because, while it wasn't necessarily on a frequent basis, whenever the occasional indiscriminate love suicide did occur, a random justifiable self-defense followed almost in retaliation. It was like a ghetto turf war complete with the drive-bys.

Unlike the first case, the trials of subsequent justifiable self-defense killers were long and drawn-out. If they were found not guilty, the "turf war" was bound to escalate, and if they were found guilty, then we'd be left to rely on an incompetent government that couldn't control the indiscriminate love suicides. There was nothing anyone could do about what was, in effect, a state of lawlessness. Most people understood that and anticipated the coming of whatever future catastrophes they imagined, but no one talked about it. Rather, they remained shut in and shut up.

I was exhausted. Things weren't easy as it was with all the shopping day worries and stresses of my work for the mountain retreat, but on top of all that, I had to wear a new hat, a farmer's. In early spring, Mokuren cleared some land near the lodge and the stream that had good sunlight and soil, and she planted some vegetables there. I was responsible for tending the fields. Vegetable gardening on the reservation didn't spark any passion for "self reliance" in me. But Mokuren didn't care and said, "We have to do whatever we can on our own, because the reality is that it will only get harder and harder to buy stuff in town."

"Iroha, how much longer are you going to dwell on the world below? You have too much time on your hands. You have all that free time, and so you check the news, obsess over everything, and that's why you're always jittery, right? Well, farming is the perfect solution. You'll be too tired and won't have time to surf the net anymore."

Sure enough, I was exhausted.

But I still have found the time for my daily visits to the spring without missing a day since April 1. The time of day isn't always the same. When I take my walk there in the morning, stepping into the woods alone is enough for me to feel enveloped by the water. Aside from the birdsongs and cicada cries, it's completely still. Not even the wind blows. The surface of the water is placid, like a stationary sheet of obsidian, as it wakes up refreshed and full of life. By afternoon, the water is transparent and infused with green from the algae below and the tree leaves reflected on the surface. In the evening, the air and light dissolve into a kind of thickness. That thickness mixes with the water and makes it look gray. At dusk, the trees fall under a purple shadow, and the wind calls up thin trails of waves on the water. Striped mosquitoes flit about the restless spring. And in the lapis sky, scattered clouds flow like red lava from a blazing sun, making the spring below a shiny copper.

I continued to film that water, which was never the same from moment to moment. I wanted to document it in all its openness and vulnerability even when I wasn't there, so much so that I thought of installing the surveillance cameras.

Regardless of how the spring looks when I peer down into it, Miko and Inoue are still there. They raise voices like the wind, laughing and joking, arguing, and singing. Sometimes when I hear them, I chime in with my two cents, pick an argument, nod along, get angry, or fall deep into thought. Then, when the time comes for the water to turn gold or orange, they draw far away from me and lie down in the depths. I watch helplessly as the knife shreds their flesh.

On the hottest day of that summer, the thermometer in the garden registered over 100 degrees. I was done in from weeding and watering in the garden that morning. But at the spring, Miko and Inoue were completely unaffected by the heat and waxing philosophic. I couldn't tell whether they were being projected onto or suspended in the water, but they were cool like fish. I, on the other hand, was burning up even under the shade of trees and took it out on them with some choice words, "Where do you two get off acting all comfortable and cool like that?"

"We can't help it. We've got no flesh," Miko replied.

"Yeah, we wish we could get hot with you," Inoue added.

"Iroha, why don't you come in here with us? If your skin touches the water, maybe you'll forget about the heat?"

"Is that a dare?"

"No, not at all. It's not as if we'll really be able to together, but if you get in, the three of us will at least be in the same spring, in a way."

"Well, more like three people looking into a three-way mirror." I was compelled, even while saying that, and jumped into the water with all my clothes on.

The coolness of the water was arousing. Just like that, my body contracted, my head woke up, and my old juices started flowing. The water was too deep for me to stand, so I rested my arm on a rock along the edge and let the rest of my body float like seaweed. Just like Miko said, I felt as though my body was melting and spreading out into the water.

My flesh disturbed the water, so I couldn't see Miko and Inoue clearly. But I could sense their presence and their voices on my skin. The instruments making that sound pressed directly up against my body, and I heard their sound not with my ears, but resonating through my skin and bones. Maybe Miko and Inoue were waves, waves that rocked and responded to the particles that make up my body. I rubbed back and touched the water directly, gasping for air while my massage strokes raised bubbles and waves.

After I got out of the water, I felt pleasantly exhausted and returned to the little cabin, where I slept like I was being sucked into the floor. I woke up around the time the sun turned amber like a hard candy. Recovered from the summer heat, I felt all my energy return.

Then when I went to the spring the next day, there were people already there. A man and two women who were staying at the lodge were sitting on the edge of the spring in bathing suits, drinking beer. The women were around thirty, and the man must have been about my age. I yelled out, "That area is off-limits!"

"Whatever," one of the women yelled back. "We're only doing exactly what you did yesterday."

"Mokuren said it was okay for us to come here," the man said.

"Really? We'll see about that. But for now, please go back to the lodge. That is a very important water source for this reservation." I refused to discuss it further and forced them out of there.

That's not all. They complained to Mokuren, but she had my back and told them if the manager said so, then there must be a good reason. End of discussion. They were out of here that night.

After that episode, Mokuren increased the budget to allow me to install surveillance cameras in the trees surrounding the spring. That way, the spring could be recorded twenty-four hours a day without interruption not just so that I could watch it whenever I wanted, but so we could also keep an eye out for trespassers.

Of all the people in the world, the first trespasser caught on film was Mokuren. In the monitor, dyed jet-black by the gloom, the water moved in ways it didn't when rippled by the wind, and because I knew how to see in the dim and diffuse moonlight, I made a beeline straight for the spring.

Out of the darkness along with the water sounds came Mokuren's voice, "Well, come on in."

"Please tell me you did *not* take alcohol in there too."

"That was a good idea you had. This is a great way to cool off." Her words were followed by the telltale sounds of a can of beer being drunk.

"This isn't a hot springs resort, you know."

"Yeah, the water's cool."

"Please get out."

"What about if, instead of saying that, you got in and joined me?"

"Are you *trying* to annoy me?"

"If you want me to get out, bring my clothes and towel over here."

"You really are treating this like a bath, huh?" I groped around for her towel and handed it to her. Mokuren took it without saying a word and maintained the silent treatment for a bit while she dried herself off. Then I heard her put on her shorts, step into her dress, and zip up the back. The sounds of bugs overeager for autumn to come resonated throughout the woods like metal being scratched. Mokuren moved closer to me and pushed me in the water as she said, "Why don't you get in too?" For a moment, I lost all sense of direction and swallowed water when I tried to breathe. Once I thought about how Miko and Inoue were probably there laughing at me too, I settled down and stopped fighting, waiting for my body to float.

I couldn't tell where her voice was coming from, but I heard Mokuren warn me to watch out, "You're gonna hit the edge like that." Her voice moved closer to me. "You're completely vulnerable, like you're there, just ready for something to happen to you."

"You mean I can't rely on myself to survive?"

"You're so pathetic. Why don't you go back home with your mom? You two are so alike. You'll read a book you know is trashy and still get upset and affected by it. Nobody here is saying anything about survival or self-reliance."

"Okay, so then why did you say I was vulnerable?"

"Because you're like a recluse, monitoring the spring, driving off anyone who comes here, and acting pretty defensive. All you have is free time on your hands. What are you protecting?"

"I'm not protecting anything. It's like going to pray at a shrine. Maybe this spring is just a regular old watering hole to other people, but it has a very special meaning for me."

"And you're not going to tell me what this very special meaning is?"

"You're too insensitive."

"Too insensitive?"

"Even if I tell you, you won't understand."

"Oh," she sighed, the dejection in her voice palpable. "I feel like I want to cry."

"Seriously?"

"Always."

We didn't talk. Then, after a while, I heard Mokuren's footsteps, and she said, "Let's go back."

I followed along after her, feeling miserable, and said, "I'm sorry."

"What the fuck?" Mokuren came to a halt with those threatening words. "Why do you have to apologize? What for? Did you do anything to me you have to feel sorry about? Or, are you going to? Are you going to kill me? Are you not sure you won't kill me?"

"Because I'm an idiot. It's just that you're protecting me…"

"Whatever. Just cut the self-deprecating routine, because I don't have the time to baby you. Shit is already going down, and it's only going to get harder, so, please, at least trust me."

As I write, I still am plagued by pointless thoughts. In terms of proof that five years have passed, all I have are records of incidents in the world below, none of which are real for me. Like my mom, I've adjusted my internal clock to match the mainstream time of this Island Country by keeping up with the news. In that sense, my five years of memories and feelings are a story produced by the media images, sounds, and fonts that have encroached on my life. If I hadn't felt such a need to stay on top of the news, I'd probably remember these months and years only as time I spent on my own in the lodge, at the spring, and in the woods. That time is different from the mainstream. It just starts and stops and winds around, but it's richer, more real, and priceless compared to the mainstream five years. I've continued my visits with Miko and Inoue, who linger on the divide between death and life. One thing I know for sure is that I've been shaped by those two separate, but tangled times.

I soon understood what Mokuren meant when she said, "shit is already going down" and that she wanted me to trust her. She took out the following provocative advertisement in *Sun Rising*.

I Won't Kill

I decided to publicize my declaration in the newspaper because I want at least my friends and acquaintances to trust me as they have up until now.

I'm not killing anybody.

I don't have a voucher to give you. These words are your only guarantee. But is there any greater assurance than that? Is there any other way to trust people than to take them at their word?

I will not say you should trust me unconditionally. I am writing so that you can judge whether my words are trust-worthy and then decide whether to believe me.

Some may think it's strange for me to announce I'm not killing anyone, but I don't think so. I don't think it's uncalled for to declare I will not kill because not killing is supposed to be natural. There are many possible worlds where not killing would be unnatural. It's happened, and it's happening now. My declaration is that no matter what becomes of the world, I am not killing. Not killing is not conventional wisdom, so you won't understand what I'm thinking if I don't explain myself clearly, and that is why I need to spell this out. If it's important, I don't think any-thing is too obvious to express carefully.

By contrast, the idea of justifiable self-defense is taken as a given, but I definitely do not think that is natural. I read an op-ed somewhere about how "I don't care if I die" means "I don't care if I'm killed," and "I don't care if I'm killed" means "I don't care if I kill," and "I don't care if I kill" means "I don't care if I die." I have a better grip on reality than that.

Let me say, at the risk of seeming ridiculous, that those who commit murder in the name of so-called justifiable self-defense are guided by those very sentiments. Thinking more in terms of possible than actual motives, who's to say people who stab other people to death are not dreaming of capital punishment and craving, even if unconsciously, an unortho-dox double-death? Let us then imagine those same people are not sentenced to death. No matter how alive and vital they might claim to feel, they will still be suicide failures for the rest of their lives, and that has to feel terrible. In fact, simply imagining that lonesome sadness is enough to make me want to die.

My sense is that there are an awful lot of very unhappy people unaware of their own double-death wishes among those drawn to justifiable self-defense. I think that says a lot about the true nature of the fear running rampant in society, because otherwise there would be no reason to live in terror every day that a huge bloodbath was coming.

Please take a good, hard look at reality. There is no mass destruction or carnage happening to justify the sensational use of expressions like "survivor" or "survival." Since early April of last year, there have been a total of fifty-eight incidents of this type. Slightly fewer than one-hundred people have died. Of course, these are not merely numbers, but we have to examine the meaning we invest in them. After all, more people die in traffic accidents. If we set aside unnecessary fears, which lead to unnecessary panic, and look at this cooly and calmly, the chances of experiencing such an incident are very slim. If everyone stopped preparing for the unlikely possibility, the numbers of these incidents would naturally decrease in turn.

But the terror remains compelling, so there must be a lot of people identifying with the perpetrators at some level. Even those on the bench expect the real killing will begin once they are moved to action. As long as we think that way, we only make it harder to suppress the desire to perpetrate.

There must also be many of you who want to say, "not me!" Me too. However, I cannot vouch for it. I cannot deny that maybe I am that kind of person too.

But even if I am, I still will not kill. Why not? Because I have a community of friends who are not trying to kill me, and I trust their intentions. To the extent that I trust them, I will not kill either. And they surely feel the same.

I will not kill. We all make this declaration to one other. We put our faith in these words. In times like these when nothing is predictable, I do not know what we can trust in others if not their words. Choosing whether or not to trust someone's words is one of our responsibilities. And I choose to trust my friends. More than people might think, trusting in one another's words will deter further incidents.

I pray friendships such as ours will flourish.

Mokuren Haku

This advertisement appeared prominently in the society section of the morning edition, taking up the lower half of an entire page. It must have cost a small fortune to get that much space. Where Mokuren's money and power come from is a mystery to me.

I felt betrayed and like my whole body filled with bile when I saw the characters for "white magnolia" in the byline, the name "Mokuren Haku." That feeling was exactly like the one I had that night when I read Inoue's document. Where did she get off writing such an irritating message without even discussing it with me?

What on earth was she thinking? It was obvious at first that the message was intended for Kisaragi, whose whereabouts were unknown, but Mokuren must have had an additional purpose to lay down such a challenge. If she simply wanted to critique "justifiable self-defense," she wouldn't have had to spend so much money.

Protests were bound to emerge from the murderous contingent in society. Was it inevitable that I be counted among them? Mokuren was spurring me to action. But what was I supposed to do and how was I supposed to do it? What did Mokuren expect me to do?

But I didn't have the time to slip into a melancholic despair. Within twenty-four hours of the advertisement's appearance, its effects were apparent. The lodge was deluged with email messages and calls from people connected to Mokuren. They all seemed to be taking the ad as a personal message from Mokuren that she was opening the door in an act of mutual trust. Some wanted to arrive the same night or very next morning. The sudden population surge would mean I'd have to assign several people to each room. My mind was filled with to-do lists: making sure there was enough bedding, food in the pantry, and adequate security precautions in place as quickly as possible.

Basically, those were the actions I was meant to undertake. As long as I was busy with clearly defined matters of calculation, the blues couldn't stick around. I accepted my calling, quickly rallied my strength, got the 'okay' from

Mokuren, and set out on a shopping trip right away. I wondered if Mokuren's vegetable planting had been for this too.

Kisaragi also got the message. Five days later, she showed up with Udzuki. She didn't seem weak or give the impression of having been a wreck, and, in fact, it was as if they had only been away for a few nights rather than a whole year. They were so casual in their return that they lost no time in preparing a meal for us.

I listened to their report from the world below while we ate dinner, and all the while my feeling that I should be making preparations grew stronger.

"It's like they're devotees of the Grim Reaper or something. On the surface everyone seems normal, but even when they act as if they aren't nervous, their eyes, their nostrils, their lips, and every orifice on their body show the signs. While they are afraid of dying in their heads, you can tell they are longing for the arrival of the Grim Reaper in their hearts."

Udzuki agreed. "For me, when I don't care, I really don't care, which leaves me wide open. But I even start second-guessing whether I stick out in a crowd of high-strung people. People always avoid me in movie theaters and on trains. When I show up, everyone acts like I'm bringing the plague with me."

"He's so damned healthy that I was really afraid someone would kill him in an act of justifiable self-defense."

"Aw, you worried about me even while we were far apart. Thanks. That really helped."

Kisaragi let Udzuki's snide comment slide and told us about the furious protests over the advertisement. I'd heard a little already from Mokuren's people who'd arrived earlier, but just as I'd imagined, the outrage spiraled out of control.

"Ms. Mokuren Haku asserts it is unusual to express an intent not to kill, but premises her argument on the idea that living is natural. The kind of society we all currently occupy is not one in which we can simply live. One needs the proper strength and must pay certain dues in this harsh battlefield into which we have been thrown. Here, we are in no position to take life for granted. Rather, natural law holds that our existence is made possible only to the extent that we protect ourselves. Ms. Mokuren Haku apparently has no appreciation of her own existence, which would explain her ability to enjoy such exceptionally blessed circumstances. Alas, such circumstances appear to be beyond the realm of what we common folk can hope to create. Unfortunately, trusting the words of the happily situated Ms. Mokuren Haku is difficult. Perhaps she should venture out into the world first and get a taste of reality before spouting off at the mouth."

This commentary by a well-known writer appeared in a certain weekly online journal. He had already been in the news for building an underground shelter beneath his house so that he and his lover could survive. If I were the type of person to commit an indiscriminate love suicide, I'd pay a visit to that shelter with a bomb for that writer.

For the most part, other than listing examples of justifiable self-defense, none of the critics had anything memorable to say, just more of the same old refrains about how you have to protect yourself and how you can't selfishly rely on others for your own safety. According to them, Mokuren was a "socialist individual," a "peace freak," a "Pollyanna," a "useless chatterbox," a "hypocrite," and an "anti-self-defense-nik." There was even the following sarcastic line in the "witty bits" column of the evening edition of *The Rising Sun Gazette*: "White Magnolia, reveal your true identity! From White Peony."

This much was within the bounds of what we had expected. But Kisaragi brought us more significant news. The mass media got wind of Mokuren Haku's apparent link to Inoue's document through her friendship with me. So, she said, it was only a matter of time before a media crews arrived at the mountain retreat.

Mokuren called for her parents before the media could sniff out the location of her family home. I remembered how suffocating it was when my own house was surrounded, so I called my mom to see if she'd consider hiding out here, but she wouldn't budge and said, "It won't be any different there. If I'm going to be surrounded either way, at least I'll have more fun here. Plus, since I'll be by myself, I can slip out of sight easily." When I thought about it later, I decided it really was best if we each did our own thing.

In an eleventh-hour effort, we planted cypress and briar roses to create a three-sided barrier, installed surveillance cameras, gathered every night for fun in the salon so that everyone inside would be able to recognize one another, and packed in as many other preparations as possible. I was drinking a cup of freshly steeped chamomile tea in the kitchen when Kisaragi pointed out, "Iroha, you're really energized, huh?"

"Aren't you?"

"Well, I was exhausted in the city, and here I don't have to tread water constantly to be on guard, so it's emotionally easier. But your energy is a little different. You are so lively and on the ball when you're working. It's like you're a different person from who you were when you first came here. I was thinking how when you struggle to prepare for something, you get energized. Maybe we need some struggle, some competition to survive. Before long, it might come down to society versus the mountain retreat."

I had a strong desire to respond, but I didn't know what I should say. Kisaragi was right. The me who was jumpy back when I thought somebody might come start trouble at the lodge seemed like a lie. It didn't matter that the lodge was more crowded. What had me standing guard and looking lively was a hostile attitude towards the world below. They were coming from somewhere. I could feel it in my gut.

I laughed it off by saying, "It's like when people get a surge of foolish strength in a fire."

"It's okay. I understand. You know how creepy the media can be firsthand, so you are breaking your back to prevent that kind of intrusion. We don't know when the attacks on Mokuren will turn violent, so we have to be ready to defend ourselves by any means necessary. We can't expect the attack to come from our own ranks, and it's not as if we have weapons ready at our disposal."

My heart skipped a beat. We had purchased an arsenal of farming tools.

"You've been here the whole time, Iroha, so you don't know just how energized the world below is now. Sure, everyone is afraid and nervous, but ever since that talk about survival started, it's like a courageous vibe has been spreading. You can see it in people's eyes, the way they gleam. You could even say they sparkle. I couldn't handle it. For me, coming home from shopping without getting killed was enough to make me practically jump up and down for joy."

I remembered the image, so tiny and far from the camera, of the compliant and calm look Miko gave Inoue, even as Inoue took out the knife. I got the feeling that now I could understand the communion between the two of them in that moment, the clear-headed connection that, as quiet as it was, could be called the ultimate rush. On the other side of that extreme place, there was no sound, no wind, just blinding light shining on a clear and still sea.

"I don't think there are many people with that kind of fire and detachment. But once the fire starts to fizzle out, you really start hating yourself and wanna die. If that fire is what makes life worth living, there's no point in living anymore once it's gone, so death is preferable for the person who can't sustain the fire. It's like this world is here for the people who can sustain that fire. If this kill-or-be-killed situation continues, all someone lacking that fire can do is die. That's where the whole idea of dying preemptively comes in. After all, life and death are the big constants. Those are the kinds of thoughts that wore me down and why I lost confidence and wanted to be by myself."

"Did Her New Majesty's silence have anything to do with it?" I was finally able to get my voice out. "My mom's reaction was similar to what you're saying. She thought it was because Her New Majesty didn't say anything to denounce murder in her interview. That's why she told me to send you her best and asked me to support you."

Kisaragi cocked her head back and forth. "I dunno. I hadn't even thought about that, but now that you mention it, it was pretty discombobulating. But I was completely focused on my own issues at the time..."

"Sorry. We weren't talking about Her New Majesty, but about my current problems. It's just that..."

"What I wanted to say was that after the fire starts to fizzle, everything comes crashing down. I just wanted to say watch out for that. That energized feeling creates the hallucination that sparks the fire. I think all sorts of trouble is headed for this mountain retreat too. I want to ward that off in as matter-of-fact a way as I can. Without getting too excited…and without any disillusionment."

I barely managed to say, "I see."

Mokuren kept track of each step in the process as teams of reporters inched closer and closer to Ascension Pass. First they showed up in Shinjuku Chinese-Town, then my mom's house, next the Yokohama Chinese-Town, and they found Mokuren's parent's house too. And then about ten days after the advertisement appeared, a crew from one TV station was spotted on the pass. Just catching a glimpse of that horrible pack was enough to suck out all spirit I'd had up to that point and make me want to stay out of sight, but Mokuren didn't seem to care. She even casually went down to the foothills to do some shopping.

In an exclusive scoop, the crew that tracked down the lodge trapped Mokuren after she returned from shopping, swarming around her as she got out of the car and feverishly pointing a mic at her.

"Mokuren? You're Mokuren Haku, right?"

"Yeah, and?" Mokuren responded without a trace of ill will.

"How is Iroha?"

"Hey, so you think they're watching this broadcast live in Shanghai too?"

The crew laughed and said "c'mon, c'mon" at the way she dodged the question. Mokuren didn't laugh and elaborated in an indignant tone, "You all don't know either? If you know anything about where she is, please tell me. That's why I took out that advertisement. It was my personal missing person ad."

This time, the TV crew wasn't laughing either. They asked, "How many people are living together at the lodge?"

"That's like going to the Okura Hotel and asking them how many people are living together there."

"They aren't making oaths not to kill each other at the Okura Hotel. A group of people who've made that oath is a kind of organization, isn't it?"

"We don't do anything creepy like taking oaths. People just come on their own, stay as they please, and leave when they want. It's a regular inn."

"Alright, well then, can we stay too?"

"There's already a waiting list of first-timers praying for a spot."

"Please let us film inside."

"Isn't this a world where you never know who will get killed and where? If you were to come inside, you could be attacked in an act of justifiable self-defense. If that were to happen, I'd be responsible. So, I'll have to say no."

"Did you think of that advertisement and write it yourself?"

"I wasn't influenced by or working for anyone else. I bought it with my own money and signed my name to assume my complete responsibility for what I wrote. Who's assuming responsibility for this interview? I'm guessing it's not you guys. You can't really talk then, can you? I'm happy to talk openly about anything on a personal basis with anyone, but you haven't even introduced yourselves, so I may as well be muttering to myself. It's very lonely."

There was no TV in the lodge, so I heard about this exchange later from Mokuren (and my mom who'd watched it). I felt scared that maybe Mokuren provoked them too much. The whole country knew about the mountain retreat, so maybe some enraged person would show up here. For all they'd include and leave out, their image of us was going to be grotesque.

According to this program, I was "the woman who launched the love suicides." They didn't mention the names Inoue or Miko at all, so somewhere high up their role must already have been shifted to me without me doing a thing.

The next day, film crews ascended in multitudes. I was holding my breath to see what Mokuren would do in front of the battalions, if she would emerge like an actor making a big entrance, but she didn't go outside, and she didn't respond to reporters. TV and internet news outlets were forced to start running speculation and analysis commentaries.

The more I checked the news and gossip sites, the more my feelings spun around in circles. All the reading wore me out not only because we were facing naked aggression, but because I had to read the same passages or phrases over and over and over again. It was like a plagiarism relay with one person borrowing the words of another, who borrowed another's, and so on and so on while the clear reasoning grew hazier. Can people who parrot whatever other people say really claim to be living by their own strength? Without noticing that basic flaw in their logic, they were in a tizzy over how great "self-reliance" was. To me, all the people who came out of the woodwork to criticize us looked the same, with the same one face.

"Each age has its old guard, and what old guards do is guard their own interests. They are egoists who don't care about anyone else as long as they are fine. While Moku Haku (sic) exclaims her fine pronouncements, she and her comrades cut themselves off from the rest of humanity and stay holed up in their castle like 'lords'. They should be ashamed to be tucked away safely by themselves when the rest of us must all equally face the dangers of today. Maybe they don't understand the meaning of self-reliance? And they want us to trust their words? Ha! We aren't the ones spitting daggers. They are the ones who made it impossible for us to trust in the first place. Their crimes are huge."

Company Employee (41)
Sun Rising, Letters to the Editor

"I do not know where you came from, but is it really that fun for you to bring your chaos to this Island Country? Right when we all came together as a people, proud and united in our stand and ready to defeat the threat to our security, you cut it short. Worldly gain and love suicide are not core values of our Island Nation and its people, and we will go on living our own way. So please keep your unwanted ideas to yourself. I am not saying go back to where you came from, but just keep to yourselves, do not bother us, and we'll leave you alone too. It is customary in this country for people not to cause one another trouble. As long as you intend to stay here, I suggest you mind that custom."

—A "comment for Mokuren Haku" by a professor of Modern Asian History in "Is it enough to survive?" Special web edition of the monthly journal *Ourselves*

"My daughter threw her life away because she trusted the words of a good friend. And this woman thinks she can say my daughter died because she had a death wish? That's outrageous. How can she know what is in another person's heart? Think of all the people who trusted someone's words and are dead now. This woman must be completely oblivious to have the gall to ask us to trust her words! Does she want to see more victims? Maybe she will say it's still worth trusting words no matter the results. Well, I have had enough! I would like to think her rant was simply a joke. It is not a funny joke or one I forgive, but that would be better than thinking she was serious. I really do not want to hear or see anymore.

However, I do not want my daughter to have died in vain, so I am giving my all to face reality. The situation is desperate, and the reality around me is dangerous, but I think about what we can do to change that reality while I protect

myself. Someone like that woman who lives outside reality and in denial should keep her irresponsible and insensitive ideas to herself."
—The mother of a girl in her late teens who died in a love suicide (the same special issue of *Ourselves*)

"Irrespective of details or individual motives, those who have died on this battlefield our society has become are, for the most part, victims. We tend to be reminded of our own existence when confronted with death. A tinge of guilt accompanies such thoughts. That guilt and its attendant unremitting reminiscence are inextricably linked to the preciousness of life. This is the *esprit* that propels us forward, that which moves us and makes us live.

The mountain retreat community lacks this crucial guilt in regards to the dead.

We will surely overcome the chaos of today and forge a new age. When that time comes, it is incumbent upon us not to forget that our lives are forged upon the dead. If we fail to maintain an awareness of this structure, that which enables our existence will be obscured, and we will be susceptible to further identity crises.

An awareness of the origins of our individual power is absolutely integral to any effort to develop that power. We must recognize that which has made our power possible. The mountain retreat community denies the power of the individual and, at the same time, severs ties with the dead who have made individual power possible. They are thus myopic in both analysis and ethos. Their restrictive approach does not take into account the very structure or scope of the world. That is to say, their ethos rejects identification with the other and, thus, resurrects anxiety over the individual subject and weaves its way into the very fabric of today's chaos, without waiting for words."
—From an essay by a well-known university professor in *Critical Enquiry*

These were on the soft side and seemed written just so the authors could let off some hot air and theories, but there were TONS of slanderous attacks dripping with vicious, nasty, and hateful venom. And it wasn't just written attacks. Outside the lodge windows, loudspeakers were blaring with calls that scared off the birds.

"Get out here! Scumbags! If you've got something to say, come on out here and say it face to face. Why don't you show those of us who have to struggle what it looks like to be safe?"

"Iroha, are you in there too? You and your lovers reap what you sow! And it's harvest time, bitch!"

"Hey, hey, ho, ho – the love suicide cult has got to go!"

But an image of a pass with no people floated before my eyes. On that pass, not even I was there.

Mokuren was attacked four days after the TV crews arrived. In the middle of the afternoon, the doorbell rang. I checked the monitor, and it was a postal carrier. Udzuki, thinking it was okay, started to open the door, but Mokuren restrained him, yelling, "It's not the regular person! He's a fake!" Several men came from behind to surround the imposter, like they were going to tackle him.

The fake mailman was caught easily, and Mokuren went outside. But as soon as she did, the guy got a sudden burst of strength and broke free from the grip of the men holding him, rolled away on the ground, threw something at Mokuren, jumped for the barrier hedge, grabbing a rope he'd left there in advance, climbed over, and got away. But he landed right in the middle of a bunch of media hounds who heard all the commotion and gathered on the other side of the barrier, so he was caught anyway.

The object he threw at Mokuren was a *shuriken* throwing star. It hit her in the thigh and was laced with some kind of poison. The wound started to fester later, and Mokuren had to get around on crutches for a while.

The fake mailman was a member of a militia called the South Kantô Community Watch. The existence of the paramilitary organization itself came as a shock to the public. The militia entered the limelight for its fifteen minutes of fame. They maintained that we have to be responsible for protecting ourselves, and an organization devoted to that purpose and based on a foundation of trust was only natural. They readied themselves with routine training and espoused the notion of mutual aid in times of danger. They formed chapters from Tokyo to Kanagawa and from Chiba to Saitama. The guy who attacked Mokuren lived in Tokorozawa and was a member of the Saitama chapter, and this area fell under his precinct.

Not that it would come as any surprise at this point, but twenty days later all the charges were dropped even though he was caught red-handed in a criminal assault. They would have to turn to justifiable self-defense law, and the courts were too cowardly to come down one way or the other and create new case precedent.

In the press conference after he was exonerated, the man declared, "You can't trust a group that says they won't kill while remaining in their safe hideout." Therefore, he said, "You can't know if and when they'll launch a massive and deadly attack, so without that information, the only option is to make a preemptive strike in justifiable self-defense." As if that wasn't enough, he went on to add, "We have prepared to go head-to-head. It's like that woman says, if I have to die in the process of reaching my goal, then so be it." I was ready to lose it. The faces of the throngs of shameless assholes applauding this guy flashed before my eyes.

That was later, but on the day of the incident, I was going nuts, thinking I had to do something as the manager, so while Mokuren was taken to the hospital, I initiated talks with the prefectural police captain in charge of the investigation. A loudmouthed band of dangerous thugs threatening to do something actually did something, and I pleaded with the police that it was their responsibility to monitor the area. The chief of police turned me down pointblank. Nevertheless, apologies for the prefectural police's lack of courtesy and poor judgment did come my way, because over the next few days, federal marshals patrolled the pass. And a round-the-clock security force was stationed at the entrance to the lodge.

I was practically beside myself with joy, announcing, "the cops caved in!" But Mokuren was livid.

"You idiot! You dipshit! You moron!" She called me many more names, most of which I'd never heard before, while sitting half-up in bed. I'd never seen her that furious.

"How clueless can you be? Everything is ruined now! We'll be surrounded!"

"What are you talking about? We were already surrounded by the news. You put that advertisement out there in the first place, what did you expect?"

"You just don't get it. You're going to turn this into a conversation about how having the cops here will make us safe. You are so stupid."

"Well, maybe I'm not the sharpest knife in the drawer, but do you want things to stay dangerous around here? Do you want some creepy macho thugs out there who are pissed off at us to come around and attack us?"

"You honestly have absolutely no idea. Why do you think I spent a fortune to take out that ad? I wanted to make the point that things like love suicides and justifiable self-defense don't have to happen in a place where everybody trusts each other, like the lodge. There are other ways to protect yourself from an indiscriminate attack than knocking someone else off in a preemptive act of so-called self-defense. Having the police here to keep us safe totally defeats the whole fucking purpose!"

"Why did you have to put yourself out there like that and tell everyone love suicides don't happen here? Why couldn't you just leave well enough alone and treat our safety like it mattered instead of going to all that trouble just to disrupt it?"

"Maybe because people like you are here too. Because someone like you worries all the time about whether or not we're really safe and wonders whether someone will come here to attack us, whether something bad will happen. It's the really suspicious person who is liable to crack, to run, to strike first. I wanted you to understand, Iroha, to understand that we don't have to worry here because we have trust. I put myself out there because I wanted you to understand."

Now I was wincing. "Well, thank you very much. You're right. I'm the most dangerous character around. But you trust me enough to let me stay here anyway. That trust is the only thing that stands in the way of me going on a rampage. That's what you're saying. I see how it is. I get it now, so why don't you chase off the media, the cops, and the looky-loos? That's what you want, right?"

"Don't you at least understand that we can't stop something midstream that we already started?"

"Excuse me? We? You were the one who started this, all on your very own. You decided, and you went ahead and did it. Just you. You didn't trust me. You didn't trust anyone else either. You don't need anyone else, do you, Mokuren?"

"That really hurts. But since I guess I don't need anyone, I suppose I'll get by even if you hurt me, huh? I will be just fine even if you pout like that and don't trust me, right? You decided that's how it is, and you make it happen. Don't mind me. I don't care. Because I trust you. Call the cops or anyone else you want. You have the right as an independent person."

"Hey, watch it!" I wasn't calling her out so much as trying to give myself a chance to simmer down. "Any trust here is fragile. Neither of us trusts the other. We both are second-guessing each other. What's there to advertise to the rest of society? The biggest joke would be for us to commit a love suicide right when everyone's eyes are on us like this. After all, I'm the bitch who started this whole love suicide thing in the first place."

"Do you want to kill me?"

"Not particularly."

"Do you want to die together with me?"

"You're pissing me off now."

"It's better to ride with the tide and not waste all your energy trying to hold back the urge to do it, you know?"

"Don't start something you can't finish."

"Iroha, you're real lively, aren't you? All rosy-cheeked and eager as hell. You look just like a steamed peach bun. Kisaragi said so, didn't she? The high times are the most dangerous too."

"I'm not the one who's high!"

"I want you both to kill me, and soon!" Udzuki's rough voice cut through the cream-filled air as he stepped through the door to Mokuren's room and into our midst. "You're pathetic. You just rag on each other. Waah, you don't trust me! You can talk like that because you freakin' baby each other. You're so sugary sweet with each other. It gives me goosebumps. Peach buns or whatever the hell it is, let's just eat it and be done with it already."

"What's it to you? Udzuki, this is not your business." I understood why Mokuren said this. Udzuki perturbed me too.

"Yeah, that's right. Nothing to do with me. It's your fight. A big-fucking-deal fight just for you two. You have all that energy because you're arguing, and you damn well know it. It's the same as feeling strong and brave cuz it's coming down to the main event, the lodge versus society. You think it's gonna kill us? Please! How likely is that? But I suppose some people up and die even when it doesn't look likely to happen, which is why this joke of a world is the way it is. But you two, your joke isn't even funny. Nobody's laughing. It's a big yawn. Even so, here I am hoping you'll both just kill me."

"I'd say you're the one getting a buzz from fighting," Mokuren snapped back.

"Maybe. I'm an action junkie. I just love arguing like this. I could go on forever, because nothing I said connected with Kisaragi. Maybe she didn't trust me, but whatever, the communication wasn't happening. We were both speechless. Without the trust, if you try to be a little loving, it just comes out like a lie, and you keep pushing each other further and further away til there's no relationship left there. I hate jokes. Especially boring jokes. That's why I'd like to see you two walk the walk instead of talking out your asses with those energizer jokes. I'd like you to finish off Kisaragi, me, and all the other idiots who responded to your damned advertisement."

I felt a gaze on me, the gaze of someone who knew the ins and outs of my fate. Was I just following instep with a predetermined fate? I felt exhausted and robbed of all will, and even though I wanted to say something, I couldn't find the words. Everything had already been said, and it felt like nothing I could say would matter anyway.

"So, Udzuki, what did you want?"

"The cops are here. They're waiting for Iroha."

"I'm so sleepy." Mokuren barely could get those words out as she yawned and started to snore softly.

Two days later, a makeshift police box on par with a portable toilet that was set up next to the gate made the news, and as expected, a backlash erupted in the world below. The criticism was memorable enough to go in one ear and out the other.

Namely: Who wouldn't want round-the-clock police protection? But it's simply not feasible for the police to provide protection to every household, so we must be responsible for protecting ourselves. That's the price we pay to go on with our lives and, in a sense, our duty as residents of this Island Nation. To shirk that responsibility and claim special rights for oneself is to steal the taxpayers' money. While they pretend to live independently, that's all talk, because they are guarded by the authorities. These bastards run away, oblivious to the casualties of the war that has befallen our society … and so on.

A sudden storm arrived on Ascension Pass early the following afternoon. Black clouds covered the sky like smoke from a burning old tire, it was as dark as night, rain started pounding down like a waterfall, and the gales were powerful enough to rip through your skin. Violent changes in the weather were nothing out of the ordinary for this pass, but the defenseless press corps ran around in a state of panic. Those able to withstand the storm under a sturdy tent or make it to a car were okay, but others were balled up like turtles under the barrier tree branches. The port-o-cop-box was shaking dangerously too.

And then almost as soon as a flash of lightning shot through the black clouds, ear-splitting thunder rumbled like a bomb going off, and you could hear the sound of a tree trunk snapping in half. I looked out from the second-story balcony to see a cedar go up in flames. The air had chilled enough to freeze-dry your skin. I decided to step outside and invite the trembling reporters and camera crew inside.

I let them all take baths, made them honey-lemon tea, and told them about the plan I'd been mulling over for several days. My idea was to let those who so desired stay here for the going rate (of course, I made up the going rate) depending on the availability of rooms. Each room has a maximum occupancy, and each company would be responsible for making the necessary staff adjustments. Those who did stay would be responsible for observing the same rules as other guests. Filming was prohibited inside the lodge. They could speak with other guests only with their consent. Any coercion, and they would be asked to leave, etc., etc.

By evening, the storm had passed, and some crews returned with suitcases. The guests were, of course, even more nervous than usual, but everything went relatively smoothly. That night while we chitchatted after dinner, I told the reporters I was Iroha.

So while Mokuren slept off the fever brought on by her injury, the mass media reports from inside the mountain lodge began. I threw us into the breach and agreed to an interview.

It took place on a sunny afternoon in the garden. Reporters formed a ring around me with cameras running behind them. What made this different from the usual interview was the fact that I was also holding a camera and filming the whole time. I wanted to make them uncomfortable.

They started off with softball questions about what I'd been doing up until then, how I was feeling, and what I was up to now. I gave truthful and basic answers as to my life over the past year and a half, more or less what I've written in this document. They looked flustered when I mentioned the names of Miko and Inoue. Nevertheless, the question I'd predicted — "Were you actually lovers?" — was not followed by any creepy push for details.

When we got to the subject of the mountain retreat, one newspaper reporter started to monopolize the questioning.

"Having stayed here for several days now and had the opportunity to converse with you, I understand this is not a sect or cult. Granted, the media bears some responsibility for why you've been called a sect or a cult too, but that also has something to do with Mokuren's advertisement, specifically the line she drew between us and them. Do you agree with that opinion, Iroha?"

"As I said earlier, Mokuren is in bed with a terrible fever brought on by the attack. After she recovers, please ask her directly."

"I'm actually asking for your opinion."

"It's easy to say 'I trust you' — to talk the talk. But as far as what that really feels like, how you live it, and what it means in practice, that's a lot more difficult. Maybe it will have the braking effect Mokuren described if you believe that's my perspective."

"Because your perspective wouldn't be as rosy as Mokuren's?"

"Mokuren's isn't rosy. It's just that she has a stronger sense of trust than I do."

"That sounds rosy to me."

"People who think that way, like me, just don't have the hang of real trust yet."

"Well, I guess it all comes down to how we define our terms." That reporter got a little testy and looked impatient for a moment, but she quickly regained her composure and resumed questioning. "Another reason why this retreat has been seen as a cult is your presence here. In fact, that could very well be the biggest reason. You were witness to the beginning of the love suicides. You were deeply connected to that first incident, when we turned the sharp corner that led to this age. Your presence has colored our image of Mokuren." It felt like she was laying into me.

"I don't understand the question."

"Cutting to the chase, would it be wrong to see Mokuren's advertisement as an apology of sorts for your role in that first love suicide?"

"Mokuren wrote that ad herself. I didn't have anything to do with it. I don't understand why you're treating us like the same person. If you're going to talk about the people here like we are all the same, that will make us look like a cult."

"I'm sorry. I'll rephrase the question. Iroha, do you feel any responsibility for the love suicides? Or do you have a victim mentality?"

"That question doesn't seem to need an answer, but I'll answer anyway. I think virtually everyone bears some responsibility for the situation. In that regard, I feel some responsibility too. I don't really understand what you mean by victim mentality."

"That was a fair answer, but it might come across as being for the cameras' sake. Iroha, did you agree to this interview because there was something you wanted to communicate to the public?"

"I just wanted to lay rest to the rumors."

"Are you saying you wanted to clear up public misconceptions?"

"I just wanted you all to be able to go home."

"Well, it would seem Mokuren's advertisement was intended to draw media and public attention to this mountain retreat. For my part, I came here to inquire because I thought you wanted to show or tell us something."

"That is precisely why I said you need to ask Mokuren herself. If there are no more questions I can answer, why don't we call it quits?"

"Let me be more frank. You survived the love suicide that started all of this. Why is it, then, that you've been hidden away here where you are protected? Why didn't you want to speak out about the value of life to the rest of society?"

I felt as if my consciousness receded into the distance, like that bottomless free-fall feeling right before you wake up.

I quickly snapped out of it and said, "I didn't survive. Who in this society is surviving? Aren't we all just either dead or not dead yet?"

"Is that truly your belief? If that's the case, all that's left for those of us who are 'not dead yet' is to die? Am I wrong? That's like telling people to commit love suicide. Just as we've suspected, you really do think these developments have been necessary, don't you?"

"What the hell do you mean 'just as we've expected?' Don't twist around everything I say to suit your theories! Life is not about killing someone else so that you don't die. I honestly want to live, so I wanted space between me and places where you can kill or get killed."

"Are you saying you *can't* kill or get killed at this mountain retreat?"

"Seeing as how this place is part of the world, there is always a danger. And, in all honestly, there have been times when I was scared. I was a little sketchy myself at those times. By that I mean I was on the verge of thinking about whether I'd live or die. But hardly anyone who's stayed at this retreat thought of themselves as *survivors*. Because of that, I've been able to live here without any violent outbursts."

"Isn't the fact you don't consider yourself a 'survivor' proof that you are privileged? No one else has the luxury to think that way. Like it or not, you'll die if you are on the receiving end, so you have to do whatever you can to avoid ending up in that position. What I can't understand is how you, who survived yourself, will not try to understand what it's like for ordinary people in these circumstances."

"I haven't survived. Two people are dead. Do you understand why they died and why I'm alive? If it's supposed to be your problem too, you should get it, right?"

"That's something only the person involved can know. Only you, Iroha. To be perfectly blunt, isn't the world full of love suicides today because the person who appears to have blazed the trail did not put what she learned from that experience into words and make an appeal? If we'd had those words, I think they would have been surprisingly powerful."

"Are you criticizing me for being irresponsible?"

"The reality is that we are in this kind of world now. Therefore, everyone without exception should have to live under the same conditions. To create space between yourself and society and have it easy in a safe place while talking as if you were going it alone and independently is irresponsible! Going it alone is a much messier thing. In order to protect yourself, sometimes you have to violate your morals."

I started feeling light-headed again. I didn't understand what she was saying. I didn't even know if it was Japanese. It felt like her mouth was a noisy rapid-fire cannon spraying something like buckwheat pellets right at me.

I was fed up, as if this same reporter had been interviewing me for ages. She had always been everywhere under the sun, popping up before me as if for the first time with the same old words, same old questions, asking for the same opinions, and throwing the same criticisms at me.

But she wasn't exactly the same, the proof being that she was halfway transparent. While she continued repeating the same things on autopilot, she was actually disappearing. Her insides were all gone, and all that was left was a thin layer of skin on the surface. But no adult human being could take care of her, so any effort to re-stuff or repair her would be short-lived, because there'd be no way to make her stop saying the same words over and over again. This person is nobody. She's not even human, just something that's not dead.

It kept making noise.

"Back when I was with the international news division, I reported from the front lines. If you go to a battle-field, you'll see that all anyone can do is protect themselves. Someone like you who says pretty things would be defense-less and, before you know it, dead. On this battlefield, self-defense is survival intelligence that comes from the drive towards self-preservation."

The outline of this grandchild copy of a grandchild copy was getting fainter. If I didn't concentrate, I wouldn't understand or remember what she was saying.

"I'm sorry to tell you this is no battlefield. You get caught up in ideas like fighting, winning, losing, and surviving because you use the word battlefield." It took everything I had just to get that out. "I'm really tired. Let's end it there." I left the quiet film crews behind and withdrew to my room.

After that I felt sluggish and weak from repeated interviews until I could only answer with the same old tired phrases – "Yes, that's right" or "I'll leave it to your imagination." The reporters eventually gave up too.

The initial public reaction to our exchanges was, at first glance, sheer outrage. Still, it was nothing I hadn't already seen. "Fuck you, Iroha! You are all high and mighty, laughing while the rest of us common people have to get dirty." Or "Iroha, you didn't have the guts to go through with the first love suicide, did you? You decided to run away. Thanks to that, now the rest of us are stabbing each other in the back in this miserable killing game. We would have taken it on the chin if you'd shown some courage as the first person to blaze this trail." There were more comments echoing that reporter's words, which people tried to pass off as their own ideas. That's why even the violence stayed on message. Even the people who were yapping themselves must have been worried about that eventuality.

Actually, audience interest in the special features about us that ran on daytime talk shows was pretty dismal, and within a week public interest had shifted away from us. The new controversy was whether police efforts to guard a special group were themselves the problem and whether there were limits to self-reliance.

I felt like something had made it over the pass. I was overcome by the idea it would start an avalanche and then move on and, at the same time, filled with hateful thoughts of it cascading into bigger and different forms. I thought no one could bear these recurrent thoughts. What happens when you can't stand it anymore?

The film crews had thinned out by the time Mokuren was hobbling around the lodge on crutches. Each news outlet kept one or two people on site and replaced their topnotch seasoned reporters who'd been here before with inexperienced newbies.

Ironically, over the course of that one summer month from when Mokuren took out the ad through the arrival of the reporters, the attack, and up until my interview, there wasn't a single report of an indiscriminate love suicide. But as soon as attention turned away from the mountain retreat, an incident occurred. A guest at a youth hostel in Furano electrocuted herself and an employee to death. Each woman left behind a suicide note about how she was "tired of the lies." It was like traveling back in time for me, but the news coverage wasn't nearly as intense as before. In fact, the incident barely made the news at all. After that, three instances each of love suicides and justifiable self-defense were reported, but not one loss of life was reported with more attention than would have been given a bad traffic accident.

Like a clap of thunder in a clear sky, Her New Majesty's succession ceremony was held on September 1. The government had scheduled the date for spring, but the public lost interest, Her New Majesty was convalescing, and the press was restrained. We were finally reminded of her a few days beforehand when they started airing special features.

I was glued to the internet despite myself, but compared to the number of people who watched her interview on the anniversary of her brother's death, the ratings for this ceremony looked pretty bleak. Maybe people couldn't stomach the idea of having to listen to another one of her canned speeches.

After the ceremonial parade was over and she returned to the Palace, Her New Majesty, like her brother, began to speak extemporaneously. Without any notes or prompts, she looked straight into the cameras and began talking.

"I am not following my brother and predecessor's example by speaking to you in this fashion because I want to respond to the people's hopes as he did. Leaving aside all hopes and expectations, I first wish to express my own feelings.

I deeply respect my predecessor's mission. Having been called forth as Majesty, I wondered how an unconventional successor such as myself might take up his mission, which was cut so regrettably short.

I am certain that many of you wondered why I offered no words of comfort when havoc was wreaked on these islands after my predecessor's death. How could I not be pained when looking at such devastation?

And yet I could not understand why people committed such acts after my predecessor was taken from us. He did not choose to die. Without such understanding, I had no words to say. While remembering my Predecessor, I continued to reflect on his bequest and the people's actions.

People invested hope in my predecessor because he was so different from his predecessors. Rather than a mere continuation of the roles assumed by Their Previous Majesties, he called for a new era, one in which we would strive to live as individuals and cultivate ourselves as individuals, even while upholding tradition.

My predecessor tried to be the beginning. I believe that is natural for us as people. We all carry on the wisdom and spirit of our ancestors and yet are uniquely different beings. We are, after all, our individual selves in the end. My predecessor was trying to be himself.

The suicidal trend destroying these islands is the exact opposite of what my predecessor intended. For people to reenact the actions that led to earlier deaths is nothing more than imitation. Can such a death even be called one's own? If even your own death, an event that comes to each of us only once, is modeled on another's, for what purpose were you granted the light of life in this world? My predecessor must be rolling over in his grave. I think his sadness deepens with every empty imitation.

I am a new Majesty. I am a different person from my predecessor. I cannot serve as a substitute for him. What I can do is take up his bequest in my own way. I pray that I can persevere, living my life as myself. I want the ancestral spirit called Wisdom to become a part of me, to find its way into the pieces of my heart. Perhaps in doing so, that spirit can be reawakened. My predecessor's death was his own. I want everyone, when the time comes, to die in his or her own way."

Her speech stole my words. A strange feeling welled up deep inside me, but it seems useless to try and describe it. There was something deep down in my body like optimism and also like an enormous sense of futility. But as soon as I try to render it into words like this, it loses meaning. Any words I could think of would only be puny imitations of what Her Majesty said.

Her Majesty's speech also seemed similar to Inoue's document. If so, was this simply a surprising coincidence or had Her Majesty read Inoue's document? I imagined Inoue and Miko as having been the warm-up act just so Her Majesty could shine like a star with her speech that day.

I expected the worst as I headed to the spring. I was relieved when the visions of Miko and Inoue appeared, and I tried to tell them about Her Majesty's speech. But in the middle of trying, I felt like I'd already recited these lines to them many times before, so I stopped without finishing. I also felt sick of the imaginary conversations with them I'd been creating in my head, and I started running my camera as I wished them into mere light and sound. I zoned out for a bit. Then Miko and Inoue were gone. What did it mean for Miko and Inoue, who botched their deaths, to disappear? Had they really finally died? Or had the Majesty-less world Inoue predicted come to pass and the two of them been reborn? Those words feel meaningless to me too.

The speech was rebroadcast many times and brought calm to the streets too. After several days of chewing on Her New Majesty's words, people were struggling to change into flesh and blood and in agony over what they should do now. Exactly like after His Previous Majesty's death. So much so that not even my mom picked up the phone to call.

However, in this lodge with no TV and just my one radio, Her New Majesty's succession speech went away with the wind, and life was unchanged, as quiet and colorful as ever. Having bid good riddance to the film crews, the lodgers could return to their routines, birds flocked to the garden birdbath and chirped away, and across from them people sitting in the rattan deck chairs and swinging in the hammock soaked up the breeze. You could hear the grass murmuring, and the trees let out sighs for the benefit of human beings.

After lunchtime on September 4, Kisaragi headed to her room for her usual nap. Only this time, the person waiting for her there was not Udzuki, but a young reporter who'd arrived only a week earlier. He had a length of thick cotton rope in his hands. It was the same rope he used to tie up Udzuki, who was bound inside the sliding door closet. The reporter closed the door and announced he wanted Kisaragi to die with him. That guy didn't understand. You're the one who wrote that letter to the editor, aren't you? You'd understand me. If you do, then I can end this without being alone, and if I can't end it all with a moment when I'm not alone, I'll have to return to an unbearably lonely existence, you're tired, rest quietly, you don't have to say you'll stay with me after we die, each person goes on to their own afterlife, I can end it without the loneliness as long as you understand me.

Kisaragi listened to him without stirring until he finished and then asked him what he'd been doing the past week. The reporter answered that he'd walked around the woods and came to this conclusion while walking, so he wasn't being impulsive. Kisaragi apparently felt flames rising all over her body. And then she laid into him.

Is imitating other people the best you can do? I want to die my own death so I say hell no to imitating anyone else's. If you still want to die, you're going to have to use force. Because I definitely will not understand, and I will resist you to the very end.

Then she walked straight up to him and snatched the rope out of his hands. In my eyes, you're not even there. A copy imitating a person isn't human, just scenery, so go ahead and try. And she handed the rope out to him.

The reporter was stiff and couldn't move. We heard Kisaragi's yelling and came running. We held him down while he was still frozen and unable to respond. He was arrested by the round-the-clock security cop for intent to kill. I don't suppose there are many cases where the word "intent" fits quite so well. He passionately wanted to do it, but he couldn't follow through.

The reporters still stationed at the lodge were relating this incident via live telecast in no time. They made Kisaragi look quite the heroine for her firm stand and determination. Her face during the interview was a radiant postpartum red, her eyes were sparkling, and her voice rang out as clear and resonant as if she were singing an aria. She was, in a word, divine. The phrase that came out of her mouth and echoed out in the world was "a copy imitating a person isn't human, just scenery." Many people's spirits rose when they heard those words. They agreed and were emboldened and resolved. This mountain lodge was called things like "The Hall of Courage," and for a little while the whole world wanted to visit Kisaragi.

That was the last attempt at a love suicide. After that, love suicides began to seem impossible, and the uneasiness in people's hearts disappeared. Society returned to "normal." People who took a defiant attitude like Kisaragi and refused to "imitate others" conquered their fears, and they were filled from head to toe with the confidence that her high spirits could be theirs too. The media called the end of the age of love suicides the "snow-melt" and pronounced that spring was on its way.

It goes without saying that it's been a while since the "snow-melt." That much you all know. So, I don't need to go into more longwinded explanations about everything that's happened these past three years. This is already too long.

But if I had to leave off by saying just one thing, it would be that the snow hasn't melted for me.

As you know, in the "election to change the world" held immediately after the "snow-melt," Terujirô Kishi, the student from the first justifiable self-defense incident back when the war began, was serving as Secretary General for the new political party, which became the dominant party ruling the coalition government. "Those of us who are here today survived because we were meant to survive. We should forge ahead, confident in our fate and our ability with a zest for life, as we set about creating a proud, healthy society." That appeal of his resonated with you all, didn't it? With a strong push forward for the stability of law and order everyone desperately wanted, they took over and absorbed all the other parties and established rock-solid leadership. Kishi assumed the prime minister-ship in no time at all and was celebrated as "The Winning Team's Premier."

Well, as I've written more than once already, our mountain retreat was under surveillance. Even after the "snow-melt," the police remained on the grounds that the danger of another attack on the lodge had not passed. If anything, the police presence increased, and everyone visiting the retreat was, without exception, subjected to intense security checks. Most of the lodgers were annoyed by all the intrusions and went back down the mountain never to return. And that's why now it's a forgotten "reservation."

Because of Inoue's mistaken approach, the holes in this screen we call society get filled with cheap pride whenever they become visible, and the projector starts back up. The post-love suicide era Kisaragi rang in with her shining declaration is nothing more than a gargantuan remake. In order to deny the reality that it's a shoddy imitation, people voluntarily become screens and believe the film projected onto them is really them. All the individual does is weave and press the screen called society. Who can say they are really living their own lives?

On the other side of the screen, reserved in taboo confines, I have lived with painful thoughts these past three years. I also have a bad feeling that if we keep going like this, we'll see another era of love suicides.

And that's why I'm breaking the taboo. I want to expose how it's all just movies projected on the surface of the moon and that, just like before, no one exists, and no one is participating in the world. As a start, I'm copying and dis-seminating Inoue's document.

I got back from my business trip to Shanghai, and Iroha wasn't here. According to Udzuki, she uploaded Inoue's document and her additional file and then turned herself in at the gate police-box. I can imagine how dazed and confused Officer Murai must have been. His strong sense of duty to protect the lodge is so cute and sincere. When Iroha suddenly showed up saying she'd committed a crime, asking to be arrested, and handing over the evidence, he must have had no clue what to do. He probably went along with it more because she was so eager than because he was focused on carrying out his duties. That's how good-natured he is. The poor guy.

That woman! She really took advantage of my absence. She did it all without sharing or discussing anything with me. She better not have been trying to make fun of my self-righteousness. And she better have known she'd get chewed out if she told me.

I was bitching like that as Udzuki gave me the low-down. Then he said, "The document part is nothing," and he took me to her room.

On the other side of the door was a fake room. Directly in front of us, the afternoon sun was shining through the sliding glass door to the terrace (it was, by the way, evening at the time), and beyond the terrace was the mountain range. You could see the trees in the garden from the western window. But there was nothing on the eastern wall, or to be more precise, there was just a white sheet hanging there.

"That projector is kaput. Iroha didn't catch that one," Udzuki explained.

Sure enough, the southern terrace and western window were just movies Iroha made that were being projected on the walls. If you took away the screens hung there, you'd see the identical real things, the terrace or the window.

A human figure appeared at the far end of the terrace. It was Iroha. She walked towards the glass door with a cup and saucer in her hand, looking off and occasionally back this way, and she was saying something. She'd start laughing and stagger off balance too. But there was no sound.

A figure crossed the western window too. Then it came back. Somehow it was me.

Udzuki said, "I'm not in this. I feel so unwanted."

Iroha faced us and walked into the room from the terrace. You couldn't read her expression because of the backlighting. There was something a little menacing and powerful in her movements. Just when I unconsciously backed away, Iroha disappeared. She must have stepped out of the camera's range.

"Don't get mad in this next part and just keep watching," Udzuki warned.

No one was left on the terrace, and everything was bathed in orange like time had passed or maybe the sun suddenly sunk. That scene was frozen for a minute and then the orange tone that was spreading out in thin rays of light from the edges of the landscape shattered into particles that fell like sand in an hourglass. The scene in the room collapsed. Nothing was projected after things fell apart. Just one of those screen saver thingies.

When the bits of color had all fallen down, the room went dark. She must have lined the sheet she used for a screen with blackout paper. I couldn't tell where Udzuki was.

Eventually, a faint light began to rise up from the floor. A gentle lemon-colored arc of light.

"Oh no, tell me that's not what I think it is."

"It's what you think it is."

"As if this was a planetarium."

It was the surface of the moon. And it stopped when it covered the lower third of the screen. I stood on the lunar surface, gazing out at the horizon, to the west and to the south. The horizon divided the light from the darkness. You could even see the pits and rocks on the surface. And she'd carefully made sure stars floated in blue space on the western wall. How did she get her hands on that film?

The light of the lunar surface gradually grew stronger. From lemon to silver to a blinding white. At the same time, the darkness deepened until it was a pure jet black. The contrast sharpened until finally the lunar surface was a high-contrast black and white. Then the close-ups of the black and white surface began. It was like riding in some kind of spaceship at light speed above the surface. I felt a little woozy.

The brakes slammed on and the close-up came to a crawl. And then it was clear. All those little black specs were words. They covered the screen like a swarm of bugs. When they were close enough to be a legible size, I realized it was Inoue's document.

The rest is predictable. Iroha's text gets mixed in there, right? And then the words start to move and scramble until they turn into meaningless black and white dots. I didn't want to imagine what form those black and white dots were going to take.

I switched on the lights. Then I turned off the projector and tore the sheets off the wall. I pulled the real sliding glass door wide open. The smell of dead leaves rushed in with the cool air. I inhaled deeply. I got goosebumps. The mountains were purple, and the sky above painted a deep indigo.

I'm not wasting my time to analyze it. To do that and draw some kind of meaning from this "work of film" would be playing right into Iroha's hands. By creating all this and writing her statement, Iroha was already getting played herself, caught up in someone else's trap (Inoue's or Miko's or the media's). I'm not getting played for a second-hand fool.

She should have just filmed it and shown it. She was actually doing okay and hanging in there, but then she got carried away by those big ideas. When she just filmed while worrying whether she was a fake or whether she was simply some device that records light and sound, she was sensual, loose, and clever. But as soon as she tried to express that fakeness, she became nasty, tight, and boring.

Why does everyone get all worked up about "self-expression?" Iroha hated all those documents and manifestos, but she went and wrote one herself. She made that dumbass movie that only Udzuki and I saw. It's pathetic. If you're a fake, that's fine. Be a fake. There are faky ways of living for fakes. If you don't feel geared up for life, then that's proof you're living. It's like back when everyone was whining about allergies and they cut down the cedars up here and replaced them with a transplanted fake variety forest. Human activity creates the bad pollution that makes the sky purple.

People get hung up on "self-expression" because they want the real thing, the big essential truth. When you start to think there's some true meaning out there and that it's hidden, you fixate on it, you struggle for it, and you try every trick in the book to say, "I've got it. This is the real thing."

Maybe there is a real thing, and maybe there isn't. Even if there is, I am not going to know what it is. And if there isn't, what's there to know? So, no matter how you look at it, it's beyond human comprehension. And I enjoy a very satisfying life without knowing.

People searching for the real thing are not living satisfying lives. They suffer from some kind of lack. To make up for that lack, they invent the real thing. And then they start "expressing" themselves.

What I want to say to the Iroha who just films and shows her films is that you yourself are expression. When I watch the films you made, I feel moved. To have those feelings and be satisfied with life is my expression. It's okay to try and communicate that, and it's okay not to. We can communicate it when we can and can't when we can't. But there's nothing that is impossible to communicate.

Making a movie of the lunar surface (which you probably want to say is the real thing), putting the document out in public, and turning yourself in like that follows the same pattern as what Inoue did. Iroha, you do see that, don't you? When you come back, I'm going to read you the riot act.

September 30

I got to see Inoue's parents. It was the first time we'd met, of course. They arrived without reservations, and I told them I could have gone to pick them up or at least arranged for them to pass through security without all the nuisance. They said their calls wouldn't go through and that they did send a letter, but hadn't received a reply, so they decided to just come. Communications must have been shut down because of Iroha's arrest.

Communications were a pain for a little while after the "snow-melt" when the police were strict. But it was a slow time for the lodge, and if they weren't going to pay attention to individuals connected to my friends, then the surveillance was just for show. They must have been checking on my activities some other way.

Inoue's parents had come to collect his old document that Iroha put up on the net. They said it would be impossible to recover everything, because even if Iroha's site could be shut down, lots of copies were probably being stored in different places. That threw me for a loop. The site she made wasn't deleted even after her arrest. It had been a week since her arrest, and you could still access Inoue's document and her story.

In a quiet voice Inoue's dad said, "I understand. We just want to do as much as we can. If you can understand how we feel. If it stays out there like this and wakes the sleeping children, we just couldn't bear it."

Inoue's mom said, "We finally have some peace, but this could start it all up again. Why did Iroha do this?"

"It's a mystery to me too. I have some questions for her too," I replied.

Inoue's dad said, "All this time, it's been tearing us apart to think about our responsibility as parents and the reality of how your kid is his own independent person even though he came from you. Even now, we still don't know what we should do. But now that things have settled down, we're trying quietly to get on with our lives."

"I lost my job. And we had to move. I had to leave behind everything from my life up until then, and I'd just found my second life," his mom said.

"Even though we say it's our second life, it's filled with grief over our son's mistake. We simply want it to be our own personal grief. But having the document available like that puts us back in the public. Are we supposed to be seen as failures in the eyes of the public forever?"

"Have you two ever met Iroha?"

Inoue's parents shook their heads.

"Please, at least this once, talk to her directly. After she decides how to handle everything, I'll get in touch with you."

"If Iroha refuses to shut it down, we can sue for copyright infringement," Inoue's dad said. Inoue wrote in the document that he wanted it to be copied and circulated, so I thought it would be considered open source material, but at that point I simply told them I understood.

They'd come all the way here, so I took them on a tour to show off our fabulous sunset. We walked down the path to the pass when Inoue's mom asked, "Is Yellow Hell Spring far from here?"

"The only person who calls it that is Iroha. Do you want to see it? It's a bit of a walk."

"No, no, it's okay," she replied. She was quiet for a bit and then asked, "What is Iroha like?"

I started out by saying, "She's sweet and attractive."

"Do you think she's perhaps too sweet or maybe comes across as a little overly impressionable?"

"Don't get the wrong idea. She pretty much keeps to herself. But there are aspects of her like that."

"Forgive me for asking, but it's been on my mind so much since I read what she wrote. It's just that, well that, that part about the dead coming back to life. Were those eerie rumors what influenced her to write it all? I'm probably making too much out of this." It looked like Inoue's mom for the most part believed Iroha had been affected by the rumors.

The rumors were related to The Majesties. On September 30, around one month after her succession ceremony, at the end of a fertility festival performance, Her New Majesty, citing poor health, announced she would take a break from her official duties, and she stopped appearing in public. But more recently, rumors that maybe her predecessor, His Young Majesty, came back to life began to swirl around the gossip papers and on the net. Those blew up into bigger rumors that spread about how everyone who died in the love suicide era had not only been resurrected, but were now "driving the living off to be "spirited away" and that more and more people were disappearing.

"She rejected that idea at the beginning of her document when she wrote about how she doesn't believe in ghosts and that her experiences at the spring were personal and ultimately figments of her imagination."

"I hope so. But she also wrote several things like how the spring is a shrine or something to that effect. I wondered if maybe she was into the occult."

We got back to the lodge, had some of Udzuki's famous savory rice made with our own homegrown mushrooms, and talked a lot. They spoke openly about their feelings and conflicts, about what it's been like since they lost their son. Maybe there was no one else they could talk to like that. Their softly spoken stories were never-ending.

"We knew about Iroha before. We were looking forward to meeting her. Our boy talked to us about everything, so we'd heard a lot about her. Well, he was honest about whatever he did talk about, but it feels like he was also a person we didn't know. It was as if all of a sudden he'd been replaced with someone else who looked exactly like him. That's why it doesn't feel real. It's like that other person caused that incident. We tried to respect his opinions and give him space, but it ended up creating this strange barrier between us. We were trying to think from his point of view, but now it's clear that we only drove him further away. That attitude came out of our fears about not wanting to make any mistakes with our son. That's why there's no end to our sadness. There's nothing worse that knowing you messed up in raising your child. It's as if the value of your existence just evaporated. It's unbearable."

The conversation lasted through the night, so I had them sleep over, and they left shortly after noon today. When they asked if they could come back, I said, "You are always welcome here."

October 3

According to information from a friend connected to the mass media, the charges against Iroha were dropped and she is expected to be released. Inoue's document isn't considered dangerous material anymore. That's a no-brainer. The files Iroha put up on the net hardly got a response. And the only newspaper coverage was one teeny article in the evening edition about her arrest. In a world fully armed with a strong sense of "total health" (Terujirô Kishi coined that phrase), not even a document like that can carry any weight. The situation now is too different from the time when Inoue wrote his document. If you think you can create a sensation the same way, serve time in jail, and stir the world up into a frenzy, then you are the most naive dreamer the world has ever known.

I didn't mention this when Inoue's parents asked, but Iroha did react a bit after she first heard the rumors of people coming back from the dead. She got angry and said the rumors showed that people who considered themselves "survivors of the love suicide era" were really just hiding their guilty consciences.

"Being scared shitless and powerless back then and acting like all they could do was watch people die was plainly and simply shameful. There's no value in surviving that. And yet they forget all about that shame and the dead people and the ones who were spirited away like more water under the bridge, and now they're enjoying safe lives, so they feel guilty. They'll start thinking they were attacked by zombies and want to strike back, so they'll kill somebody. An incident like that is bound to happen. They'll probably even call it justifiable self-defense. Another killing age is on its way. If they are gonna call up the spirits of the dead like that, then they'll just have to kill the dead all over again. Fuck me, but I'm not having any of it."

She always talked like that. Three years ago, the two of us went at it over the same issues.

I suppose that's another way of taking rumors seriously. At any rate, the origins of the rumor weren't exactly what Iroha had in mind. As I mentioned earlier, they had to do with The Majesties.

The Current Majesty didn't give any signs she'd return from her medical leave. At first, disturbing rumors abounded that an evil spirit appeared during the fertility festival when the mystical rites were being performed and said she was a fake Majesty and unfit to succeed. But after half a year or so, people had lost interest, and she was all but forgotten. Then, out of that lull burst the question of an heir. The current Majesty wasn't married, and those around her didn't seem to be pressuring her to find someone. People thought this was strange and wondered whether something was being hidden from them. The theory that The Previous Majesty was alive apparently developed from that idea.

A friend who works at a communications company told me about the unspoken understanding within the Imperial Household National Press Club that Her New Majesty was, in actuality, quite healthy. There was considerable rancor with the government over various opinions and views, with each side holding fast without giving an inch, and Her Majesty was sort of relieved of her duties. However, that was also what Her Majesty wanted. She ventured out on walks and enjoyed her anonymity. Even the prickly Imperial Household Affairs cooperated with the police and acquiesced to her not showing up in public. According to my friend, there were reports that Her Majesty was disguising herself as a man and that maybe the sightings of His Young Majesty were just her in men's clothing.

But Iroha didn't know any of that. When I heard how angry she was, I thought she wanted the love suicide era to come back with a vengeance.

If I were to hazard a guess, Iroha's feelings would go something like this:

She's not hoping for love suicides or for us all to die, but if this façade of shining peace and stability is going to

continue, she'd rather we went back to the dangerous love suicide days when no one trusted anyone else. At least in those
chaotic times, to use her words (or, more accurately, the words
she borrowed from Inoue), you could see the fraying edges of
society through holes in the screen. You could glimpse the
real thing, the true nature, the "essence," of this world.

The holes Inoue and Mikoto did such a fine job of opening had been filled in. And along with them, Inoue, Mikoto,
and even Iroha herself were buried alive and left forgotten.
Given the circumstances, the only thing to do would be force
back the hands of the clock to the moment when Inoue
decided to die and His Young Majesty was truly buried.

That's why Iroha took actions that put her smack into
Inoue's shoes. Maybe she was trying to be a reincarnation
of Inoue. And maybe in that sense she was also processing
her yearning and sadness over it having been Inoue and not
herself who committed love suicide with Mikoto. The very
person who warned another bloody age would come if people
kept up this same attitude was herself on the verge of setting
off a love suicide ticking time bomb.

I really should have taken her, even kicking and scream-
ing, with me to Shanghai, but hindsight is twenty-twenty. I'd
invited her time and time again, but she wasn't interested, so
I dropped it. But she reached her limit after never going anywhere and staying holed up in her little room with nothing
to do but keep that threesome going. And three years of that
was enough to turn her into a deluded dreamer completely
out of touch with the world.

Yes, it was also the same three years when "the
Winning Team's Premier" Terujirô Kishi, burst through the
mainstream and, before you knew it, popularized his message
of pride in being one of the "superior people who survived"
and stuck the label "total health" on it. In the blink of an eye,
he'd enacted martial law, and since there weren't enough soldiers to make that happen, he opened the door to citizenship
for foreigners on the condition they served in the military.
And with the relief over law and order in the background,
he reached out for support to legalize euthanasia in order to

reduce the number of old people, which fueled the elderly exodus abroad. And he cooked up that dominant gene myth too. Nevertheless, since it seems like the peace has been secured now, nobody gives a rip what Terujirô Kishi does.

Udzuki started Chinese-Language studies, and now he helps me. He's no whiz when it comes to foreign languages, and I have to help him out a lot, but he's finally gotten to the point where he can read newspaper clippings.

Either she really is slow on the uptake or isn't interested, but Iroha doesn't know what my real job is. The restaurant manager gigs in the Shinjuku and Yokohama Chinese-Towns were real jobs too, but I make my real money placing workers. I find above-board job opportunities for those from the continent looking for work on these islands and those from these islands who want to cross over to the continent. Obviously, all the work involved in that process is more than I can do on my own. People like me shuttle from here to there and there and back delivering human resources. The world's a big bathtub full of people, and our job is to stir it up. I used money I made that way to pay for the advertisement.

Even though my role in the process is completely legal, after they cross, some of the people I place commit crimes. That's why the Feds have their eyes on me. I think they set up police surveillance at the mountain retreat so they could check on the comings and goings of myself and those close to me. Because I had those suspicions, I placed the ad and caused the big commotion. I thought that would increase the flow of people (boy, did that backfire!).

I brought people crossing to the continent, looking to immigrate, or coming over from the continent here to stay at the lodge. When the "snow-melt" hit and almost everyone left, they didn't just go back down the mountain, but many of them crossed over to the continent for good. Or, in my mind, they flew the coop. One reason for seeing the hand of the state in all this is the coastal surveillance. Ascension Pass is a kind of harbor in the sky, so it's only fitting that the police would arrive here too.

In that sense, a hole did open up. But there's no real thing on the other side.

I'm probably seen as a necessary evil on these islands, where fewer babies are being born, and on the continent too. Actually, I'm getting fat off Terujiro Kishi calling for foreigners to join the military and scaring the elderly overseas. That's not all. Terujirô Kishi is putting his own head in the noose.

October 3, again

Iroha's mom called. She'd met with the lawyer, and it looked like the prosecution wouldn't be pursuing the case against Iroha. She called to ask what we should do. Her voice was as bouncy and breathless as ever. I answered, "Let's set up a family court trial for her welcome home party." We joked around about how we'd give Iroha a hard time, and it felt good.

I had a fight with Udzuki. A fight so bad even a dog wouldn't eat it. So, what kind of classy fight would that be? It's nutritious. And even if it isn't, it tastes good. Hardly. Fighting with Udzuki isn't nutritious or delicious. I dish it out for myself, and still it doesn't agree with me.

Yet again, the subject was children. Apparently it wasn't okay for me to say the lack of people and quiet must have had a negative impact on Iroha. Because Udzuki then said, "That's exactly why I'm asking you to think about having children."

Udzuki and I are together now. He and Kisaragi broke up. Kisaragi went back down the mountain. It was back when people were leaving the retreat – like the annoying surveillance was plucking them away one at a time like strands of hair. Kisaragi announced, "The mountain retreat is going down." I had no idea what she was talking about. That's what you say when whatever it was that drew people together for the same purpose ends up collapsing. Like this island nation is going down, or Down With the Tokugawa Clan, or the East Harajuku Projects are going down, or taking Western

Aoyama down to the ground. Don't talk like that, I told her. Iroha and Udzuki nodded in agreement. And then Kisaragi said, "It's time to join society."

She went on. "Anybody can be themselves when no one else is around. For people who can't take care of themselves beyond that, it's fine to be holed up in isolation. But now the whole world has rejected imitating other people. People want to live life in their own individual way. So, you don't have to hole yourself up to be yourself anymore. Nowadays, you can be yourself out in the open. I think I'll have a more authentic sense of myself by putting myself into the mix and interacting with other people."

Udzuki's biting response: "Isn't it still imitating other people if everyone's acting like they're not imitating anyone?" Kisaragi blew up at him and insisted the experience of almost being killed made a huge difference in her life. She called him a "spoiled brat." Udzuki's comeback: "Yeah, that's right. I keep whining and I won't let up. I'm a fucking idiot. My lover goes fucking crazy, fucking scary, and still I don't give up. I keep coming back for more. I'm impossible." For days on end, they fought like that until Kisaragi had finally had enough and went down the mountain and back home.

There wasn't anything the least surprising about her departure. For one thing, Kisaragi's famous line rang in the "snow-melt," just like Iroha pointed out, and seeing as how she was the catalyst for the new "snow-melt" era, it was only natural that Kisaragi felt a kind of responsibility to it. Everyone was looking to her as a model for overcoming the love suicide era fears. Or at least for thinking they already had. Kisaragi felt like she had to be there with everyone. Now she's renting an apartment in the building Iroha's mom manages, and she's got a kid too.

Time passed, and before I knew it my room and Udzuki's room became the same, and we consciously decided to create a partnership. As we sorted through all the ins and outs of living together, we didn't encounter any major points of disagreement. The only issue where we didn't see eye to eye was children.

Udzuki said he wanted to have children someday. I said I didn't know. I honestly don't know what I want in terms of kids. Udzuki couldn't accept that. But that's his personality. He wouldn't relent. Why don't you know? When you say you don't know, can you be more precise and tell me how you feel? Those kinds of questions. I couldn't satisfy him with the kind of answers he wanted. If he asked me whether I wanted children, I'd answer that I wasn't interested in having any now. He'd ask if "I don't know" was just a roundabout way of saying I didn't want any, and I would be speechless. If adoption is a viable option, would you consider it? In theory we weren't supposed to have any troubles, but we ran into one.

After the "snow-melt," society moved onto the "one child policy." In order to compensate for the population lost during the love suicide era, the plan was for people to pair off in couples and then for each couple to have at least one kid. Various incentives were introduced to promote this. And outrageous slogans told us we survivors would bear children ready to survive, children born strong and in total health, so we shouldn't worry and just do it.

But the one child policy wasn't particularly effective. Most couples didn't try to have kids, and, more than that, there weren't many couples, particularly couples that stayed together very long.

Udzuki asked whether I was being influenced by those trends. I told him I didn't think so. We didn't fit the conventional definition of a couple after all.

"Maybe this environment is too comfortable, and you don't want to risk ruining anything?"

My life with Udzuki was, in all honesty, too cozy for comfort. We didn't get tangled up in any of that annoying falling in love business, but we shared tender feelings, enjoyed a rich sex life, and maintained a good power balance. Our efforts paid off for both of us. If the situation were to change, couldn't we simply adjust the nature of our efforts to compensate? We'd been pretty flexible up until now. That's precisely why I answered, "Probably not."

"Are you worried about how Iroha would feel?"

"No way. She'd be thrilled if there was a kid here. She'd be excited to babysit too."

"My thoughts exactly."

For a moment, I felt like I was experiencing the exclusion Iroha herself felt while Udzuki and I were having that conversation. The relationship among the three of us may have been one of the reasons for her actions. Or maybe the fact that I was worrying was a bad sign that we'd get caught up in a romantic power game.

And then today, Udzuki asks me this, "You want us to hit a dead end, don't you? I figured it out when I was reading the files Iroha put up. In Inoue's document, it says, 'the world wants to die'. Those are Mikoto's words. You feel the same way. You want it to end with you, don't you?"

When he said that, I remembered how children were a bone of contention with Iroha and Mikoto. But it wasn't as if Mikoto wanted children. Without thinking, I let slip, "You're insensitive, Udzuki." Iroha let slip the same words to me once too. "That's a romantic way to say it, that the world 'wants' to die. How on earth can I sympathize with that? If I wanted it to end with my generation, adoption would be okay, wouldn't it? So something else is holding me back, I think."

"What can I do, Mokuren? It's weird that you can't analyze some parts of yourself. What with you picking over my issues all the time the way you do."

"I hardly ever analyze myself. You really don't know me very well."

"Tell me you're not worrying that your business might go under if there's a baby boom."

The rest was a bargain basement trade war of words. I feel bad about it.

It just occurred to me that there's something about children that smells authentic. Maybe I'm put off by whatever that smell is, like the essence of human divinity or something. And that smell seems artificial to me.

In that case, maybe I'd be okay with a fake kid. But what in the hell would a fake kid be like? Iroha's idea of an "island of children" is swimming around my brain.

Yikes! Am I starting to feel the curse of real-thing-consciousness?

October 4

She's back. Iroha came back. And she was carrying on as if nothing had happened.

She opened the door, looked at me, and while panting (elated really) said, "It finally started. The Love Suicide Era!" I didn't say anything, but just looked at her skeptically, and she insisted, "I'm serious. It's the truth. On my way back, I saw a couple up at the top of Mount Morokami. They held hands and looked down below. They looked really serious. Then they suddenly embraced each other. That's a love suicide."

"Oh really?" I halfway believed her.

When we got to the spot and saw a middle-aged couple sitting back and enjoying rice balls on the mountaintop, I wanted to needle Iroha and say, "Yeah, it really looks like they're itching to die." We were out of breath, huffing and puffing, when the couple spotted us and came up to ask, "Sorry to bother you when you're in such a hurry, but would you mind taking a picture for us?"

I deferred to Iroha, the professional after all. When Iroha had their camera ready, they sat up close to each other, took off their sunglasses, and smiled. I recognized their faces from somewhere. Were they actors?

Iroha returned the camera, and they politely bowed their heads and said, "You were obviously in a hurry, and we hated to bother you. Thanks so much."

I said, "Don't worry. We were rushing because we saw you." Iroha went pale and glared at me. "We're actually out to solicit guests, for that little log cabin over there," I pointed beyond the ridge. I had finally realized who the woman was, and by hook or by crook, I wanted her to stay at the lodge. "Where are you staying tonight?"

"We'd just planned to make it a day trip. I wonder if that's too short."

"Yes, that's definitely too short."

"She says it's too short," the woman said to the man. "And I want to stay here a little longer. Let's spend the night."

The man objected in a hushed voice, "But Chichibu is waiting for us."

The woman pulled a cell phone out of her fanny pack and said, "Why not send for Chichibu? If Chichibu can't come, we can always cancel."

"You're not going to get any reception up here in the middle of the mountains."

"I won't know until I try. There might be cellular coverage up here on the summit with nothing in the way."

While the woman was calling, the man asked, "We don't need reservations?"

"It's not the most spectacular mountain, so we don't get many guests."

Then Iroha had to butt in and say, "Well, we do screen our clientele a bit."

"You're right. There's no reception."

With a relieved expression, the man looked at the woman and said, "They screen their clientele? That doesn't sound so good. Why don't we save it for another time?"

The woman gave up and replied, "We're so close, but I can't get through, so I suppose that's the way it goes. We'll stay next time if you'll have us."

"Oh," I let my disappointment show. I was actually disappointed. Even so, I tried to sustain the conversation by asking, "Do you go mountain-hiking often?"

The woman looked me in the eye and said, "Yes, I actually came here a long time ago. It's changed a lot since then."

"When was that?"

"Oh, ages ago. Your lodge looked much older then."

"You knew it before? Did you stay there?"

The woman shook her head. "I wanted to stay over then too, but I was just passing through." Then she drew a breath and whispered, "I was really keen on staying tonight, but we'd already made plans with someone, so we have to go back."

"I don't know what it was like back then." I couldn't contain myself. The weather has changed so drastically, and I heard it used to be an ordeal to cross the pass. That it wasn't unusual to find the bodies of people who didn't make it. I heard that's how it got the name Ascension Pass."

She laughed and said, "That was a long time before I came here, before the shake-up in the government. It seems like even though the name stayed the same, the meaning changed to fit the times. Over a hundred years ago, a famous writer jumped with his secret lover, and for a while it was famous as a place where troubled youth came to kill themselves. It must have been hard on the people living around here."

"To be honest, when we saw you two standing at the edge of the cliff, we thought the worst and came running." I finally said it. Iroha, who'd been quiet this whole time, looked ready to pass out.

The woman broke into a lighthearted laugh. "If you see someone looking down from Ascension Pass, you wouldn't be able to stop them anyway."

"What did it feel like when you looked down?"

"It felt good, like I was ascending to heaven." The man grimaced at her joke. I could tell he did that to keep from laughing.

"You really can fly. All the way to Shanghai. It must have something to do with the air currents. Next time you come back, why don't you give it a try and see? If you don't prepare a little, you'll come crashing down before you make the ascent to heaven though." My smile was earnest.

She laughed and said, "Crashing down sounds like it could be interesting too." He couldn't keep up his poker face this time and joined in the laughter.

But a stone-faced Iroha threw water on our slightly cryptic, but pleasant mood by saying, "Ascension Pass is that way. This is Mount Morokami."

"When the famous author jumped off the cliff, it must have been slightly confusing for him." Judging that it was time to leave, I segued into parting words, "Well, enjoy your-selves, at least until sunset."

"I thoroughly enjoyed visiting with you. Next time we'll definitely stay the night. Take care of yourselves," she said. I told them to do the same and took Iroha's hand, and we quickly made our way back down the ridge.

I broke the silence by whispering, "That was Her Majesty, huh?"

Iroha snorted as if to mock me. "Please! That was just an ordinary middle-aged woman."

"Wasn't Her Majesty already an ordinary middle-aged woman before?"

"That's disgusting. Was she on her Roman Holiday?"

"It doesn't matter if you think it's disgusting. It's true."

"Mokuren, then you know what?"

"What?"

"You didn't figure it out?"

"Figure out what?"

"If that woman was Her New Majesty, then the man with her was her older brother, His Young Majesty."

"What the hell are you talking about?"

"Even a sparrow would notice. Those two looked exactly alike. Both of them had double lids on their right eyes. Having two lids on only the right eye is a characteristic of that family."

"It's just a coincidence. I would have recognized him if he'd been His Young Majesty. Sure, now that you mention it, they look alike, but it wasn't him. Let me put it this way, His Young Majesty's hair was a little thinner."

"Now they can make it grow back. That's no reason."

"Well, neither of us can know for sure, so why don't we each believe what we want?"

"That's okay for you, Mokuren. Because if you think she was out hiking with her secret lover, all that means is that her medical leave is a lie and that she's living it up. But if that woman was Her Majesty and the man was His Young Majesty, there's a lot more involved in what I have to imagine."

"You mean that the rumors were right and His New Majesty came back from the dead?"

"Or maybe that he never died. You have to think about what it all means. Like what's up with their relationship, and what they intend to do, and what will happen to Their Majesty's family, and so on and so on until your head starts spinning."

"Iroha, you don't have to worry about any of that. That's for the two of them, the government that makes the institution, and Parliament to think about. Even if we do worry about it, that kind of conversation will not happen out in the open. And if you do obsess over it, you'll be caught in a trap, like Mikoto."

Iroha looked dazed and muttered, "That's true."

After waiting a bit, I told her that Inoue's parents had visited and that they wanted her to erase the document. "What will you do?"

"Erase it."

"That's irresponsible. Think about all the people who've read it. Don't you at least want to give people an explanation?"

"Mokuren, you write it. You're already writing anyway, like a diary. Udzuki told me. That you're writing your opinions about us all."

"I don't think it's anywhere near as exciting as what you wrote."

"That's why you should write it."

"I'll pass. Other than that, Inoue's parents want to meet you. How about it?"

"Okay. Invite them up. You're having a welcome home party for me, right? I heard you're putting me on trial too, huh?"

"Call them yourself."

Iroha didn't answer. I couldn't tell if it was rage or rapture, but I was seized by an intense feeling, and, in a loud voice, I asked, "Wanna jump?" Before Iroha could reply, I yelled, "Let's jump." And again, "Let's jump already." Three times, I pushed my voice to its limit, and I thought I was pretty clever. I felt like a flying horse.

A reporter friend said this as a joke. Until they get the matter of an heir resolved, they could keep Her Majesty alive for one hundred or even two hundred years even if she physically died. I don't know if any mysterious plans have been laid, and assuming there haven't, even if she died, they could say she was still on medical leave, so she'd continue to exist as The Current Majesty. In effect, she'd be The Last Majesty. And I seem to recall a certain someone having a dream about a Land of Majesty without a Majesty. He willingly and passionately laid his life on the line for that dream. He was a great person.

Her Majesty opted out with that in mind. It's as if she said, "Sorry parents of these islands, but I'm not playing mommy." Or did she stop to blend in with all the other ordinary people? Maybe she became another one of the children?

I know the answer. I found it in the conversation I just shared, along with my faith.

So come on, Iroha, let's jump. Come jump with me. I'll be waiting at the bottom.

October 7

AUTHOR AND TRANSLATOR Q & A

The following questions and answers were exchanged over email between January of 2007 and November of 2008.

Hurley: Before PM embraced this novel, it took us a while to find a publisher for the English translation. Along the way, we found a few professionals in the U.S. publishing world who loved the first chapter, but were bothered by the ending. We even were asked to change the ending or publish only the first chapter. I was shocked to learn that some noted contemporary Japanese writers have agreed to have the endings of their works changed for the U.S. (and by extension English-language) marketplace. While I shared my frustrations and thoughts on all this with you and we both refused such changes, I never asked you what it felt like for you to be faced with that kind of response and request.

Hoshino: It felt like Iraq or Iran.
"The Middle East is really selling now!"
"Well, let's see…. You're right. It sure is. But Iraq is a little hard to understand. I think it will sell better if you change Iraq. Can you change Iraq?"
"You're joking, right?"
"No, I'm serious. Change it."
It felt like that. I'm very glad my work wasn't changed.
(Continued)
"I changed Iraq, but it's still not selling that well."
"Maybe you didn't change it right. Yes, that's it. It would have been better if you'd changed Iran. Try changing Iran."
"But if we go that far, it's not really going to be the Middle East anymore."
"It's okay. As long as it sells. Alright then? Let's change Iran."

Hurley: My students and I like to discuss what doesn't appear in this novel, like the U.S. (Perhaps our inquiries are structured by the arrogance of U.S. imperialism and its claims to universal relevance.) Aside from the aquarium scene from *The Lady from Shanghai*, almost no mention is made of anything related to what my students call "the Western world," and they like to speculate, "where did it go?" After all, much of the modern and contemporary Japanese literature they encounter invokes "the West" more overtly. In writing a novel that addresses questions of borders, sovereignty, migration, and security involving nations, what did the absence of the U.S. mean for you? Does the U.S. empire have to disappear (or be abolished) before the Japanese emperor system can?

Hoshino: Yukio Mishima and Yasunari Kawabata wrote a number of "Japanese" works. Foreign (especially Western) readers experienced these works as "very Japanese" and proclaimed you could find "Japanese beauty" in them. This was to be expected. Mishima and Kawabata depicted images of Japan that Western eyes wanted to see.

But Japanese readers who were aware of such assessments followed suit, saying these works were written with a sense of "Japanese beauty that even a Westerner could admire" and that "Japan had the kind of culture written about in these novels."

This was how value judgments about "Japaneseness" were shaped.

Foreign readers who only find value in the first chapter of this novel must still have those Western eyes.

Paradoxically, foreign readers today seem to respond to Japanese literature with a lot of "American-ness" as universal and, at the same time, as "Japanese." Perhaps "Japanese" novels subtly and gently exoticize American problems.

When I read that sort of novel, I feel like I'm reading fantasy fiction and wonder, "Where is this tale from?"

I didn't intend to eliminate American references from *Lonely Hearts Killer*. It's not explicit, but I think of it as covered by America's shadow. The effort to put out the nationalist fire in the first chapter is also an effort to get out from under the shadow of America. After all, Japan's reality after the end of World War II and ever since the American Occupation has been that of "America above the Emperor."

Hurley: Your novels have helped me think about the deleterious effects of "unification." The word is so often used to describe something we are supposed to see as positive, as is the case with the various efforts to unify North and South Korea (divided primarily because of the U.S.), but you really spell out the dangers inherent in attempts to create a unified sense of national, cultural, gender, or ethnic identity. What kinds of resistance have you met when expressing your thoughts on the unification of a national or any other identity or ethos?

Hoshino: In the spring of 2006, the World Baseball Classic was held in the United States. Japan won and people across the country were excited. But the excitement took on a very nationalistic character because the leader of the Japanese team, Ichirô Suzuki, made multiple statements that were heavily loaded with nationalism.

So I wrote an essay for a newspaper about the discriminatory content of Ichirô's words and how the Japanese society that was so fired up by them seemed very aggressive to me. Now, I know to expect a certain amount of bashing for taking on a charismatic figure like Ichirô. I was in fact bashed quite a bit on the internet.

I wasn't actually trying to criticize Ichirô so much as throw some cold water on the fanatical fire. I thought it was important to point out that some people didn't share in the enthusiasm. Otherwise, it could look like every Japanese person was expected to be elated over the victory, and if you weren't excited, you weren't really Japanese. Eventually, people who had doubts would disappear altogether.

I am afraid of individual violence, but the violence of a fanatical group is much more frightening to me. People who distinguish what's wrong from what's right disappear when everyone turns to violence. That kind of group is formed with a sense of "unity." And that "unity" sets up some fictional enemy against whom the aggression builds.

Unification is homogenizing. Everyone must be the same, and differences can't be tolerated. That is to say, the aggression directed at "something different" or "something that isn't the same" escalates. Words like unification and assimilation might evoke an image of different people living side by side together, but in reality, I think what we see is a society fiercely intolerant of even the tiniest differences.

Hurley: I love the setting of the second and third chapters. The remote mountain lodge calls up images not only of idyllic mountain resorts, but also of the Aum movement's headquarters, the Chichibu Rebellion of 1884, the Umemura Rebellion in Hida, the Asama Sanso Incident, and especially (at least to me) United Red Army (*Rengô sekigun*) figures such as Hiroko Nagata. But the setting's significance isn't limited to Japanese histories and contexts. Iroha's use of the phrase "reservation," themes of self-governance and autonomy, and the title of the final chapter, drawing on Luis Buñuel's 1951 film *Subida al cielo*, invoke multiple landscapes and histories. Where did your own journey into the mountains of *Lonely Hearts Killer* begin and what do the mountains mean to you?

Hoshino: My first clue for the secluded mountain setting for Iroha and the others came from Buñuel's film *Subida al Cielo* ("Ascent to Heaven" in Japanese). The mountain reaching up to heaven is a threshold place that carries an image of death mixed with utopia. In the first chapter, Mikoto et. al. develop the vision of everyone dying for a utopian society. Ascension or "Ascent to Heaven" is the name for precisely this vision. However, the people holed up on the mountain are Iroha and others who commit to living and try to distance themselves, running away from Mikoto et. al.'s vision. I wanted to put the brakes on the escalation, and this ironical situation effectively neutralized the vision of death and utopia

That was the impetus for the mountain, which also relates to an image in the third chapter. You ascend from the mountain and migrate to a different place; but even though you cross the border, you aren't entering the world of the dead, but moving to another kind of life. I set up the mountain as that kind of three-dimensional threshold. Iroha and the others are definitely holed up on the mountain, but the mountain isn't a dead-end. Depending on your changing perspective, it links to a different latitude or culture. Before they were surrounded, they had the possibility of coexistence, not "unification." Underlying that possibility is an image of a reservation with autonomy. I think the groups of rebels who historically entrenched themselves in the mountains had similar visions.

One other factor was Japanese mountain worship. In Japanese animism, each mountain is a different god. With the arrival of the emperor system, they were forcibly unified. However, in this novel the people who look like *okami* ("Majesties") "come down" from the mountaintop. In other words, they stop being *okami*. They abdicate "unification."

Hurley: The most heated arguments in my classes usually focus on Mokuren and what her "real job" is. Some students see her as an opportunist whose money is made through human trafficking. Others interpret her as working to place people in strategic industries and positions on the "mainland" and in the "Island Nation" for more revolutionary purposes. Still others see her work as a much less dramatic form of labor recruitment and placement consulting. As an educator, I revel in the room you've left for my students to pursue these different interpretive lines. This may be an unfair question, but what did you want her "real job" to be?

Hoshino: As the writer, it makes me very happy that they come up with so many interpretations about Mokuren. I also want the reader to think about Mokuren's way of looking at the world. I'm still thinking about it. So I don't have an answer.

I entrusted the interpretation to the reader because thinking about Mokuren's meaning is connected to thinking about how we can break through this impasse in our actual world. That's why I felt very strongly that I wanted people to see possibilities in Mokuren. It thrills me to think she is plotting something with a magnificent vision of overcoming the nation. But because that possibility isn't fantasy, it involves considerable risk too. Becoming a cold opportunist is one such risk. I want us to imagine the many risks and think about how we might work with the possibilities.

Hurley: You often explore grief and death in your work. *Lonely Hearts Killer* begins with a moment of collective grief, but we also encounter a more intimate grief in Iroha's visits to Yellow Hell Spring. In both cases, you invite readers into feeling states with your characteristic detailed descriptions of atmosphere, location, sights, and sounds. To be honest, I often felt depressed when translating such sections, and many of my students have felt depressed while reading the novel too. And yet, many of us ultimately experience the novel as hopeful and as holding onto possibilities. As a writer, do you feel a responsibility to engender hope? Are we simply inserting our own yearnings into how we interpret the ending of this novel, for example?

Hoshino: The interpretation behind this question is precisely the kind of reading I'd hoped for. I wanted readers to experience the sadness Iroha feels as if it were their own, and I wrote it in a way that is laden with sensory descriptions to invest some immediacy in it, as if it was happening here and now.

As far as the meaning of the third chapter goes, I basically want readers to think about it for themselves, but for my part, I wrote it with the intention of making it a very hopeful ending. To reach that hope, I had to start with very deep depression and navigate through a great deal of negative feelings. People who embrace powerfully positive feelings are at the same time people who also have known what it's like to feel helplessly or hopelessly negative. You can't get to real hope by ignoring or denying the negative. People who are numb can't feel hope or happiness either. We can experience the real value of hope to the extent that we engage negative events or feelings head-on, whether inside us or in society.

Hurley: As serious, sobering, and often heart-breaking as this novel is, it is also quite funny. I don't think of you as a "comic" writer and yet some parts are absolutely hilarious. What has enabled you to find the humor in patriarchy, xenophobia, policing, and even personal anguish, for example? And how do you stay funny without making light of human suffering or surrendering to the maudlin (or self-indulgent)?

Hoshino: In situations where what's right in front of you—whether it's human beings, the earth, the universe, or anything else no matter what it is – is completely destroyed, I think people are more likely to find it hilarious than hideous or horrifying. The most extreme actions don't scare people so much as crack them up. However, things like the great massacres that come with war or "ethnic cleansing" fundamentally differ from what I mean by "complete destruction" in that they are nothing more than selfish endeavors for personal advantage and vile economic interests. I don't think there's an exception when the baseness underwriting such vile actions gets blown to smithereens; that destruction also produces laughter. I think it would be nice if the humor or silliness aimed for in my novel is something like that.

Hurley: None of the main characters in *Lonely Hearts Killer* are clearly anarchists. Yet it can be read as an anarchist novel. (I like to read it that way.) Does this bother you?

Hoshino: It makes me happy. If these characters are anarchists, then I suppose I am an anarchist too.

Hurley: You don't shy away from exploring the limits and possibilities of gender identity and sexual expression in your work. But you don't simply celebrate alternative sexualities and difference. Gender and sex are rarely if ever easy in your work. It seems like the most authentic questions of desire and connection you explore have nothing to do with prescribed gender roles and even transcend or are unrelated to conventional notions of sexual intimacy. And, honestly, men aren't usually very attractive in your works either. When clichéd images of patriarchal or macho sexuality appear in your work, they seem ridiculous. This makes your work radically different from two (male) Japanese writers to whom you are sometimes compared: Yukio Mishima and Kenji Nakagami. All this leads me to my next (loaded) question: how do you see yourself as a man, as Japanese, and as a writer?

Hoshino: I'm an oddball on each count, but I could engage myself through my work on novels. I'm heterosexual, but I dropped out of the prescribed image of the everyday hetero male. What's "normal" for the hetero male is not normal for me; it's a role that takes effort to play (of course, there's a cumulative aspect, but…). But I'm also not female or transgender. There is no place for my sexual identity within the existing categories. But that doesn't mean I plan to develop a new and appropriate category for myself. That's because categories intended to make discrimination or oppression visible can serve necessary political purposes. In reality, individual people are bound to have subtle differences in their various gender identities. At least that's how I see it. If you have a billion people, it's fine to have a billion sexual identities. I'm not trying to categorize anything, and so I want to treat gender identity as hard to describe in my work in order to show how routinely vague and flooded with microscopic differences it is.

The same goes for national identity. I grew up in Japan in the 1970s and 1980s, so I've been influenced by the customs of those times and that place too. My concept of values and how I think about things are definitely inextricably linked to those times and that place. But that's completely different from having a national identity that involves thinking "I'm a

Japanese." Just like I didn't have to end up conforming to the hetero male standard even though I was born a heterosexual male, it doesn't mean I have to adhere to the standard of a Japanese person just because I was born to Japanese parents, have Japanese citizenship, or was raised in Japan. I used to try to hide the fact that I was born in the U.S., had American citizenship too, and was told from my childhood that I was also American. Since I only lived in the U.S. until I was two and a half, I don't have any memories of America. But even though by appearance, language, and behavior I'm not different from other Japanese people, I was documented as simultaneously Japanese and American. This was a complex. It's what made me a "Japanese" drop out. I didn't have a national identity where I believed and never doubted I was a Japanese person. Rather, I felt like someone who simply happened to have Japanese citizenship. In this way, I turned into someone who doesn't see identity in hard and fast terms, which is why I think words are so important to me.

Regardless of whether or not it's conscious, majorities are made up of people who put a lot of faith in "conformity." So the language there basically functions to "conform" and "discipline." By contrast, the ultimate minority is the individual. The words of the individual are monologues that don't conform or discipline. A complete and total monologue is for oneself and not for communicating with another. Novels, poetry, and languages bring monologues into the social language fraught with "conformity" and transform them into something that can be communicated. If we didn't have the language of novels or if they were obliterated in a way that made them inaccessible, we'd be smothered by society's words of "conformity" and "discipline." All we'd be left with would be a society without any more individual words or individual difference, like a gigantic machine. People would vanish. This is not an extreme characterization. I feel like we're getting closer and closer to that kind of world, which is why I want to keep sallying forth the words of novels.

So, I don't really think of myself as a writer. It doesn't matter if it's sexual identity or national identity; all single individuals have their own unique and loose identities, and for any of us to be able to hold onto our own words on a day to day basis, we need the language of literature. People who express themselves even when their words are different are all poets and writers. I don't think literature has any authority or privilege beyond that.

Translated by Adrienne Carey Hurley
The Q&A will continue on the PM Press website at: http:// www.pmpress.org/content/article.php/Hoshino

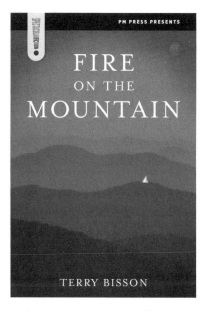

PM PRESS
SPECTACULAR FICTION

Fire on the Mountain
Terry Bisson
978-1-60486-087-0
$15.95

It's 1959 in socialist Virginia. The Deep South is an independent Black nation called Nova Africa. The second Mars expedition is about to touch down on the red planet. And a pregnant scientist is climbing the Blue Ridge in search of her great-great grandfather, a teenage slave who fought with John Brown and Harriet Tubman's guerrilla army.

Long unavailable in the US, published in France as *Nova Africa*, *Fire on the Mountain* is the story of what might have happened if John Brown's raid on Harper's Ferry had succeeded—and the Civil War had been started not by the slave owners but the abolitionists.

Reviews:
"You don't forget Bisson's characters, even well after you've finished his books. His Fire on the Mountain *does for the Civil War what Philip K. Dick's* The Man in the High Castle *did for World War Two."*
—George Alec Effinger, winner of the Hugo and Nebula awards for *Shrödinger's Kitten*, and author of the *Marîd Audran* trilogy.

"McKinley Cantor and Ward Moore move over! The South has risen again—this time as a brilliantly illuminated black utopia. Terry Bisson's novel touched my heart, brought tears to my eyes, and kept me thinking about it for days after finishing the book. It's an astonishing feat of rewriting history into something truly wonderful."
—Edward Bryant, co-author of *Phoenix Without Ashes* and winner of two Nebula awards for short stories *Stone*, and *gIANTS*.

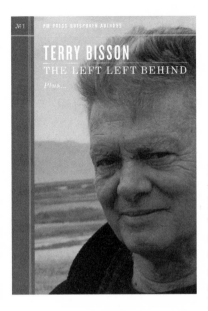

PM PRESS
OUTSPOKEN AUTHORS

The Left *Left Behind*
Terry Bisson
978-1-60486-086-3
$12

Hugo and Nebula award-winner Terry Bisson is best known for his short stories, which range from the southern sweetness of "Bears Discover Fire" to the alienated aliens of "They're Made out of Meat." He is also a 1960s' New Left vet with a history of activism and an intact (if battered) radical ideology.

The *Left Behind* novels (about the so-called "Rapture" in which all the born-agains ascend straight to heaven) are among the bestselling Christian books in the US, describing in lurid detail the adventures of those "left behind" to battle the Anti-Christ. Put Bisson and the Born-Agains together, and what do you get? *The* Left *Left Behind*-a sardonic, merciless, tasteless, take-no-prisoners satire of the entire apocalyptic enterprise that spares no one-predatory preachers, goth lingerie, Pacifica radio, Indian casinos, gangsta rap, and even "art cars" at Burning Man.

Plus: "Special Relativity," a one-act drama that answers the question: When Albert Einstein, Paul Robeson, J. Edgar Hoover are raised from the dead at an anti-Bush rally, which one wears the dress? As with all Outspoken Author books, there is a deep interview and autobiography: at length, in-depth, no-holds-barred and all-bets off: an extended tour though the mind and work, the history and politics of our Outspoken Author. Surprises are promised.

PM PRESS
OUTSPOKEN AUTHORS

The Lucky Strike
Kim Stanley Robinson
978-1-60486-085-6
$12

Combining dazzling speculation with a profoundly humanist vision, Kim Stanley Robinson is known as not only the most literary but also the most progressive (read "radical") of today's top rank SF authors. His best-selling "Mars Trilogy" tells the epic story of the future colonization of the red planet, and the revolution that inevitably follows. His latest novel, *Galileo's Dream*, is a stunning combination of historical drama and far-flung space opera, in which the ten dimensions of the universe itself are rewoven to ensnare history's most notorious torturers.

The Lucky Strike, the classic and controversial story Robinson has chosen for PM's new Outspoken Authors series, begins on a lonely Pacific island, where a crew of untested men are about to take off in an untried aircraft with a deadly payload that will change our world forever. Until something goes wonderfully wrong.

Plus: *A Sensitive Dependence on Initial Conditions*, in which Robinson dramatically deconstructs "alternate history" to explore what might have been if things had gone differently over Hiroshima that day.

As with all Outspoken Author books, there is a deep interview and autobiography: at length, in-depth, no-holds-barred and all-bets off: an extended tour though the mind and work, the history and politics of our Outspoken Author. Surprises are promised.

FRIENDS OF

PM

In the year since its founding – and on a mere shoestring – PM Press has risen to the formidable challenge of publishing and distributing knowledge and entertainment for the struggles ahead. With over 40 releases in 2009, we have published an impressive and stimulating array of literature, art, music, politics, and culture. Using every available medium, we've succeeded in connecting those hungry for ideas and information to those putting them into practice.

Friends of PM allows you to directly help impact, amplify, and revitalize the discourse and actions of radical writers, filmmakers, and artists. It provides us with a stable foundation from which we can build upon our early successes and provides a much-needed subsidy for the materials that can't necessarily pay their own way. You can help make that happen—and receive every new title automatically delivered to your door once a month—by joining as a Friend of PM Press. Here are your options:

- $25 a month: Get all books and pamphlets plus 50% discount on all webstore purchases.
- $25 a month: Get all CDs and DVDs plus 50% discount on all webstore purchases.
- $40 a month: Get all PM Press releases plus 50% discount on all webstore purchases
- $100 a month: Sustainer. - Everything plus PM merchandise, free downloads, and 50% discount on all webstore purchases.

Just go to WWW.PMPRESS.ORG to sign up. Your card will be billed once a month, until you tell us to stop. Or until our efforts succeed in bringing the revolution around. Or the financial meltdown of Capital makes plastic redundant. Whichever comes first.

PM Press was founded at the end of 2007 by a small collection of folks with decades of publishing, media, and organizing experience. PM cofounder Ramsey Kanaan started AK Press as a young teenager in Scotland almost 30 years ago and, together with his fellow PM Press coconspirators, has published and distributed hundreds of books, pamphlets, CDs, and DVDs. Members of PM have founded enduring book fairs, spearheaded victorious tenant organizing campaigns, and worked closely with bookstores, academic conferences, and even rock bands to deliver political and challenging ideas to all walks of life. We're old enough to know what we're doing and young enough to know what's at stake.

We seek to create radical and stimulating fiction and nonfiction books, pamphlets, t-shirts, visual and audio materials to entertain, educate and inspire you. We aim to distribute these through every available channel with every available technology - whether that means you are seeing anarchist classics at our bookfair stalls; reading our latest vegan cookbook at the café; downloading geeky fiction e-books; or digging new music and timely videos from our website.

PM Press is always on the lookout for talented and skilled volunteers, artists, activists and writers to work with. If you have a great idea for a project or can contribute in some way, please get in touch.

PM Press
PO Box 23912
Oakland CA 94623
510-658-3906
www.pmpress.org